ALMOST A WHISPER

ALMOST A WHISPER

Priscilla Masters

SEVERN
HOUSE

First world edition published in Great Britain in 2021 and the USA in 2022
by Severn House, an imprint of Canongate Books Ltd,
14 High Street, Edinburgh EH1 1TE.

Trade paperback edition first published in Great Britain and the USA in 2022
by Severn House, an imprint of Canongate Books Ltd.

severnhouse.com

British Library Cataloguing-in-Publication Data
A CIP catalogue record for this title is available from the British Library.

ISBN-13: 978-0-7278-5083-6 (cased)
ISBN-13: 978-1-4483-0721-0 (trade paper)
ISBN-13: 978-1-4483-0720-3 (e-book)

All Severn House titles are printed on acid-free paper.

MIX
Paper from
responsible sources
FSC® C013056

Typeset by Palimpsest Book Production Ltd.,
Falkirk, Stirlingshire
Printed and bound in Great Britain by
TJ Books, Padstow, Cornwall.

ONE

'*Noooo!*' His scream rolled down the empty valley as he processed what he was seeing. His first instinct had been disbelief. But his eyes hadn't deceived him. The young woman was edging the pushchair nearer the drop and he screamed again, searching the landscape for someone to heed his call. But no one was there. He scanned the nearest road, more than a mile away, an empty ribbon of grey gleaming in the rain as it sliced through scrub, bracken and the odd bush. He watched, paralysed, as the figure, silhouetted against a tumbling grey sky, took another, dangerous step.

'*Noooo!*' he screamed again.

She didn't seem to hear him against the howling wind. Her head didn't turn and there was no acknowledgement in the rigid body, bent forward, arms stretched out to the pushchair.

He raced across soft, boggy ground, trying to decide what was the best course of action, whether to make an attempt to climb the rock face and grab her from behind or run beneath and try to break the inevitable fall of the child. Or should he scrabble over the rocks to the side, try to jerk her into responding to his screams and move back from the edge?

He made his decision.

Keeping one eye on the woman, he scrambled up the slope directly behind her, praying he'd be in time.

She was still holding the pushchair in front of her, arms stiffly outstretched. He heard the wheels scraping, stones loosening and tumbling down the scree, a warning of what would happen if she let go or pushed only another inch or two. He kept running, scrambling up the slope, his hands reaching out now as he climbed over larger rocks, gaining momentum just as the pushchair tipped forward. In desperation Jeremy Western made another decision – to take a risky shortcut. If he could sneak up the Hargreaves Chimney, he might just reach her before . . .

Don't even think about it. Just do it.

His senses were screaming at him, registering that there was no sound or movement from the child. Maybe he or she was already dead and this was a bizarre body disposal.

He wedged himself into the narrow crack of the infamous 'Chimney', his bottom tight against sharp granite, his hands scrambling to find purchase. He inched upwards, looking only up, towards the gaping sky. To look down would have been to invite disaster. He couldn't see her now. At any moment he expected to hear the final rumble of pushchair wheels or the scream of the child as it bumped over rocks and stones, thudding to the bottom. The rocks were damp; his feet slipped and for a moment it was his own safety he was concerned about. No one ascended the 'Chimney', a narrow fissure in the gritstone, ninety feet high, without a safety harness. It was a fool's journey. 'Except in an emergency,' he muttered. His hands found a hold on a rock that wasn't loose and at last he hauled himself to the top.

She was still there, her shape black against the sky, still bent forward, reminding him of the wooden figurehead on the prow of a ship, searching open sea, a hand shielding her eyes instead of poised on the very edge of a potentially fatal drop. Crouching low now, like a beater in a shoot, he raced across soft heather, his feet sinking into dark, peaty moorland mud. Eight more steps and he would be there. 'No, please,' he begged, one last time. Now, distracted, she finally looked at him. He saw a calm, young face, registering slight puzzlement. Confusion. Disorientation rather than malice or intent.

He'd reached her now and grabbed the handle of the pushchair tight enough to yank it backwards.

And then he fell down.

Just before he did so, he'd peered into her face. He'd expected some demonic person who might snarl and scream, but she'd continued to look puzzled, eyeing him with wide, questioning eyes, tawny as a tiger's.

He stood up now, regained his dignity and pulled the pushchair further back, safely away from the edge, and now for the first time he saw the child inside. Bundled up in a blue anorak, hood up against the wind, which tugged sharply at dungarees flapping against his legs. A toddler, two years old at most, who watched him placidly through big, blue eyes.

He addressed the young woman. 'What on earth were you thinking? What are you doing here? You could have . . .' He corrected himself, 'You *would* have . . .' And stopped when he realized nothing was registering. Her face was blank.

She was still staring at him, a confused frown on her face as though she could neither process his presence or his questions. Her lips moved as though she wanted to speak, maybe explain, but nothing came out. She looked down at the child with the same measure of confusion. As though she didn't know who he was.

Jeremy looked down, past her, and shuddered. The drop was almost a sheer cliff lined with projections as sharp and potentially lethal as sharks' teeth. His mind skittered along the likely scenario. The pushchair would have bumped and rattled and torn its way to the bottom, probably ejecting the child halfway down, abandoning it to injury, possibly death. Had *she* planned to follow it?

She reached out as though to grab the pushchair again but he was much stronger. He was in the way and he was not going to let go. The child's big, round, blue eyes regarded them both curiously. Without any fear. Not crying or making any sound.

But now he had a problem. What to do next?

He switched his attention back to the woman and tried again to squeeze out some sort of explanation. 'What were you doing? What were you thinking of? Do you know how far down it is? The child. He . . . she . . . could have been . . .' His voice trailed away as he realized this was pointless. He wasn't getting through. Nothing was registering. She was regarding him with mild interest, head tilted to one side. He could have been someone she'd just passed in the street.

He tried again, touching her bare arm now which was as cold as a corpse's. 'Who are you? Where have you come from? How did you get here?'

The young woman simply shook her head with apparent bemusement.

He stared at her, uncertain what to do next.

There was, in this lonely spot, just the three of them, the child now kicking in his pushchair, the silent woman and the uncertain Jeremy Western who had just been out for his morning constitutional.

He turned his attention back to her, trying to glean something that gave him a clue, answers to his questions. She had light brown hair, straight and fine, which hung in dripping rats' tails around a face which was as pale as a vampire's starved of blood. She wore a long brown cardigan over a red dress, possibly a uniform. A nanny then, or a nurse? Her feet were encased in olive green wellingtons which ended just below the knee. Her legs were bare, her arms bare to the elbows as though she had found the cardigan too warm and had pushed them up though the morning was actually cold and the wind still blew ice along the ground. She'd dressed in a hurry, he thought. No coat? Again he looked around him, scanning 360 degrees of the landscape for some assistance or to give him a cue as to what to do next. But the three of them were still alone – himself, the woman and the child – and he felt a sudden frisson of fear, cold fingers on his neck. She looked strange to him. Not quite the full ticket, he thought. Maybe she was an escapee from a mental hospital and had abducted the child. He scolded himself. There was no mental hospital anywhere near here. In fact, there was nothing anywhere near except a few isolated farms, a restaurant closed since the virus and a pub, also closed. He hadn't noticed another car when he had parked his.

She was still looking at him, or rather looking *to* him for a resolution to this situation but he had none. He was in a dream – floating through a nightmare – where nothing made any sense. This felt out of kilter, surreal as a scene from a nightmare film, but there was no one else to help and so he focussed on the practical. 'How did you get here?' He added, 'Miss?'

No response. Nothing but that blank, unsettling look, the eyes flickering over him not even displaying curiosity. And he was left with the thought: what now?

TWO

8.15 a.m.
Leek police station

'You look awful, Jo.'

'Well, thanks for that,' DI Joanna Piercy snapped. The realities of parenthood were draining her spirit. 'You try feeding a bloody baby at two a.m., then again at six a.m., changing its nappy and trying to get to work for eight o'clock.'

DC Alan King smirked. 'Who's got him today?'

'His father,' she said shortly. Then she couldn't help but smirk. 'He's experiencing the wonderful joys of fatherhood.'

She could have added more. The word, 'doting', for a start, the fact that this was what Matthew had wanted, his heart's desire, and now he'd got it. The son he had lusted over, like Henry VIII. Instead all she managed was a mighty, all-encompassing yawn, her chin on her hands as she waited for her computer to fire up. In truth she was ready for one thing only. When had a few more hours' sleep been worth a pot of gold?

Sergeant George Alderley burst in. 'Sorry, Jo,' he said. 'But there's someone in reception.'

She lifted her head with difficulty. 'And?'

'We can't make out what's going on.'

'So . . .?' She was about to add the classic Hollywood response: *And that's my problem because . . .?* But stopped herself. Since when had she become so prickly, so sarcastic? Was it motherhood? Missing Mike? She gave in, almost apologizing to Sergeant Alderley. George was in his late fifties. Weeks off retirement. He'd done his thirty years and he knew when something was important. He didn't need her showing him up. He wouldn't have asked her to intervene unless he'd felt it warranted her involvement.

'Sorry, George.'

His response was to grin forgiveness at her. Typical of this thoroughly decent officer. She'd put twenty pounds into his retirement fund.

She followed him out to the front desk to see a slim man in his thirties dressed in hiking gear. He was hyperventilating and shifting his weight from foot to foot with an air of extreme anxiety.

He swivelled around as Joanna approached him, holding out her hand and managing a tight smile. 'I'm Detective Inspector Joanna Piercy,' she said. 'What can I do for you?'

He looked wild, dressed in khaki walking trousers and a parka; muddy hiking boots marking a trail behind him. He carried in the fresh, open-air scent of the moorlands. 'I'm really sorry,' he said, his eyes still wild. 'I'm so sorry. I just didn't know where to go. What to do with her.'

She tried to soothe him, speaking slowly. 'O-*kay*,' she said. 'What's the problem?'

He jerked his thumb behind him. 'I've left them in the car.' He repeated himself. 'I just didn't know what to do with them. Where to take them.'

She asked the obvious question. 'Who?'

He didn't answer her but, like many members of the public, launched into a narrative, seeming to feel he needed to fill her in on the background. She'd learnt to be patient. 'I was out for an early morning walk.'

Her eyes drifted towards the window. Rain spattered the glass with staccato taps. Even through the glass she could sense the cold. Not the loveliest of weathers but hikers in this part of the county had all-weather gear and prided themselves with being able to cope with all that Mother Nature might hurl at them. She jigged him along. 'And?'

'She was up there. At the top of The Roaches. She had the pushchair. She was about to push it . . .' He passed his hand across his face as though he still couldn't quite believe it. 'Over the edge.' His tone now was less panicky, more incredulous. 'There was a kid in there. I thought she was going to tip him out.'

There was plenty to alarm her now. The words 'kid' and 'pushchair', the phrase 'over the edge', a precipice well-known to her and the fact that this man was still white with shock and hyperventilating.

'You'd better sit down, I think.' And, to one of the PCs watching curiously while pretending not to, she said, 'Hot, sweet tea, please.'

The man sank into a seat, his face still ashen.

'Your car's in our car park?'

He nodded.

'What make is your car?'

'Ford Fiesta,' he said, and after fumbling in his pocket held out a bunch of keys which she passed to George Alderley. 'Go and see if anyone's in it, will you?' As Alderley shot out through the doors she turned her attention back to the shocked man.

She waited while he sipped the steaming liquid and some colour returned to his cheeks. His breathing slowed and he made a brave attempt at a smile and an apology. 'I'm sorry,' he said. 'You must think I'm an absolute . . .'

Joanna shook her head and sat down beside him. 'Maybe,' she suggested gently, 'you should start at the beginning? Your name?'

His voice trailed away. 'Jeremy,' he said. 'Jeremy Western. I live in a cottage in Flash.'

Flash, she thought, her mind wandering towards the highest village in England. 'Good.'

Jeremy Western still seemed to think further background was necessary. 'I run – or walk – most days up there in that area.' He swallowed and turned a pair of blue-grey eyes on her. 'The peace, you know. It's lovely.'

Joanna nodded. She loved the place herself but . . .

'I saw her standing on the edge of the rocks.' He looked up. 'Silhouetted against the sky.' He gave a nervous laugh. She resisted the urge to push him along with another *and?*

'She had her hands on the pushchair. I couldn't even see the child. Not then. She was inching towards the edge. I knew what she was going to do. Push it over. With the little kiddie in it. It's a steep drop. A long drop. The kiddie could have been—' He couldn't quite say it but half closed his eyes against the vision. 'I called out. And then I worried I'd startle her and she'd— But it was as though she hadn't heard me. It was as though she was on autopilot or in a trance or something. It was weird, Inspector. In the end I scrambled up the Chimney and reached her before . . .'

He closed his eyes. His colour had leached out again. He was about to faint.

'Put your head down between your knees.'

He did that. There was a muffled, gulping noise. *Please*, Joanna thought, *don't throw up all over the floor. Thanks to little Jakob I've had enough sick to last me a lifetime.*

She waited for him to recover.

Eventually he lifted his head and continued where he'd left off. 'I shouted at her but it was as if she didn't hear me. She didn't respond. She didn't look around – or anything.' He was still struggling with what he had seen.

Alderley came back in then, a small child, swathed in a thick blue anorak and denim dungarees, in his arms. Joanna raised her eyebrows and waited for an explanation. The toddler was watching her with big, round, blue eyes.

'The lady has stayed in the car,' Alderley said.

'Did she say anything?'

He shook his head. 'Couldn't get any response out of her. Sorry.'

'OK. Right.'

Joanna glanced back at Mr Western. 'We'd like you to stay here and make a statement. Is there anyone you want us to call?'

'My wife.' His voice was muffled as he spoke because he'd put his head back down. He handed her his phone. 'Celia,' he said.

The desk sergeant looked helplessly at the child in his arms and then back to Joanna. 'What shall I do with . . .?'

That was when Joanna focussed her attention on the child who seemed content to stay in the desk sergeant's arms. George was a grandfather. He had plenty of form dealing with wriggling, lively, noisy toddlers. Except this one wasn't wriggling or screaming. He was quiet, observing all that was going on around him – or her.

She detailed PC Paul Ruthin who was watching from the side-lines. 'You stay here with Mr Western and take a statement. You can ring his wife and suggest she come and pick him up. He can leave his car here. I'll be outside. I'm going to talk to the woman.'

A bitter wind nipped her as she stepped outside and the rain spat in her face. Not exactly the weather she would have chosen to climb The Roaches, she thought. Bleak and cool except in the very warmest weather, they were slippery and dangerous in the wet. She glanced back at the station and wondered.

It was not difficult to see which was Western's car. A dirty red Ford Fiesta was slewed across two parking spaces, side lights left on. Joanna could see the woman in the passenger seat, staring through the windscreen. The wipers gave a feeble swipe and she saw the woman clearer. A pale face stared ahead, face expressionless, apparently taking no notice of anything around her. Maybe she too was in shock. Joanna walked around to the passenger side and opened the door, a friendly smile pasted on her face as she squatted.

She breathed in deeply: damp, humid, heathery, the scent of the moors clinging to the interior, the air captured. 'Hello there, I'm Detective Inspector Joanna Piercy. Do you want to come inside and get warm?'

The young woman didn't give any sign that she'd heard, not even turning her head. Her only movement was a shiver. She was thin, somewhere in her twenties, hair straggling down her back, still dripping. She was dressed in a dark red dress that reached over scrawny thighs, ending in pale bare legs and wellingtons, a long brown cardigan soggy and misshapen completing the ensemble. Joanna put her hand on the woman's arm which felt as cold as a frozen chicken wing. 'You're wet,' she said, smiling. 'You need to dry out. Get warm.' She borrowed one of her grandmother's useful phrases. Said with another smile. 'You'll catch your death.'

There was still no response from the girl who, apart from the occasional shudder, sat as still as a robot. Joanna tugged at her arm now. 'Come inside,' she urged, and the young woman allowed herself to be pulled out and led, stumbling as though in a daze. Joanna searched for an explanation and appropriate response. Drugs? Would a doctor be more appropriate? A social worker? They'd need one for the child anyway, temporarily, until they found out what the situation was. And then she noticed a small stain on the skirt of the girl's dress and a larger stain on the soggy cardigan. As she'd stood up the rain that dripped down her bare legs from both dress and cardigan was pink and watery. Blood?

While it was possible that either the woman or the child had suffered a minor injury or the girl was having a period, combining the story Jeremy Western had brought in with this finding, Joanna shuddered at the other alternative.

THREE

She left the door of the interview room open and George Alderley, who must have handed the toddler over to a colleague, obliged with cups of tea.

As Joanna sat down opposite the woman she decided to be circumspect in her questioning rather than going in all guns blazing. 'First of all,' she said, her voice brisk, neutral and matter of fact, 'I need your name.'

The woman seemed to look right through her.

Joanna looked right back. The girl had tawny eyes, brown flecked with yellow. They were cat-like and yet surprisingly candid. Her lashes were long and she was wearing no trace of make-up, as though she'd just got out of bed. Her skin was very pale, almost anaemically white, and she was chewing her lips but saying nothing.

'Your name,' Joanna repeated.

This time the woman shifted her gaze to focus on Joanna, but she still made no attempt to respond. She didn't even open her mouth.

Joanna tried a different approach. 'We should really get you out of those wet clothes.'

The woman seemed to shrink away from her into the chair.

'Do you want to use the bathroom to change? We can lend you some clothes.'

There was no response. Not even a shake of her head, nothing but this fixed, blank stare.

Joanna waited for a while before standing up, decision made. 'We have some clothes you can change into. One of the female officers will give you a hand.'

She opened the door. PC Dawn Critchlow appeared, as though by magic, a pile of clothes in her arms. If anyone could coax the woman to speak it would be Dawn. She had a natural talent for persuading people to trust her and confide in her. With a smile Dawn held out her hand and the young woman rose from the chair, following her meekly.

As they passed Joanna spoke in the officer's ear. 'Bag up those clothes.'

Dawn nodded.

Ten minutes later they both reappeared, the girl now wearing loose grey jogging pants and a cream sweatshirt. Her hair had been partially dried but was still lank and damp. Joanna spoke softly to Dawn. 'Does she have any obvious injury?'

Dawn shook her head. The woman was standing, looking from one to the other, perhaps waiting for direction. Joanna indicated for her to sit down again.

And tried a gentler approach. 'We do need your name.'

The girl continued to stare at her, her eyes fixed and unresponsive. It was hard to work out whether this was deliberate obstinacy, a natural reluctance, or her silence was due to some other factor. Whatever the reason Joanna felt unnerved. What was going on in her mind? Was she unable to process the request? Like Jeremy Western before her she ran through various possibilities. Was she deaf? Dumb? Didn't understand English?

Joanna repeated slowly, 'What's your name?'

The woman gave no sign that she had heard, let alone understood the question. Joanna tried another approach accompanied by a friendly, almost conspiratorial smile. 'And the child? A little boy, isn't he? Is he *your* little boy?'

The eyes never dropped their steady gaze on her but there was not a flicker of response. The pupils remained constricted.

Joanna indicated the cup set on the table. 'Drink your tea before it goes cold.'

Obediently the girl lifted the cup, answering three tacit questions. She heard, understood, and could process a simple direction. As she drank, her eyes were fixed on Joanna's face. But whether they held appeal or stubbornness was impossible to decide.

Joanna picked up her pen. 'Whatever lay behind the circumstances in which you came to our attention I hope to be able to help you. But first of all I do need some basic details. You understand what I've just said?'

No response.

Joanna looked around her, met Dawn Critchlow's eyes, gave a slight, frustrated shake of her head and tried again. 'Do you know where you are?'

This time the girl's eyes moved slowly around the room as though committing it to memory. Her lips moved now, forming silent words. This, Joanna reflected wryly, was turning into a very one-sided interview.

She tried another approach. 'There was what looked like blood on your dress and cardigan. Have you been in an accident?'

There was a slight shake of the woman's head.

Joanna tried again. 'Or the little boy?' This time she could have sworn a spasm of pain crossed the girl's face. 'Is the child yours?'

The response this time was a widening of her eyes, as though she felt panicked. Maybe she was concerned for the child.

The child it seemed she'd wanted to hurt or kill?

Didn't make sense. Joanna had never thought there would be anything less informative than a 'no comment' interview. But this was breaking all records.

She asked slowly, 'Can you hear me all right?'

Still just that blind, unnerving stare.

Running out of options, Joanna sat back and thought. Then she tried again. 'Your name?'

The slightest movement of her head.

'Would you find it easier to write it down?' Joanna pushed a pen and pad towards her.

The woman picked up the pen and studied it for a moment before putting it down again neatly and precisely at the side of the pad.

Joanna was beginning to feel really irritated. Whatever the backstory to these events, this was turning out to be a waste of time. 'At the very least,' she said, 'let us have your name, please?'

She might have imagined it, but it seemed to her that the woman pressed her lips together even tighter – as though to prevent her name from accidentally escaping.

Joanna gave her a moment to think about it before trying in yet another direction. 'Is there anyone you'd like me to contact? Your parents? Someone who can look after you?' This time the response looked more like grim humour freezing the girl's features and making her eyes look even more predatory. There was even a ghost of a smile.

Joanna waited for a while as the silence lengthened and then she stood up. This was no good. The girl was not going to respond to any of her questions. Whether that was from guilt or embarrassment, an impediment or sheer stubbornness, Joanna wasn't going to get any answers. She left the room and found Dawn in the corridor. Her expression was troubled. 'I've put her clothes in an evidence bag. I think it's blood on the dress, Jo. And on the sleeve of the cardigan.'

'That's what I thought. We'll send it to the lab. And you say there was no sign of injury on her?'

'No. And she wasn't having a period either.'

'How did she respond to you stripping her off and changing her clothes?'

'She was fairly compliant, even helping me. There was no problem getting her out of her wet clothes and into the jogging pants and top.'

'I don't suppose you found any ID on her?'

'No.'

'A bag, a purse, maybe in the car?'

'No. They've had a look. And Alan King asked Mr Western, the walker, if he'd seen anything that might have identified her when he'd found her. Nothing.'

'They've examined the pushchair?'

'Yeah. Nothing there either.'

'And the child? I suppose he's too young to be telling us who he is.'

Dawn nodded then smiled. 'George is enjoying showing his granddaddy skills. He's having the time of his life.'

Joanna was smiling too – she knew about doting grandfathers. The smile lasted until she turned back towards the room where, through the open door, she could still see the girl, sitting motionless, shoulders slumped, staring ahead. There was something bleakly defeatist in her attitude. Joanna watched her for a while before turning back to Dawn.

'We'll send a couple of uniforms up to The Roaches to take a look around. See if a car's there, maybe a purse or handbag, some form of ID.' With a sense of dread she recalled Jeremy Western's panicked description of the circumstances in which he had found the woman together with the bloodstains on her dress and cardigan. 'See if there's any sign of anyone else up there. Maybe someone's hurt. If necessary they can take the dogs. And if we do find a car at least we'll have some idea of who she and the little boy are.'

'Will do.'

'Until we know who she is we're a bit stuck. We certainly can't charge her with anything. Not even Intent to Cause . . . And the child will need taking care of too. Properly.'

She returned to the interview room. The woman still hadn't moved but she turned her head as Joanna entered. Her eyes followed the DI as Joanna took her seat and tried again to question her.

'Is the little boy yours?'

Her eyes remained cold and she continued to stare straight ahead.

'Don't worry. We're looking after him. He'll be safe with us.'

The woman dropped her eyelids as though they were very heavy and she could give in to her exhaustion now she'd handed over responsibility for the child. She gave a slight shudder which passed through the thin body.

Joanna watched her for a moment. This was a challenge. Without any sort of response from the girl, together with the troubling story from Jeremy Western, she was having to glean all she could from the clues given out by the girl's body language. And she wasn't getting far. 'We'll be sending a team out to The Roaches. Did you leave your car there?'

The woman looked confused now, internalizing, as though scouring her memory for an answer.

'It must have still been dark when you dragged the pushchair all the way up to the top. Quite a climb. I've done it myself, though not dragging a pushchair. It was very early. Why did you go up there? Was it really to hurt the little boy? Why? Why would you want to hurt him? He's only about two years old. He can't tell us anything.'

No response.

'How did you get there?'

The woman's gaze settled on her.

'Did you drive? Park in the layby? At the side of the road? Surely you didn't walk all the way from the town?'

The blankness of the girl's gaze was unsettling. Had she been subject to trauma herself?

'You're not in trouble, you know. But we can help you better when we know who you are. We can contact your friends, family. Make sure your little boy is with people who can look after him. Make sure he's safe. Be reunited with his family.'

There had been quite a pool of blood on the woman's right sleeve and a spattering on the lower skirt of the dress. Dawn had said the girl had no injury. And George would have told her if the little boy was injured. So now her worry was intensifying. Who was she? Why had she gone there? Was she suffering from some strange mental condition? Had she abducted the child? There had been no reports of a child abduction but she needed to know whose blood it was – urgently. Was someone lying out there, injured? At this very moment, while this woman remained tight-lipped, was someone's life ebbing away, someone's life which could or should have been saved? Had the woman witnessed – or inflicted – some trauma? Would she really have hurt the child in such a cruel way? Jeremy Western had believed so and had left her with the problem of what to do with the girl and toddler. Or what if she and the child were victims and she'd fled, somehow ending up on the rocks? And now, because of her ordeal, she couldn't speak and had blanked it out? As Joanna's frustration and impatience increased her voice grew more strident.

'Where have you come from? Who *are* you?'

The girl was chewing on her lip now but her eyes still held that faraway look. Jeremy Western's statement had indicated that he had believed this young woman had been prepared to hurl the little boy over a precipice. Western had not struck her as someone prone to exaggeration and he had delivered his statement without drama or coercion. They could have been looking at a case of murder or attempted murder of a child. And this girl was saying nothing?

'Does anyone need to know where you are? Can we make a phone call for you?'

But the blank, empty expression in the woman's eyes didn't change, though behind that was something that looked like cynicism. It was pointless continuing to direct these questions to her. Joanna may as well have asked the toddler. For some reason, whether connected with trauma or mental incapacity, either deliberately or because she couldn't, she was not going to respond. The woman was, in equal parts, irritating and intriguing her.

Or maybe it was simply another version of the 'no comment' interview.

She laced her fingers together and reflected. What she would have done to have had DS Mike Korpanski by her side. Maybe he could have extracted something.

As it was, all she had was a woman who refused to or was unable to speak, a child and bloodstained clothes. Questions but no answers.

FOUR

10 a.m.

There are clear directives in the police force, ways to deal with every situation – almost. This one was stumping Joanna. Was this a medical problem? Stubbornness? Was this unnamed woman even fit to be questioned? She didn't know. Neither could an ordinary GP turned forensic medical examiner, she suspected, but it was a start. And she had to start somewhere. Her overriding question was if it was blood that stained the girl's clothes then whose was it?

'Who's the duty FME?'

DC Alan King looked up from the computer screen where he'd been running through missing persons. 'Dr Shilton.'

'OK, we'd better ask him to come in and assess our silent girl.'

She drew up a chair and studied the screen alongside him. 'Anything coming up from missing persons?'

'No,' he said. 'Not so far, anyway. No young woman and/or child have been reported missing in this area and I've extended it to Derbyshire, Cheshire and Shropshire.'

Joanna peered at the screen willing it to produce a name. 'Look countrywide, Alan. It's early days yet.'

It was vital that they identified her. Once they knew who she was they could track back to the situation she'd left behind.

Alan King continued with his widened search on the PNC, fingers flicking through details. While DS Mike Korpanski was still on sick leave following 'the accident', Joanna was getting used to working alongside the DC and his idiosyncrasies. Tall and skinny with long, gangly, seemingly uncontrollable limbs, he was constantly barging into objects. This was his downside. Around him there was always noise, a clashing and clanging, something being tipped over. He could cause chaos in the station simply by walking through, or rather into, a door. It made her twitchy and on edge. But DC King had his advantages too. He was tech-savvy, a whizz with computers and mobile phone technology. His long, bony fingers danced across the keyboard with an elegance the rest of his body couldn't possibly have matched. He could elucidate facts from technology quicker than anyone else in the station. He was also a linguist, speaking fluent French and Spanish. But he wasn't Korpanski, she thought grumpily. He didn't have Mike's wit or sarcasm – or his honesty either. And he didn't have her DS's talent for lightening the grimmest scenario with a twitch of his lips forming a smile.

'What about a lone child missing?' she suggested. 'She might have snatched him. She might not be the child's mother or any relation at all.'

He didn't even look up but shook his head. 'Nothing there either.'

Joanna frowned. She was tired and jaded from too many broken nights' sleep, thanks to her four-month-old son, Jakob Rudyard Levin. Maybe she should have taken longer maternity leave. But the truth was even Jakob, lovely little infant though he was, was no substitute for the challenge of work. Like many new mums, she felt intermittently guilty about motherhood not being wholly satisfying. But the fact was that being at home since his birth had bored her. She had chosen police work initially because it was a challenge, always a mountain to climb. Watching a baby feed and fill nappies, occasionally smile but spend much of his time sleeping, she had found stultifying. Besides, her being at work meant that his doting father took his turn, as did Matthew's parents who seemed to have turned back the clock. Rather than ageing, since having some responsibility for their new grandson, they seemed to be rejuvenating almost day by day. She suppressed her guilt with the consolation that childcare was doing them a favour.

Back to the moment. She picked up the phone.

Dr Robert Shilton, duty forensic medical examiner, listened without comment as she related the story. 'She had no ID on her?'

'Nothing. We have no idea who she is or how she got up to The Roaches. We don't even know whether the child is hers or whether she has abducted him.' She tried to laugh it off. 'So far, Doctor, we don't know very much.'

Stolidly he pursued the point. 'No handbag, purse, mobile phone?'

'Nothing,' she repeated.

'And the child?'

'A toddler. He looks about two, reasonably well nourished, while she is stick thin.'

'And you say it looked as though she was going to push the child over the edge of a drop?'

'It appeared so – according to the sole witness.'

'And she's refusing to speak?'

This was difficult. 'We're not sure whether she's refusing or whether she can't speak. She doesn't really react to any of our questions. She just blanks us.' She hesitated. 'There is something else,' she said. 'There is . . .' She erred on the side of caution. 'There is what appears to be bloodstains on the girl's clothes.'

'I'll be over right away,' he said. 'This sounds like it could be interesting.'

Joanna tried to make light of it. 'It's certainly frustrating, Doctor. It makes me long for the good old days and relatively garrulous "no comment" interviews.'

'I'll hold you to that,' Robert Shilton said, 'when next we have one of those uninformative types.' She knew he was still smiling as he put the phone down.

'Thank you.'

*   *   *

Joanna re-entered the briefing room, already setting out clear plans in her head. 'While we wait for Dr Shilton to make sure our lady is fit to detain, I want PC Kitty Sandworth and you, Austin' – she addressed PC Austin Sidwell, one of the force's stocky dog handlers – 'to take Holmes and Watson up to the moors. Search around. See if you can find anything – or anyone. Maybe a purse or a mobile phone, set of car or house keys. See if she's parked there and see if you can find the source of the apparent bloodstains on her clothes. Let me know as soon as you find anything.' The two officers nodded and she turned her attention back to the roomful of personnel. 'In the meantime, our priority is to establish the identity of both girl and child. Obviously one main clue may be how she arrived there. Most probably by car, which should quickly lead us to the girl's backstory and the source of the blood as well as securing a safe place for the little boy. If Austin and Kitty, together with the dogs, don't find a car, our search becomes a little more complicated. Did someone give her a lift up there? If so who, why, and is it someone she knows? Where did she come from? Did anyone see her before our helpful Mr Western? Is she local?' She scanned the room. 'I don't suppose anyone recognizes her – or the child?'

That resulted in a sea of shaking heads.

She continued, 'As far as her refusal or inability to speak we can leave that to the medics now. That isn't our problem. We can treat it the same as a "no comment" interview. I'll give her the chance to have a lawyer but if she fails to respond I'll take that as a no – for now.'

Since government cutbacks and a general downsizing of the force combined with centralization they no longer had a specialized Moorland Patrol. Much of the work was carried out by a Wildlife and Countryside team who covered a huge and desolate area with, thankfully, a low incidence of crime. PCs Timmis and McBrine, who had worked for years as the Moorland Patrol, had both taken early retirement. Saul McBrine now taught self-defence and 'keeping safe' in and around schools while Timmis had started up a self-protection unit which was, Joanna had learned, quite successful.

She moved to pictures of the girl's clothes, pointing out the spattering on the skirt as well as the stain on the sleeve of the cardigan. The dress itself was dark red so the spots of blood were not obvious, but the stains on the cardigan sleeve were easier to spot.

'The dress,' she pointed out, 'could be a uniform. Nanny? Nurse?'

Then she was silent, letting the assembled officers make their own conclusions. 'As neither the girl nor the child have any visible injuries we have to assume that the blood is someone else's and that *that* person possibly has a significant injury. Combining that with the fact that our girl appeared about to throw the child over a ninety-foot drop, are we searching for a crime scene?' There was a shuffling movement around the room as though each and every officer was troubled by this possibility.

'Nothing, so far, has been reported and DC King is spreading his search countrywide. So . . .' She turned her attention back to the screen. 'We have work to do. The dress has a label from Alexandra Clothing. They supply all the hospitals, private clinics, nursing homes and anyone else who wants a uniform, so this is unlikely to lead anywhere. But you could fax over a picture to check whether it's a current line. Phil,' she addressed DC Phil Scott, 'you contact the local mental health services and see if they know anyone answering this description.' That was a possibility, she realized. But it didn't account for the child.

All the time she was addressing the assembled officers she was musing, testing various scenarios and questions in her mind. Was the girl an escapee from a local mental health facility? Was she a local or someone who had travelled in? Could she have come from a holiday let? There were few houses within two miles of The Roaches. It was an isolated area, exposed to the weather and sparsely populated. People knew each other out here. Many of the properties were holiday lets but on a Tuesday morning in mid-March it would be unusual to have many visitors apart from hardy runners and hikers – like Mr Western. Their girl did not fit the profile of a hardy outdoor sort. Wrong clothes. All the same, she detailed PC Jason Spark to make a round of the holiday lets, beginning with the ones nearest The Roaches and spiralling out. 'For now,' she said, 'we'll just release to the press that a woman and child have been found in this area and anyone having any information should contact Leek Police. No pictures,' she warned. 'No details for now. I'll wait and see what the doctor says, confirm that she's fit to detain and hope she soon starts to talk.'

She broke up the briefing and returned to the interview room. Dawn was still sitting with the young woman. She shook her head as Joanna entered. The girl did look up as Joanna sat down opposite her and tried a friendly smile which provoked no response at all.

The force these days was all about 'reaching out and engaging' which was exactly what Joanna tried to do now. 'Have you come from one of the local mental health facilities?'

This provoked a look of alarm, a widening of her eyes. Joanna waited, watching the girl's face for further signs that she had heard and understood the question. Maybe now she would speak? But after a moment the woman's features settled back into bland disinterest, her native neutral expression, so Joanna proceeded.

'A police doctor is going to come and examine you,' she said, 'to decide where you should go. We don't want to keep you here. It's not as if you'd actually *committed* a crime. But there are some points that need explaining.' She was watching the woman's face very carefully as she spoke but it remained impassive as she stared ahead, breaking eye contact, neither focussing on Joanna nor Dawn but seeming to fix on a point somewhere vaguely past them. Clinging to her still was the scent of moorland heather and bracken, mixed with damp, peaty soil and mould as though her skin still hadn't dried out. Her clothes had held that same scent of cerements. And Joanna could have sworn that somewhere in the air around her was the rich smell of blood.

She tried a different approach. Even friendlier this time, acting the confidante. 'What's the little boy's name? Just tell me that.'

Something did soften in the girl's face. A hint of affection for the child? But, as before, she said nothing; tightened her lips against any words leaking out and the native bland facial expression returned.

Inwardly Joanna was sighing but she forced herself to continue in the same bright voice. 'One of our officers is looking after him.' She was scanning the girl's face for a sign of concern. Nothing. 'I want you to understand,' she said, 'that as it appeared you could have harmed him . . .'

The girl jerked her head. In denial?

'Unless or until we find another family member we may need to ask social services to place him with a foster family. Temporarily,' she added. 'We can't keep him here.'

As a mother, Joanna was puzzled. Had anyone threatened to

take Jakob away from her, mentioned the words foster family and social services, she would have fought tooth and nail to keep him with her. Screamed out '*Noooo!*'. But here this strange girl sat, like a Buddha or the Sphinx. As impassive as though she had been carved out of stone. And then she reminded herself. This girl had been prepared to throw the child, whether it was hers or not, over the edge of a cliff. Possibly before doing the same to herself. Had that been her intention? To kill them both? Was she a victim of depression? Domestic violence? Had her actions been the result of desperation or trauma? Or did the answers lie in a damaged psyche?

'Look,' she said, gentler now. 'We just want to help you.'

The girl's eyes locked into hers. Her mouth twitched into an expression of cynicism and a vague shake of her head negating the offer. She was staring down at the desk now, looking weary as though all the fight had gone out of her. Her face and shoulders sagged. She pushed her hair out of her face as though even the thin, damp rats' tails were too heavy to support. She slumped down in the chair.

After a few more moments Joanna left the room with a spark of an idea. If the girl wouldn't speak how would the little boy react to her? Would he call her 'mummy'?

George Alderley was still holding the child who seemed perfectly happy in the burly sergeant's arms.

'I've changed his nappy,' George announced proudly. 'I sent one of the PCSOs over to Aldi and they've picked up a pack of disposables. When I changed him I found this.' He indicated a smear on the little boy's dungarees and they exchanged glances. More to worry about. The dungarees were pale denim and the smear was unmistakably blood. 'He isn't injured?'

George Alderley shook his head.

'Neither is she. So . . .' She didn't need to complete the sentence.

The child didn't respond even when George handed him over to her and she carried him into the interview room. She watched the girl very carefully as she entered, holding the child. But there was no response from either. They could have been strangers to one another. Maybe they were. So where was the child's mother? Why hadn't she come forward? Was she the source of the blood? The woman had looked up briefly as they'd entered, but then, without any expression, she'd dropped her gaze again to the surface

of the desk. Apathetic and strangely unemotional. Switched off.
Joanna, still holding the child, who felt heavy in her arms compared
to Jakob, sat down, the little boy on her lap, facing forward. The
girl's shoulders twitched. But there was still no interaction between
the two. The toddler stared at the woman, who could have been
his nemesis, with nothing more than mild interest. Joanna looked
harder at the woman, then at Dawn who lifted her eyebrows and
couldn't help making a comment.

'Lovely little chap, isn't he?' She addressed the young woman.
No response.

'Is he yours?'

The girl closed her eyes in one long, weary blink, not responding
to the PC.

Joanna took over. 'Someone might be worried about both of
you.'

A look of cynicism twisted the woman's mouth. It was as
effective as if she had said, *As if.*

Still holding the little boy, Joanna switched to conversation
mode. 'What puzzles me is how did you get up there?' She'd
modified her tone to one of mild curiosity.

Joanna tried another line. She leaned in and spoke in a
no-nonsense tone. 'We found what looks like blood on your
clothes.' That provoked a sharp intake of breath. A spike of a
memory? Joanna added in a softer voice, 'And on the little boy's
dungarees.'

The response to this was a watchful flicker of the eyelids and
the girl continued to hold her breath.

The child sat between them, looking from one to the other.

'You understand as *you* have no apparent injury and neither
does this little fellow, that we need to know whose blood this is
and how it got there. It looks as if it could have come from a
significant injury.'

No response. And the girl's breathing had returned to normal.

'We need to know. Is someone hurt? Has there been an accident?
Does someone need an ambulance?'

Was she imagining it? Had the girl's mouth just twitched, as
though she found it all funny?

Joanna's voice was stern as she pursued this point. 'Has anyone
been hurt? You need to tell us.' Her voice had become more and
more strident. Her patience had completely gone and she was

worried. Something here felt edgy. It wasn't only the girl's refusal – or inability – to talk or the presence of blood on their clothes. It wasn't even the apparent threat of injury to the child. It was something else – the entire collection of facts as they knew them that felt off-kilter. Dangerous. Something extraordinary. What lay behind this odd set of circumstances? What would they find?

But it was obvious the girl was determined to stay a closed book. Joanna was convinced she had understood all her questions. It was simply that she was refusing to answer them or respond in any way. It was rare for someone to be such a successful enigma. Joanna felt this was a voluntary action overriding natural instincts. What was she, so successfully, hiding?

Luckily just as Joanna's patience was running transparently thin, George Alderley walked in. 'Dr Shilton's here,' he said. 'Come to help you out.'

She stood up, glad to hand the child back to George and leave the room. But before she exited she couldn't help saying, 'You understand we have the right to detain you until we know who you are and why you ended up here in these circumstances?'

She was tempted to bang the door behind her.

Walking along the corridor, she hoped Kitty Sandworth and Austin Sidwell, or even one of the dogs, would be providing some answers and soon. A car would be a good start, she reflected, nice and easy to trace its owner and work backwards. But there was always the chance of a bag or a purse or even better a mobile phone which was as good as having a diary with every location, contact and conversation recorded. From there they would be able to spiral out their enquiries, check on a potential crime scene and find out who the child was, track down some relatives and hand him over to someone who didn't want to tip him over a ninety-foot drop. That would be a good start.

The one-sided interview had frayed her nerves. There could be many reasons why the woman was refusing to speak and only she could fill in the blanks. What she worried about was that this delay could prove costly for someone. And all the time this vulnerable child was here and they had responsibility for him.

As she continued along the corridor, she glanced across at the little boy in Sergeant Alderley's large arms. It registered how very quiet and unresponsive the child was, being handed from one stranger to another without demur, a grizzle or any other objection.

Just looking around him with big blue eyes, taking it all in. Surely it wasn't normal? Jakob was only four months old but he took more notice of his surroundings than this little boy who was, in her estimation, around two years older. George knew more about child development than she. 'Shouldn't he be starting to talk by now?'

George stroked the blond hair. 'Yeah, he is a bit quiet, isn't he?'

'I wonder why?'

'Maybe he's traumatized, Joanna.'

It was an uncomfortable thought but one which had crossed all their minds. 'Even though he's so small?'

Sergeant Alderley met her eyes and shrugged. 'Little ones,' he said. 'They can be hard to work out.'

She had to be happy with that.

'Have we had anything back from Kitty, Austin and the dogs yet?'

He shook his head. 'As soon as we do, Jo, I'll let you know.'

Dr Shilton was waiting in the reception area. He stood up as she arrived. He was a short, plump guy with thick-framed glasses, a GP in a local practice who had been called in many times. He was, by nature, friendly and helpful, usually ready with some (bad) joke up his sleeve. Dr Shilton seemed to have one for every occasion. But, however poor the jokes were, it was hard not to join in with his infectious chuckle. Joanna had appreciated his assistance on previous occasions. She waited until they were safely in the privacy of her office before responding to his question.

'*Her* child?'

'We don't know. She hasn't uttered a single word in the time she's been here.'

'Refusing to give answers?' He looked up.

'Refusing to speak at all. I can't work out if she's traumatized or being stubborn.'

He grinned. 'Nice and quiet for you then, compared to some of the gobby drunks you usually have here.'

She smiled.

'And the child?'

'Around two years old, I'd say. Seems quite a contented little chap but he's quiet.' She stopped. It was more than that. 'He's not really responding at all. Not crying or showing any emotion. He just watches us and tolerates being passed from person to person without objection. We've contacted Karen Murphy, the duty social worker.

'We can't keep him here, Doctor, with the sergeant looking after him. He may need to be placed with a foster family if we can't find out who he is and locate his family – if our girl is not his mother. They don't seem to respond to one another at all.'

Shilton raised his eyebrows. 'As you say, Joanna. All odd. Very odd.'

'There is one other thing,' she said awkwardly, knowing this would sound melodramatic.

'Both of their clothes have blood on them. But it's not hers or the child's.'

He anticipated her next question. 'So you're anxious where it came from.'

She nodded.

He gave her an encouraging smile and a light pat on her shoulder. 'Don't you worry, Inspector Piercy,' he said. 'We'll work it out, somehow.'

Probably to further put her at her ease, he added, 'How's Korpanski these days?'

'Getting there . . . slowly.'

She could never rid herself of the guilt – that the deliberate running down of DS Mike Korpanski had somehow been her fault because it had been connected with a case she was involved in. Six operations later and enough metalwork embedded in his leg to sink a battleship, he was, at last, walking, but with crutches. A long way from the gym addict he'd been. But at least he'd kept his leg which at one point had been marked for amputation.

'I visit him a couple of times a week.' She smiled at Dr Shilton and shared a confidence. 'Much to his wife's annoyance. She complains that seeing me just makes him itchy to return to full duties before time.' And that was an understatement. Fran Korpanski watched her chat to her husband with undisguised hostility and suspicion. She had never liked Joanna and resented her husband's close friendship with his inspector. 'I miss him,' she admitted. 'It's like trying to work at half strength without his perspective.'

Dr Shilton's response was to pat her on the back. 'Well, knowing him, if he's making such a good recovery he'll soon be back.'

'Not soon enough for me. And he won't return immediately to front-line duties – if ever. He might be stuck behind a desk. Certainly for the foreseeable future.'

Shilton laughed at this. 'Can't imagine Detective Sergeant Korpanski stuck behind a desk.'

'Me neither.'

'All a big shame. Right. Time to see your lady. Lead on, Inspector.'

'Good luck. If you can just get her to speak – or at least communicate. Even by writing. I want to know where that blood's come from. I need to know who she is, Doctor. If she was prepared to injure our little chap, maybe she's hurt another child. I want to know where she's come from. What she's left behind her. What was she doing up there?'

He patted her shoulder. 'I'll do what I can, Inspector.' And he disappeared into the interview room.

FIVE

Half an hour later Dr Shilton emerged. He shrugged and gestured Joanna towards a private room, shut the door carefully behind him and spoke in a quiet, controlled voice. She sensed the underlying frustration which mirrored her own.

'She's fit to detain,' he said shortly. 'She doesn't have any *physical* injury. Pulse, blood pressure, temperature all normal.'

'She's not deaf?'

He shook his head. 'I tried signing to her, Joanna.'

'Did you get *any* response from her?'

'Not really,' he said. 'She's completely shut down.'

'Why?'

'That's anybody's guess.'

'Drugs, alcohol?'

He shook his head.

'So, give us a clue here, Doctor. I'm floundering.'

He shook his head. 'I'm sorry,' he said, 'but I got nothing. She's thin, undernourished. I would say early twenties.'

'So what's the verdict?'

'You understand, Joanna, I'm not a psychiatrist.'

She nodded.

'She appears,' he said cautiously, 'to be suffering from selective mutism.'

'Which means what exactly?'

'She is, apparently . . .' He was choosing his words very carefully. 'Unable to speak.'

'Unable,' Joanna asked sharply, 'or unwilling?'

Robert Shilton smiled. 'I understand your scepticism, but in this case I believe she is unable rather than unwilling. I don't think this is voluntary mutism.' He smiled. 'She is, almost in a Biblical sense, struck dumb.'

'So what do we do? Just wait for her to speak while God knows what happened out there?'

'Mutism is usually the result of some trauma or acute anxiety.'

'Like . . .?'

He looked awkward. 'You mentioned bloodstaining on her clothes – and those of the child.'

Joanna waited for him to continue.

'The bloodstaining – was it extensive?'

'I would say it is the result of an injury to someone. Obviously not her or the little boy. Hard to say whether it was the result of a major injury. That would be up to the experts on blood pattern analysis. Not the police. I am concerned another child could be in danger.'

'There have been no reports of any accidents or assaults in this area?'

'Nothing so far. Not on the PNC. It's a mystery.' She paused before asking, 'So what do you suggest we do with her?'

'I suggest you consult a forensic psychiatrist.'

Joanna felt waspish. This was all time delay. 'What will a forensic *psychiatrist* be able to do? Unlock the woman's speech?'

Dr Shilton ignored her ill humour. 'A psychiatrist doesn't have a magic wand,' he admitted, 'but you won't get much out of your girl here.' He looked around him. 'This is the wrong environment for her. You can't keep her here indefinitely so what will you do with her? She's obviously damaged.'

'And damaging.'

He ignored her jibe, continuing smoothly. 'She needs to be under a psychiatrist, Joanna. She needs specialist treatment.'

'And that will persuade her to talk?'

He looked even more awkward. 'It may take some time.'

'And in the meantime maybe somebody lies injured? Possibly dying? It could be another child.' An image of the child-catcher doing his horrid dance disturbed her. 'She could have abducted this little boy which is why he isn't responding to her. Because he doesn't know her. She could have murdered the mother as she very nearly killed him.'

'That's a little dramatic, isn't it?'

'Doctor. No one has come forward to report a child missing. I ask myself why not? Is there somewhere a crime scene slowly disintegrating? A body?'

He frowned.

'Put it like this. If I am right and behind this silent young woman is a crime scene, we need to uncover it as soon as possible. Until we do I am not happy for her to be released back into the community.'

'She couldn't be anyway,' he pointed out. 'She's vulnerable.'

'Yes, *she's* vulnerable,' Joanna countered, 'and so is the child she apparently wanted to hurt. Who else? We may not have time, Doctor. We just don't know, do we? We don't know who she is; we don't know where she's come from. All we know is she was about to tip a two-year-old over a ninety-foot drop.'

'If she won't speak,' he said gently, 'you don't have a lot to go on.'

'Hopefully the team I've sent over to The Roaches will find something that helps us identify her. Maybe a car or some ID. I'm hoping for a bag, a mobile phone, something discarded.'

Robert Shilton met her angry gaze. 'My professional recommendation is that you consult a forensic psychiatrist. If the psychiatrist thinks it appropriate she could be made a patient at a secure inpatient unit.'

Joanna glanced back at the door of Interview Room 1. 'OK,' she said, knowing she would have to act on the FME's recommendation. 'Can you recommend anyone?'

He looked pleased with himself. 'It so happens I can,' he said. 'There's a psychiatrist based near Hanley. She has a secure unit and quite a reputation for treating difficult pathological psychiatric cases. If you like I'll give her a call. I can discuss your lady with her and she'll contact you.'

'Thank you. That'd be great.'

'In the meantime,' he advised, 'I think you should keep her here under observation. She is very disturbed. Something has made her so.'

They shook hands and he left Joanna with that phrase. *Something has made her so.*

SIX

1 p.m.

Holmes and Watson might seem an unimaginative name for two police German Shepherds but over the years they had proved their worth and their moniker. PC Austin Sidwell, their handler, had treated them to one of the girl's wellington boots and after a prolonged sniff the dogs had looked both enthusiastic and optimistic, their tails wagging and their barking noisy as they romped across the moorland paths, heading up towards the summit where Jeremy Western had first glimpsed the woman. Sidwell and the dogs had a close relationship. Mrs Sidwell had once confided to Joanna, after a few party-sized glasses of wine, that if he could, he would have moved the dogs into their house and her into the kennels. It was an exaggeration but Joanna had smiled and seen a hint of truth behind it.

PCs Kitty Sandworth and Austin Sidwell had pulled up in the layby that served as a parking area for The Roaches. It was empty, as was the entire road. So the first question was how had the woman arrived in such a remote spot? Walked? From where? The town was nearly five miles away and this spot was a stiff climb. Had she come on the bus? One did pass on the hour heading towards Buxton. Had she been given a lift? Even so, pushing a child in a pushchair up the steep slope to the top must have been quite a feat and taken some determination or panic. Next question: why there? Even for the two officers it was a stiff climb up the soft, peaty path. Kitty was young and fit. She ran marathons but Austin Sidwell had succumbed to middle-aged spread and sported a beer belly.

They reached the summit, breathless from the exertion, and peered over the drop. It looked ominous, the rocks gleaming and slippery. A light drizzle dampened the day and blurred the expanse of moorland, grey and inhospitable, the road hardly in view, as they took the path in the other direction – just in case. But even here the dogs looked crestfallen, bounding around and finding nothing from either woman or child. The only evidence of her recent presence were the faint grooves of the pushchair wheels leading up from the road, round the back of the Chimney, to the crest of the rock.

'Nothing here,' PC Sidwell said, the words muffled in that silent, remote atmosphere.

It was almost three o'clock when they reported their results.

Meanwhile, DC Phil Scott was focussing his attention on the child's pushchair, taking samples of the dark, peaty mud which clung to the wheels and the undercarriage. He took the samples with care, labelling them clearly, knowing there was a chance that this evidence might be what led them back to a specific location and possible identification.

Joanna passed by. 'Bag the whole thing up, Phil,' she said, 'and hold on to it. We may need a plant and soil expert to try and find out where it came from.'

If the girl could not or would not tell, and the child was unable to, then maybe it would be the dumb witnesses which would yield the true facts.

This was when Joanna missed Korpanski most of all. They would have sat and discussed the case, made a clear plan, always with that touch of humour and self-deprecation that marked Korpanski's attitude to work and his superior. He wasn't shy of teasing her, mocking her, at the same time providing stolid and unwavering support. Korpanski's loyalty sometimes even amazed her. She'd never quite got used to it. DC Alan King, who worked closest with her now, was bright and clever and tech-savvy. But he wasn't Korpanski who could put a smile on her face in the darkest of moments, when cases seemed insoluble. Maybe, she thought, she'd drop in on him on her way home. Just because he was still off sick didn't mean she couldn't pick his brains.

Dr Shilton rang back at four o'clock to say that Dr Roget, the forensic psychiatrist he had mentioned, had agreed to come and see their silent girl. 'She'll be in touch,' he said, adding, 'I'm sure she'll come as soon as she can. And she *will* be a help. I promise.'

Joanna thanked him and tried to cover up the fact that she was sceptical.

Jason Spark returned to the station late afternoon and Joanna could tell from his demeanour that he'd drawn a blank. 'I'm really sorry,' he said, his natural ebullience for once suppressed. 'Most of the holiday lets are closed until Easter and the ones that are open don't have a girl and child staying.'

'The hotels?'

Leek had few hotels and none of any size. Again he shook his head. 'Drawn a blank there too,' he said glumly, adding, 'sorry.'

'No worries, Jason. You tried. She must have come from some-where nearby. I take it the house-to-house enquiries have turned up nothing either. According to Kitty and Austin there's no car parked near The Roaches so how did she get up there?' Jason 'Bright' Spark would love to have been able to answer. He looked crestfallen as it was. She took pity on him. 'OK, Jason. Thanks.'

He still looked chagrined. 'Sorry,' he said again.

She gave him a smile but the clock was ticking. They had contacted social services to take over the care of the child whose identity was still a mystery. They couldn't keep him here, being dandled by Sergeant George Alderley. He had other work to do.

DC Alan King was keeping an eye on the PNC to see whether any reports had surfaced that might be linked to their girl. He'd extended the search area countrywide but still drawn a blank.

At five thirty Karen Murphy from social services finally arrived to relieve one of their problems.

Joanna had known Karen for a number of years. Inevitably there were occasions when their paths crossed. Initially she had struck her as ineffectual with a high-pitched, squeaky voice and hesitant manner. She always seemed to put obstacles in the way of a solu-tion and appeared generally unhelpful. But during the last year something had happened. She had joined a local running club which had not only improved her physical appearance but seemed to have given her a new-found confidence and a way of dealing with problems.

Joanna gave her a potted explanation of how the girl and the toddler had come to their attention. Karen listened without comment. 'You don't even know where she comes from?'

'No. We don't think she's local but she could be from the Potteries – or anywhere. We can't keep the little boy here, Karen.'

'And you say there appears little to no rapport between the child and the woman?'

Joanna shook her head.

Karen took in a deep breath. 'I think a foster family might be the best solution for now. Just until we find out who he is and where his family are. If, as you say, the girl seemed to want to harm him we're perfectly justified in removing him from her care. Let me make a few phone calls, Joanna. Give me twenty minutes.' Then she smiled. 'I suppose I'd better take a look at him.'

Sergeant Alderley was reluctant to hand the little boy over to Karen. Over the course of the day the sergeant and the child had formed something of a bond and the little boy looked fondly at the burly policeman.

Karen sat down, the little boy on her lap. 'Hello, you,' she said. 'What's your name?'

At least the child made some gurgling noises for her, seeming to respond to the social worker's soft voice. He started pulling her hair and even laughed once or twice. He looked happy and contented as she pulled her phone out of her pocket and started talking to someone on the other end.

Minutes later she beamed at Joanna. 'Sorted,' she said. 'I'll take him round there myself. I suppose I'd better just inform the . . .' She hesitated before adding, 'Mother?'

Joanna shrugged. Who knew?

The girl appeared to be asleep. Her head, resting on her folded arms, lay flat on the desk. Her breathing was deep and regular. But she must have sensed their approach and lifted her head as they entered, her eyes registering the child in Karen's arms.

The social worker spoke to her, gently explaining that the little boy would be well looked after. The girl's eyes remained on her but it was impossible to say from her expression what effect the social worker's words were having.

Finally the girl gave one slight nod, showing she had understood, but that was all.

With a last glance back into the room, the little boy left in the arms of the social worker. But even his response was uninterpretable.

Joanna watched with a pang. She would have preferred to have seen the little boy leave, happy and responsive with a family member. Instead he was going to a halfway house, being parked there as his future was decided.

And who knew what that would be?

The entire process had taken up most of the day. Joanna held a second briefing, which was as unproductive as the first, a whole bunch of negatives to add to the girl's silence. The following day would be just as busy though hopefully bearing some result. The psychiatrist had been in touch and promised to come and see their girl, whom she already called 'her patient', in the morning. Hopefully *she* would be able to persuade her to talk and tell them her name at the very least. Otherwise they would have to use social media to appeal to the public and try and find out who she was and piece together the jigsaw.

Joanna dreaded the coming days.

For the time being their dumb girl was being housed in a cell. It wasn't ideal but with a possible charge of attempted assault of a minor hanging over her, as well as the evidence of bloodstained clothing, they had little choice. They had sent samples of her DNA to the lab together with the clothes.

By the time Joanna had written up her report it was almost nine o'clock.

But she wasn't ready to go home just yet.

SEVEN

D etective Sergeant Mike Korpanski's house was a smart, modern, detached place on an estate where he lived with his wife, Fran, and their two children, Richard (Ricky) and Jocelyn (Joss), though Ricky hoped to head off for university later this year. Fran Korpanski answered the door with a smile that failed to thaw her face. She looked tired, unhappy and strained. Maybe having her husband home all the time, as well as her work as a nurse, was proving taxing. 'Joanna,' she said, with undisguised hostility, an icicle tone and zero welcome. The two women eyed each other. How Korpanski's wife had surmised that Joanna held some responsibility for her husband's injuries was beyond her. But then in Fran Korpanski's eyes Joanna was responsible for anything bad that happened to her husband. Fran jerked her head in the direction of their lounge. From upstairs she could hear the sound of thumping music, presumably one of the children.

Korpanski was sitting on the sofa watching TV and he, at least, looked delighted to see her. 'Jo,' he said, almost jumping up to hug her, and his look of delight warmed her from head to toe. *God, she missed him.*

'Mike.' She greeted him with a hug and sat down opposite him in the armchair. His leg was propped up in front of him on a stool, some of the ironwork that was fixing the bones exposed. His face too registered the loss of weight and he looked – a word she had never thought she would apply to DS Korpanski – vulnerable. She averted her eyes from the leg and he switched the television off.

'I am so bored,' he confessed. 'Lying here is bloody well killing me.' He glanced down at his leg. 'One more operation, Jo, to take some of the pins out and then I can start bearing some of my weight.' He aimed a venomous glance into the corner. 'Off those ruddy crutches. Then a few more weeks and I'll be fully weight-bearing.' He grinned. 'Can't wait. And then, a few sessions at the gym and I'll quickly be back to normal.'

She pretended to swallow the fable. 'Yeah.' But the look they exchanged told a different story. Of concern and unhappiness, apprehension and pain. Still, they clung to the fantasy.

'So?' he prompted, sensing there was a purpose behind her visit. 'What is it?'

'Actually, Mike,' she said, 'I haven't come on a sick visit. No grapes or flowers, I'm afraid. I've come to pick your brains.'

'Just the therapy I need,' he said and leaned back, his arms folded behind his head.

She filled him in, about the child and the dumb woman who, it appeared, had tried to harm the child, the fact that she wouldn't or couldn't speak, the remoteness of the location combined with the absence of a vehicle nearby and lastly about the blood spatter on both their clothes.

He looked interested. 'So what have you done with her?'

'We have her at the station under police protection and we've called in a forensic psychiatrist.'

'A psychiatrist?' He couldn't conceal the grin that was spreading across his face.

'Well, what else?' she snapped and then apologized. 'Sorry.' She followed that up with a sigh. 'When did I acquire such a short fuse?'

'You've always had a short fuse, Jo.'

She shot him a look but his mouth was softened with humour rather than with criticism.

'And the little boy?'

'He's being placed with a foster family.'

Korpanski was silent for a moment, his face screwed up in concentration, while Joanna waited. Half Polish by descent, his features were blunt, his head almost square and his build decidedly muscular – though less so since the accident. Before, he had been a regular at the gym, preserving a powerful physique. He looked vulnerable since the accident. Korpanski had been run over deliberately by a driver intent on taking him out of the equation of a planned crime, to wreak vengeance on the DI who had put a felon behind bars. As the crime had largely involved Joanna she felt responsible. He had nearly lost his leg and, looking at him now, she realized it would be a long time before he regained that muscular build for which he was renowned and made criminals think twice before taking him on. Korpanski had always felt protective towards her and she missed having him around.

She eyed him. He might have been injured. He might be thinner, part of his muscly bulk temporarily reduced. But his thick, black, wiry hair and the dark eyes which could light up with amusement were the same. That big, square face still looked strong and his sense of humour undamaged. He and Joanna might have started out on the wrong foot, but over the years this had morphed into a respect for each other, which in turn had resulted in regard and ultimately affection. He might have lost some of his physically powerful presence but underneath he was the same stubborn but clear-thinking detective sergeant. Logical, pedantic, loyal and experienced. Joanna felt a huge impulse to hug him to her and will him back to the station. But these injuries would not heal in a hurry. The leg, with its exposed external fixation, had been shattered in the accident. For a time there had been a question of its being amputated. Looking at it, Joanna still shuddered at the thought.

'So,' he ventured. 'Either your quiet lady is the child's mother which you say seems unlikely as the little one expresses more affection for George.' He chuckled at the thought before sobering up quickly. 'But if she's not the kiddy's mother has she abducted him?'

She waited.

'But if he's been abducted how come his mother hasn't reported him missing?'

'It's worrying me,' she admitted.

His frown deepened. 'Could he be kidnapped and the mother's keeping quiet in the hope that a ransom gets him back safely?'

'She doesn't look like a kidnapper.'

Korpanski raised his eyebrows. 'So kidnappers have a "look"?'

Chastened, she returned to the facts. 'Besides, chucking him over a ledge is hardly the action of a kidnapper, is it?'

Korpanski shook his head then proffered another potential explanation. 'Did you say she could have been wearing a nanny's uniform?'

Joanna thought about this suggestion but only for a moment. 'Maybe.'

Korpanski was silent for a minute, a frown deeply scoring his forehead. 'Could she be a vengeful mistress?'

This time it was she who raised her eyebrows.

Korpanski continued. 'I don't mean to be hard, but chucking a kid off a remote cliff seems a weird way to want to polish him off. I mean, it's unreliable. For a start, someone might see her.'

'Someone did,' she said.

'And that' – Korpanski wagged his finger at her – 'is exactly what I mean. Almost advertising her intent. The child could have lain there, seriously hurt, for days. No. It wasn't an attempt on the little one's life. It can't have been. It was something else.'

'What?'

'I don't know. Drawing attention to something?'

She tried to turn it into a joke. 'Why not just ring one oh one?'

'Hmm.' He was running out of ideas so changed the subject. 'How's little Jakob?'

She shook her head. 'A handful. How the heck do people have more than one child, Mike? He's up at night, wakeful, wants to be held twenty-four seven, preferably by his grandparents or doting father rather than his mother.'

Korpanski's eyes were alert. He knew that throughout the preg-
nancy Joanna had been worried she and the baby might not bond.

Joanna continued as though she hadn't noticed Korpanski's
concerned expression. 'He screams if he doesn't get the attention
he wants. He's permanently hungry.' She stopped. 'That wasn't
what you were asking, was it?'

He shook his head and omitted to speak the word out loud.
Bonding.

'It's taking time,' she admitted. 'I'm not quite there yet.'

That provoked another grin. 'You will get there, Jo.'

'Matthew loves him enough for both of us.'

'Never,' he said firmly. 'Doesn't work like that.'

'If you say so.'

'So then. About this girl and the little boy. What's your next
step?'

'Wait and see what the psychiatrist has to say, I suppose. See
if she can get the girl to talk. She's promised to come over
tomorrow.'

Korpanski leaned back on the sofa. He was beginning to look
tired and she saw that he was nowhere as close to a full recovery
as he'd made out. She watched him silently for a moment as his
eyelids drooped.

'We can do this another time, Mike.'

His eyes jerked open. 'Sorry.'

'No, I'm sorry. I shouldn't be . . .'

'Don't worry,' he said. 'Fran'll chuck you out as soon as she
can.' It was the first time he had acknowledged the hostility between
his wife and his DI. And, as with all admissions, it put them on
a new footing, almost fellow conspirators rather than colleagues.

And then he returned to the questions that had brought her here,
into the lion's den. 'Intriguing little case, isn't it?'

'The case might not be so little if those bloodstains mean
anything.'

Korpanski nodded. 'Yeah, you're right. Apart from the obvious:
who is she? Who is the child? Are they related? How did she get
up there? Why did she go up *there* in particular? I suspect that
what you're really wondering is what is the backstory. Where has
she come from? Has a crime been committed?' He looked
thoughtful. 'How much blood was there?'

'Quite a bit on the cardigan sleeve. Just spattering on the skirt of her dress. And there was spatter on the little boy's dungarees too. Whatever happened he or at least his clothing was in the vicinity when an injury was inflicted.'

'Worrying,' he said. 'A crime scene waiting for you to unearth and you're not getting much help, are you? And then there's the sixty-four-million-dollar question. Why has no one reported a girl and a child missing? Is it because someone is injured or dead? Are they the source of the blood? If so, has she committed the assault? What purpose could have been achieved by heading up to The Roaches and hurling him off the edge? Temporary madness? Alcohol? Drugs?'

She shook her head.

'Why is she mute? Why won't she speak? Your psychiatrist should be able to shine a light on all these questions. Maybe by tomorrow you'll have *all* the answers.' He gave another tired grin accompanied by a wide yawn. 'I wish I was back at work, Jo, getting my teeth into this one.'

Right on cue, the door opened. Fran stood back against it and waited. Joanna could take a hint. She rose, thanked Mike, rejected the impulse to kiss him and left. As she passed Fran gave her a withering look which Joanna returned with a blandly neutral half-smile. At the door she paused, turned back and spoke impulsively, 'Can't wait to have you back.'

His eyes were already closed.

Korpanski looked vulnerable.

Fran saw her out, accusation and dislike firing her eyes right up until she slammed the front door behind her.

EIGHT

10.05 p.m.

The house was quiet as she let herself in. The lights in the sitting room had been dimmed. She tiptoed inside. Matthew was sprawled on his back, asleep on the sofa, his blond hair ruffled, glinting in the light. His mouth was open as he exhaled with a shallow snore. Across his chest lay Jakob in blue Babygro, plump-faced and with Matthew's blond curls, his face turned to the side, equally unconscious to the world. She sat back on the chair opposite and watched them, not wanting to break the spell, feeling a swell of love for the pair of them. The quiet peace of a father with his child. Such trust in those two lives entwincd. But it turned her thoughts back to the little boy in the pushchair. Who had he trusted? The enigmatic girl who had appeared to want to hurt him? From what she had seen of the little boy he had appeared trustful – perhaps too trustful – but is that necessarily a good thing? Is not trust preserved for close family, parents, grandparents, a familiar childminder – a mechanism of self-protection? An instinct that keeps them safe?

Neither Matthew nor Jakob was aware of her presence as she continued musing.

What a shame that the child was too young to tell them his tale, leaving them to unearth any evidence or a crime scene.

She shifted her attention back to the scene playing out in front of her. Matthew's long legs were stretched out in front of him. Although he was asleep his arm held his son tightly and she knew if she touched either of them that both would be instantly alert. But for now neither stirred. Both chests rising and falling, in unison, it seemed, father and the son Matthew had longed for, both exhausted and relaxed. She was reluctant to disturb either of them.

And then the inevitable happened. Perhaps belatedly sensing her presence, Matthew stirred and then Jakob came to with a loud roar.

'Hey.' Matthew was addressing his son, not her. He kissed the soft, blond head. Jakob would have his father's colouring. The blond hair and maybe his father's green eyes too unless he retained her blue eyes.

Now Matthew settled his son and turned his attention to her. 'Hey,' he said again. 'How's your day been?'

As was usual with her, instead of launching into what would have been a long and complicated narrative, she went straight to the heart of her curiosity. 'Matt,' she said, crossing the room, bending down and kissing his mouth, then the top of her son's head, 'what do you know about mutism?'

He sat up, gave a little chuckle, his smile creasing the corners of his wide, generous mouth. 'As I'm a pathologist, my darling, my patients are *necessarily* mute. Does that answer your question? I suspect not,' he said, mischief lighting his eyes as Jakob watched them both, agog.

'No, it does not.'

He gave the matter a little more serious thought. 'Well, if it isn't a lifelong condition you'd probably need to talk to a psychiatrist. If it isn't organic or due to injury or insult – and by that I mean disease, a stroke or something – then it's usually hysterical. Or stubbornness. I'd expect a psychiatrist to sort it out. Not the police.'

'One's coming over tomorrow.'

He looked intrigued. 'How come you've got involved at all?'

She gave him a potted version of the circumstances of the girl being brought to the police station.

'Weird,' he said. 'Poor little chap. What's happened to him?'

'Social services have placed him with a foster family.'

'So you'll know all tomorrow.' He bent and kissed his son's head. 'Clever mummy,' he said. 'Not only going to solve an impossible crime but now working with a psychiatrist.'

She couldn't help but laugh. 'Not exactly. Talking about tomorrow, are you at work?'

'Yeah.'

'So . . .?' Jakob was watching them both now with large, round, serious eyes flitting from one to the other.

'Mum and Dad.'

Matthew's parents had moved to a bungalow minutes away from them and took on more than their fair share of childcare. Initially blaming Joanna for breaking up their son's first marriage, they had resented her, not even thawing when she and Matthew had married. But with Matthew's father retiring from his job as a GP, they had moved nearer and their grandson had papered over the cracks in their relationship with their second daughter-in-law. All had been forgiven, though they would never be close friends. Joanna's place was, in their view, the home, with the little boy. This devotion to her career was the source of some pursing of the lips and silent scolding. But the upside was that they had much to do with their grandson's care. And little Jake? He adored his paternal grandparents – which was a good thing as Joanna's own mother was not maternal. And her father, Christopher, or 'Kit' Piercy, who had left when she'd been young, had died of a heart attack, brought on, her mother insisted, by the young 'floozy' he'd subsequently set himself up with. Christopher Piercy had always insisted he never wanted to grow old. And he hadn't.

She picked Jakob off his father's chest to a protest but it was only mild and accompanied by a fist in his mouth which didn't quite smother the yawn. 'Has he had his last feed?'

Matthew shook his head.

The next three-quarters of an hour were spent with a feed, a change of nappy and some crooning of his favourite lullaby sung by both mother and father. Not exactly Brahms or particularly melodic, it was their rendition of Mary Poppins' 'Feed the Birds'.

Eventually Jakob's eyelids were too heavy for him to hold open. His whole body relaxed and Joanna put him into his cot with a kiss. 'Goodnight, little fellow.'

Matthew was wide awake when she returned to the sitting room – and curious. She gave him a few further details ending with, 'I expect I'll have a lecture about it tomorrow from the psychiatrist so I'll be able to fill you in.'

Matthew's eyes still held the sparkle of mischief. 'After all the "no comment" interviews I'd have thought you would have been used to silence.'

She shook her head.

He couldn't resist further pulling of her leg. 'Some men,' he said, smirking and dropping his arm around her, 'would pay a lot of money for a few hours of mutism.'

She satisfied herself with her reply. 'Some women too.'

They were quits.

NINE

Wednesday 17 March, 6 a.m.

They were woken by the usual human alarm clock – Jakob stirring – and in less than five minutes it had turned into a loud holler for his breakfast. Early morning pillow talk had stopped from the moment he'd been born.

Joanna, yawning, picked him up while she heated the bottle,

watching his face, that beautiful smooth skin, cheeks still flushed from the warmth of his cot, plump as they sucked the milk. Joanna had felt very proud of herself that she had breastfed this greedy little boy for almost three months before succumbing to the bottle and facing the fact that for her to return to work it was a necessity. Immediately life had become easier, times between feeds stretching nearer to the recommended four hours and the evening feed gradually morphing towards lasting until morning.

How could anyone want to hurt a child like this? Jakob's still-blue eyes stared up at her, fixing into her own with a trusting gaze. They say that a mother's, father's or carer's face imprints into a baby's memory. So what about the little boy? What had imprinted into *his* memory?

She finished the feed, changed his nappy and sat him in a baby chair while she ate her breakfast. Jakob played with a line of plastic pigs stretched across the front of the chair, though whether it was by accident or design that he sent them spinning was almost impossible to tell. Certainly the movement made him chuckle.

Matthew emerged in a navy suit, still knotting his tie. 'Court,' he explained. 'Evidence in a granny neglect case.' He poured himself a large mug of coffee. 'Carer,' he explained further, 'paid by the family.' He rounded the breakfast bar to plant a kiss on his son's head. 'They paid the bills,' he said, looking momentarily despondent, 'but they never visited. Never checked up on the old girl.'

With no understanding of what his father was saying, Jakob started chuckling. Matthew wagged a finger at him. 'And here is the model, little boy,' he said severely. 'It's not enough just to pay the carers. You need to watch over them too.'

Inexplicably, with the unpredictability of a baby, Jakob's face screwed up and he looked on the verge of one of his speciality howls.

'Mum and Dad will be here in a minute.' Matthew kissed her on the mouth. 'Mmmm,' he said. 'Marmite?' And he was gone, his car reversing down the drive.

Matthew's parents, or Peter and Charlotte, as they liked to be called, turned up five minutes later and took over the childcare, barely disguising their disapproval as Joanna flew out of the door. 'Sorry. Have to go. Busy case. And Matthew's in court.'

To be fair to Peter and Charlotte, they held Jakob to the window,

waving goodbye as she too backed down the drive. She flashed
her lights and waved back before she manoeuvred out onto the
main road, heading into town. Before Jakob had been born,
actually while she'd been pregnant, she'd cycled the couple of
miles into the police station. Now she always felt she was on catch
up, in a hurry, should be somewhere else. Late, late. Always late.
Like Alice's White Rabbit.

Her first duty was to visit the girl, make sure she was all right.
She'd been housed overnight in a cell. It was relatively comfortable with a flushing loo and plenty of blankets but the girl had
still been locked in. It wasn't ideal. Joanna peeped in through the
Judas window and wondered what time the psychiatrist would
arrive. The girl was sitting on the edge of the bed, staring at the
wall opposite. Her face was expressionless. Joanna unlocked
the door and entered, beginning by asking her whether she'd slept
OK. She didn't really expect a reply. The girl's eyes on her felt
cold and unresponsive and she was, as anticipated, silent.

Joanna was beginning to get used to the fact that there was no
verbal response – whatever questions she posed. It was up to her
to *imagine* what the girl might be thinking. But her expression
was certainly guarded, watchful and wary as Joanna sat beside her
in the cell and began with an apology.

'I'm really sorry about this, keeping you here overnight. We
didn't know where else you could be kept and this way seemed
safest.' The girl blinked but otherwise there was no response.

'We've arranged for a psychiatrist to come and interview' – *was
that even the right word?* – 'you sometime this morning to see if
she can help.' *Unlock your tongue.* This time the girl's mouth
definitely twisted into an expression of cynicism as though she
mocked the idea. Her eyes remained trained on Joanna's face as
though trying to guess what she would say next. She still looked
pale, colourless, anaemic. Ill. But Joanna reassured herself with
the fact that she had been seen by a doctor who had passed her
as fit to detain.

'We're hoping that the psychiatrist can help us to decide what
to do with you next.' She tried out a smile. 'Where you should
go and if any treatment or therapy is suggested.'

She was playing a game. Joanna was sure of it.

'You see,' she continued smoothly, playing this 'game' alongside

her, 'we do have a quandary here. First of all there is the suggestion that you could have harmed the little boy.' There was a slight
shrug of the thin shoulders. Indicating a denial? 'As we don't know
who you are, neither do we know who the child is, whether you
are related or not, you understand our concern? And then there is
the question of the blood we found on some of your clothing.
It suggests you might have been involved in some sort of incident . . .' She scoured the girl's face for any sign of unease or
guilt. 'There is always the possibility that the blood is the result
of an assault. A crime.' She paused, aware that this suggestion
might provoke a response.

But the girl's face remained impassive. A waxwork who now
was looking past her, somewhere into the distance. Joanna was
beginning to realize that the way this girl dealt with the situation
was to abstract herself. Shut it all out.

'You see we don't even know how you got out there to The
Roaches or even where you came from.' She moved an inch or
so closer and the girl flinched. 'Why there? What were you going
to do to him?'

Without warning the girl began to shake. It was barely percep-
tible at first, little more than a shiver but it continued and increased
as did her breathing rate. Her jaw tightened and she seemed to
draw herself in, rocking now, backwards and forwards. At the same
time she opened her mouth and gave sharp inhalations. It was like
a panic attack. Her mouth clamped shut, tighter than before. And
then she controlled it; her breathing rate slowed and her cat's eyes
resumed their watchful, wary look. And Joanna knew she would
not extract one single word from her. But she'd realized something
else. This girl might be giving an outward appearance of being
simply un-cooperative but inside she was in turmoil. Maybe a
psychiatrist was the right choice.

Reluctantly she rose feeling the girl's eyes follow her to the
door with something of an appeal as though she was silently
reaching out. Her hand on the door Joanna turned and waited but
after a moment the girl's eyes dropped and Joanna left.

Back in her office she rang Karen Murphy to see how the place-
ment of the little boy had gone. Karen responded in her chirpy
voice, speaking quickly.

'He's fine. He's well settled with a local family who have much experience in this sort of thing. We've used them loads of times before in emergencies. They're a great couple. He seems happy enough. They say he's eating well and he can stay there for as long as it takes. Until we find his family or find out who he is.'

'I don't suppose there's any clue as to his identity?'

'No-o. Hasn't anyone come forward, reported him missing?'

'No.' And Joanna felt that familiar anxiety. Someone should have reported him missing. The child's mother, father, grandparent, childminder, aunt, uncle. Anyone related to him. A neighbour, perhaps? She took a punt. 'You have lots to do with various families. I don't suppose you've any idea who he is?'

Karen, newly confident nowadays, was not above pulling Joanna's leg. 'You want me to do your job for you, Jo?'

'If you're offering. I don't seem to be getting very far.'

That drew a tight little chuckle. 'It's early days yet, Jo. And just for the record, I'm definitely not offering to do your bit as well as mine. How is the mother?'

'We don't know she is the mother.'

'No – sorry. An assumption. You know who I mean. How is she? Is she talking yet?'

'Not a bloody word.'

'I'll keep you updated as to the little boy. Keep in touch and if you find out who he is we can maybe reunite him with his family.'

'That's our hope. In the meantime your foster family can keep him safe.'

'Yes. And you'll keep me up to date?'

'Of course.'

'I'll tell you what I will do, Joanna, that might bear fruit. I'll contact other social workers in the area. Considering what the child's fate could have been it's possible that there has been contact between the family and social services in the past. We may be able to find something out that way.'

'Thanks.'

11 a.m.

It was time to brief the few officers she had assigned to work on the case. So far it was a small team. This would be increased if needed but at the moment she had a sufficient force. DC Alan King remained at her side.

'OK,' she began. 'Well, to revise what we know, or rather what we don't know, let's focus on two areas. One: who is this girl whose identity remains crucial? We hope a forensic psychiatrist will attend sometime today and give us her opinion on why she isn't talking and what can be done about it. Until we know who she is any questions about her circumstances remain unanswered. Two: what is her relationship to the child? Did she really mean to harm him? What took her to such a remote spot and how did she get there? And then there's the question of the bloodstained clothes. I don't need to spell out to you why this is an area of interest.

'PCs Kitty Sandworth and Austin have taken the dogs up to the area surrounding The Roaches but have found nothing, not even a car.' She turned to the map reflected on the screen. 'It's a few miles from Leek town centre and more than ten miles from Buxton. There is a bus from Hanley calling in at Leek that goes past The Roaches, but the first bus would have reached The Roaches at round nine. She was spotted by our walker at seven thirty a.m. – too early for her to have caught that bus. There are earlier ones from Hanley but they stop at Leek. Although her clothes were damp they weren't soaked; neither were the little boy's dungarees and there was heavy rain on Monday night. So she must have had shelter overnight, arriving at The Roaches early Tuesday morning. She was wearing a dress that could easily be a nurse or nanny's uniform but no coat.'

She paused and addressed PC Bridget Anderton. 'Bridget, maybe you could go round the taxis. See if she got up there using a local firm. If you get no joy there maybe try the Potteries or Buxton. She could have come from either direction.'

Bridget flashed one of her warm smiles and bent her head over her notebook. She was a hardworking, reliable woman, conscientious in her work.

Joanna continued. 'Apart from finding out who the girl is and who the child is our concern is where did that blood come from? Is there a crime scene somewhere? An accident? Was she running away? Jason's already checked out the holiday lets and the hotels and drawn a blank and a nearby house-to-house has also drawn a negative. What troubles me is this: if someone is simply injured why haven't they reported it? And why has no one reported either the girl or the child missing? As far as we *know* she hasn't committed a crime. We can't charge her with anything.' She couldn't stop herself from adding, 'Yet.'

She had their full attention. 'So . . .'

She scanned the room, giving the assembled officers a chance to air any thoughts, before turning back to the whiteboard and making another attempt to lighten their mood. 'If you're wondering what I'm going to do with *my* day' – that provoked a few smiles – 'at one thirty this afternoon I'm speaking to local radio and press and at some point our psychiatrist will arrive.' She couldn't resist a smile. 'Maybe she can persuade our Jane Doe to speak.' She paused. 'And DC King will, as usual, be playing with the computer and seeing if he can get it to cough out the girl – or the child's – identity. Now. Any questions?'

There were some dubious looks but it was left to DC Gino Salvi, their half Italian newish recruit, to voice them. Somehow he thought that occasionally bringing in food from his parents' restaurant gave him licence to voice questions for all of them.

'Are you sending that bloodstained dress off for forensic analysis?'

'Yes. Done.' She paused. 'We're waiting for the results of the swab to see whether they are mother and child.'

She didn't yet share her instinct.

DC Salvi was nothing if not persistent. 'If it isn't *her* blood . . .'

'We'll soon know for certain.'

Salvi nodded and gave one of his broad Mediterranean grins.

TEN

Midday

It seemed a good omen that the psychiatrist arrived before the scheduled press conference.

George Alderley announced her. 'The shrink's here,' he said with a wink.

Joanna could only hope the psychiatrist couldn't hear.

Her wish was not granted. Two steps behind him walked a

slight, slim woman dressed in a pair of cream trousers and a black silk shirt. She had straight brown hair and a pale complexion. And from the straight line of her mouth she hadn't appreciated being called a 'shrink'.

'DI Piercy?' Her tone was soft and uncertain.

Joanna stepped forward and grasped her hand. 'Dr Roget. Am I glad to see you.'

The psychiatrist relaxed. 'That's nice,' she said. 'And my name is Claire.'

'Joanna.'

'Great.' Claire drew out a notebook. 'Dr Shilton has filled me in with some sketchy details. Is your girl still mute?'

'Yes.'

She gave a hint of a smile. 'So I can't begin with a name, can I?'

Joanna shook her head. 'I don't know how much Dr Shilton told you but she was found on the edge of The Roaches about to push a toddler in a pushchair over a ninety-foot drop.'

'Wow. Where is the child now?'

'Social services have taken him to a foster family.'

'Right. Well, I have *something* to write at least.' She scribbled for a moment or two before looking up, waiting for the rest.

'She was wearing wellington boots and a dark red dress that looked like a uniform. Nurse or nanny. The skirt of the dress had blood on it and there was blood on the sleeve of her cardigan. She wasn't wearing a coat.'

The psychiatrist's face changed as she absorbed this detail. Joanna read alarm in the pale face. 'A significant amount of blood?'

Joanna nodded.

'And on the child?'

'He looks about two years old. There was some blood spray on his dungarees.'

'Has any crime been reported?'

'No. Nothing's shown up on the PNC. No reports of a woman and child missing or of an assault. We don't know how she got up there. It was too early for her to have travelled by bus from Leek; similarly too early to have caught the first bus from Buxton and there's no sign of her having driven a car up there. Her clothes were damp but not that wet. We don't think she slept rough but she got there somehow.'

'Maybe someone dropped her off?'

'So far no one's come forward. I'm making a public appeal later today.'

Claire nodded.

'We're checking the taxi firms but no luck so far. We don't know why she went there.'

Claire looked sharply at her but was silent for a moment, absorbing all the information. Then she said, 'Do you want the good news or the bad?'

Joanna shrugged.

'The good news is that statistically this mute state is likely to be temporary.'

Joanna could guess the bad.

'Reversal is likely to take some time if it's due, as is suggested . . .' She looked apologetically at Joanna. 'If it's connected to some trauma.'

And a psychiatrist's time frame was likely to be far more generous than the police's.

'Well, she's all yours.'

Joanna led her to the interview room and returned to her desk.

Officers were reporting in with information all the time and Joanna was marking it down.

Taxis – negative.

Hospitals – negative.

Holiday lets and hotels and surrounding properties – negative.

No reports on the police computer that could be connected.

And Alexandra Clothing had practically laughed when Hannah Beardmore had questioned them about the girl's uniform. 'They sell thousands of them in a year both online and in their retail outlets to all sorts of people. There's no way they could narrow it down to a specific outlet.'

So Joanna knew that to focus on this point would be a waste of time and resources.

This was the woman who didn't speak and didn't exist and the source of the blood the same. Didn't happen, didn't exist. No one missed either of them . . . No one who was able to report it.

An hour later the psychiatrist emerged and Joanna waited anxiously for her opinion.

She closed the office door behind her before asking, 'We-ell?'

The psychiatrist was in no hurry. 'Let's sit down, shall we?' She opened her notebook to a page with writing scribbled across it.

What had the psychiatrist learnt that she had not?

Then Claire looked across and smiled at her. 'I could do with starting with a brief explanatory note.'

If you must. Joanna was struggling to hide her impatience.

'Selective mutism is usually an attempt to blank out some trauma, a memory. In blanking out that memory the subject withdraws from reality.'

'Is this what she is doing?'

'Very possibly. The circumstances in which she was found, together with the state of her clothing, would indicate this is the case. And it would be an explanation for her silence. An extreme experience can, in some subjects, cause anxiety so debilitating that the subject is literally unable to either voice their thoughts or even formulate them inside their head, which means they can't even write their words down. The words simply don't come in any sort of sense or order but scramble inside their head.'

'Are you saying after an hour that you got *nothing* out of her?'

The psychiatrist was unruffled. 'I got no verbal response; neither did she write anything down.'

'So?'

'I had some non-verbal indications when I spoke about various subjects.'

'Is she on drugs?'

'I don't think so,' Claire Roget said. 'She seems alert; her pupils look normal. There's no sluggishness in her manner. We can, of course, test her blood for various substances, but I don't think she's drugged.' She hesitated before uttering her next sentence. 'I think she's deeply traumatized.'

'Which leaves us with a quandary. If she's traumatized somewhere, there is an incident which caused this. You see my problem, Dr Roget?'

'Claire,' she corrected. 'And of course I do.' She hesitated. 'I daresay you have other means of finding out what that trauma is?'

'It would be a lot easier if she simply told us,' Joanna snapped. 'We could waste days waiting for her to speak. And in the meantime what can we do? Just wait until she decides to tell us what has happened while possibly someone is bleeding to death or lying injured? What do we do with her? What do we do with the child?'

Claire Roget managed a smile. 'Honestly, Joanna, I'll do what I can.' She hesitated before proffering her next sentence. 'I do have a suggestion.'

'I'm all ears,' Joanna said through gritted teeth.

'I can admit her to the secure ward at Greatbach Psychiatric Unit.'

'And?'

'And start treatment.'

'What treatment?' Joanna asked curiously.

'Start her on a course of anxiolytics and some psychotherapy. It's going to take a few weeks for them to kick in.'

'OK, well if that's your recommendation I'm with it.' Joanna was already formulating a plan. 'I suppose in the meantime I can put out an appeal through the media. We can get some results on the girl's clothing, a soil expert on any debris on the pushchair wheels. Take a look at the child's clothing.' She couldn't resist a cynical chuckle to herself. 'I wonder who'll speak first – the child or our mute.'

The psychiatrist gave her a polite smile.

'One question, Claire: is she likely to be a danger to others?'

'To be honest – I don't know. I'm not a clairvoyant. I can't know – not for certain. I can't even tell you whether she actually would have pushed that child's pushchair over the edge. Until we know a bit more about her, who she is and what her backstory is, I can't tell you anything, but I very much doubt that she'll be a danger to the wider community. I'm not really worried on that score.'

Joanna gave a sigh of resignation. 'Well, you do your bit and I'll do mine. Between us perhaps we can get at the truth.'

Claire stood up and shook her hand. 'We'll send a car for her this afternoon and admit her to Greatbach.' She ended politely by saying, 'It's nice to have met you.'

'You too.'

In one way Joanna was relieved to have someone else take responsibility for their silent girl. But when the psychiatrist had gone frustration took over. They had still achieved nothing and even though her degree was in psychology, her degree of faith in the powers of psychiatry to solve their problem was not high.

For a while she stood in front of the map of Staffordshire and its borders, Cheshire and Derbyshire. It was a vast area, from town to city, moorland to streets, hills, valleys, reservoirs. If only she could hover, like a drone, and find out what lay beneath.

And now it was time to harness the power of the media.

ELEVEN

1.30 p.m.

They were waiting for her, cameras at the ready, plenty of mobile phones recording her words, fewer notepads these days. There were some familiar stalwarts, faces she recognized from previous encounters. Richard Corby, crime reporter from the *Sentinel*, two others from the *Manchester Evening News*, a couple from the *Birmingham Post* and others, presumably from the nationals, whom she did not recognize, plus a camera from *Midlands Today*.

She launched in without preamble and gave them the bare bones.

'Early on the morning of Tuesday the sixteenth this woman . . .'

She paused before making her appeal. 'We are naturally concerned for this lady, the little boy and the circumstances which led up to these events.'

She was aware that she'd hidden behind a euphemism: *the circumstances*. But the details you omit from an investigation can be just as important as the details you reveal. Someone out there could make the connection.

There was a plethora of questions – who, when, what, where, why? – all of which Joanna fended off with her media training.

But when she turned back to view the face on the screen in detail, absorbing the girl's pale, bedraggled look of anxiety, her involuntary thought was that this was the face of a victim rather than a villain.

'Where is the girl now?' The question came from the back of the room, a female reporter, Asian, with silky black hair, one of those she did not recognize.

'She's being transferred to a secure psychiatric unit for the time being for some treatment in the hope that her speech might return.'

That provoked another question, this time from Richard Corby, the *Sentinel* reporter, whose question was, as usual, blunt. 'What treatment?'

She side stepped him. 'I'm leaving that part of it to the professionals.'

'Do you think her speech will return? Is it a deliberate evasion of answers to your questions?' The *Birmingham Post* this time. A blonde woman with large, black-rimmed glasses.

'Obviously I can't answer that.' She felt compelled to add, 'We hope that at some point her speech will return and she can . . .' She hesitated, rejecting the phrase *help us with our enquiries* as sounding too accusatory. Instead, she said, 'Recover her power of speech.' After all, what could they charge her with?

One of the older reporters sitting on the front row spoke. 'Do you believe her reluctance to speak is the result of trauma or a crime?'

This was a little too near the truth. Joanna answered cautiously. 'I can't comment. It would be pure conjecture. We are hoping the forensic psychiatrist will be able to answer all our questions in time. For the moment we want any member of the public who recognizes our lady or the little boy to contact us. Please.'

A girl sitting near the back, in ripped jeans and grey hoodie, asked the next question. 'Where is the child now?'

'He is currently being cared for by a foster family and under the responsibility of social services.' She turned back to the image. 'We don't have a name for him. All I can tell you is he appears Caucasian, about two years old, in good health, and is being well cared for. He is safe. We have taken the decision to release his photograph in the hope that he will be reunited with his family.'

The girl in the ripped jeans gave Joanna a sharp look. 'Why isn't he with the girl? Isn't she his mother?'

That was more difficult to answer but Joanna fended it neatly. 'We're checking their DNA to see if they're related. If the girl is the child's mother we want her to be well before resuming her son's care.'

Richard Corby from the *Sentinel* gave her a look of incredulity. 'Are you saying this girl has said nothing? Nothing?' he repeated.

'Not spoken a single word.'

'And is this her condition? I mean is she normally mute?'

'We don't know that,' Joanna said testily. 'The psychiatrist's opinion is that her apparent inability to speak is the result of anxiety or some trauma. We can only know for certain if or when the psychiatrist ventures an opinion after spending some time assessing her. Or . . .' She hesitated. 'We discover the girl and the little boy's backstory.'

Looking round the sea of faces, she could read them. Many were dubious; some reflected her own scepticism. All were curious. As was she. Good. The more column inches or soundbites they put out there the sooner they would have some answers.

She thanked them all for coming and slowly the reporters dispersed, probably already penning their headlines.

By the time she left the room word came through that their mystery girl had been successfully transferred to the psychiatric unit in the centre of Hanley.

TWELVE

Greatbach Secure Psychiatric Unit was renowned for taking some of the most complex psychiatric cases. While most of their work was routine: depression, personality disorders, patients with bipolar disorder as well as a progressive unit for patients with schizophrenia, psychosis and a plethora of other psychiatric diagnoses, they also treated patients whose psychiatric condition had resulted in crime.

So Joanna had handed over the two main characters in the drama to other agencies which left her with a void but it wasn't making her role any easier. She still had to work out the backstory.

There was no point in being impatient with the forensic lab for results. The scientists would do their bit in their own time however much she tried to hurry them. Sometimes she could almost convince herself that the more impatience she displayed the slower they worked. A day could seem like a month while you waited. When the results leaked through they would start to unravel the answers. Paramount, in her mind, was the question of the relationship between the child and the girl. In the meantime they could only hope that the psychiatrist's skill would unlock the girl's mouth. That would be the swiftest route to solving their case. The first reports should appear on the news channels this afternoon and make it into the main six o'clock news bulletins.

By seven o'clock they had received more than three hundred calls which seemed to be mainly from grandmothers who hadn't seen their estranged daughters-in-law and grandchildren in months – sometimes years. It simply rubbed in the fact that many young women sever relationships with their in-laws when their marriages break up. When questioned most of the callers had been vague as to whether the child and/or woman bore any resemblance to the missing people. Many could be resolved with a quick phone call but other leads had to be followed up which would cost man hours. Added to that apparently hundreds of girls leave home every year and simply disappear. Joanna and the team worked late into the night and through the following day.

The breakthrough came early on the Friday.

The warden from a children's home in Shropshire rang and said the girl looked very much like a girl who had been in their care until four years ago.

Joanna spoke to him at length. The lead sounded promising enough for her to take a car together with DC Alan King and drive over to Market Drayton, a small town in Shropshire served by a canal and known for its deference to Robert Clive, otherwise known as Clive of India, who had attended Market Drayton Grammar School. Currently perceived in a less favourable light as a plunderer, being partly responsible for the formation of the British Raj, he was out of favour these days.

The children's home was on the edge of the town. A Georgian house, slightly rundown, with peeling paint and a worn front door but a pleasingly symmetrical Georgian façade. The door was answered by a man in his forties with a ponytail and a broad grin who introduced himself as Stuart Manning, the person who had contacted them. He led them into a shabby sitting room with bulky green sofas and a carpet that had seen better days before wine spills and cigarette burns. He closed the door behind him with deliberation. He didn't want anyone listening in.

'I'm not absolutely sure that it *is* her,' he said, frowning apologetically. 'I hope you haven't come here on a wild goose chase.'

Joanna tried to put him at his ease. 'It wouldn't be the first time.' She raised her eyebrows, cueing him in.

'We haven't seen Dodie for around four years. And as you know girls change very quickly between fifteen and twenty.' Something sad crossed his face. 'Particularly if they have developed a drugs or alcohol habit, or if they've been sleeping rough or got hauled into prostitution. I'm afraid many of our youngsters go down that road.' His face sagged as he faced reality. He looked worn and terribly tired. 'But we do our best.'

Stuart Manning scratched his head then looked at his fingers as though they might hold an answer to the itching. 'We do our best,' he repeated, 'but it isn't enough. It's never enough. We're no substitute for . . .'

Joanna might have sympathized but she was hoping this visit would provide them with some answers, so she cut in. 'Do you have a picture of Dodie? What was her second name?'

'MacFarlane,' Manning supplied. 'Yes. I fished it out for you from her records.' He gave a sad smile. 'We always hope, you know, that they'll come back one day, thank us for what we did – or tried to do.' He looked rueful. 'It hasn't happened yet.'

He flipped a photograph onto a small table which stood in the centre of the room. At the same time Joanna produced the photograph of their silent girl and put them side by side. She, Manning and Alan King pored over them, trying to decide. The picture was of a thin-faced girl, rebellion, hatred and resentment beaming out of her every pore. Even from the photograph Joanna sensed she would have been a difficult girl to manage.

'You were here then?'

'Yeah. She was always running away,' Stuart Manning said, scratching the corner of his mouth now. 'She just couldn't settle.'

'Can I keep this?'

'I'll make you a copy.'

'And this was taken when?'

'About four years ago. She was fifteen and disappeared every week – sometimes twice in a week. She was usually gone for a week or so. Sometimes almost a month. We rarely knew where she'd been or how she'd survived and she didn't want to tell us. This picture was taken a month or so before she left for good. The police were sick of looking for her. Have you any idea how many youngsters in care go missing every day?'

'Unfortunately I do. They keep us busy.'

'She came back when she felt like it. And then one day she didn't come back. Not ever.'

Joanna scrutinized the picture again. The hair was the same – long, thin, straight, mid-brown. The eyes were the same, tired of life. It was difficult to see whether they had the same amber flecks that made her eyes look cat-like but the shape of the face and skin tones were similar. She stood back, holding the picture at arm's length and narrowing her eyes. She couldn't be sure. It could be the girl. It might not be. They could use facial recognition techniques but they weren't a magic bullet. And the photo wasn't great.

'What were her circumstances?'

'She was taken into care when her mother died of a drugs overdose when Dodie was ten. She had been on the radar from six months old when she was found playing with a syringe and a packet of cigarettes. I'm only surprised she hadn't been taken into care from birth. She was born with Foetal Alcohol Syndrome. But then every opportunity is taken to keep the child with its natural parents – until it just gets too difficult and dangerous. But when Dodie's mother was clean she was a good mum.' Honesty compelled him to add, 'Considering.'

Joanna hardly needed to ask the next question but she did anyway. 'Father?'

Stuart Manning simply shook his head and that was answer enough.

'She went missing for the last time when?'

'Just over four years ago. We did inform the police. She was just fifteen.'

'So she'd be nearly twenty now.'

He bent down and scrutinized the two photographs again. 'I couldn't say for definite,' he said, looking up now, 'but they do look similar, don't they?'

Joanna could have cried at the hope in his voice; not that she was in a predicament but that she was still alive.

'Did she have any mental health problems?'

He blew out his cheeks. 'They all do, Inspector.'

'And problems with speech?'

That provoked a cynical huff. 'Not her. Think hind leg off a donkey. She never bloody shut up.'

'Had she ever been pregnant?'

Stuart Manning shook his head. 'No – that was one blessing. Half the girls here have to have a contraceptive injection every twelve weeks or we'd be inundated with abortions or babies. But Dodie – no. She showed nothing but contempt for boys.' He laughed. 'I actually saw her take a swing at a boy who got a bit too close for comfort once. She was a stroppy little thing. Character of iron. You couldn't help but admire her.' Honesty compelled him to qualify the statement. 'Sometimes.'

Joanna looked again at the photograph, handing it to Alan King who took it and regarded it without comment before handing it back to her, a frown puzzling his eyebrows. Joanna tried to read his expression – and failed. It was hard to describe the girl who had been in their custody as having a character of iron. It was hard to describe her as anything.

Joanna was silent while she thought. The story Stuart Manning was relating was hardly unexpected or unusual. The kids placed in care often were troubled individuals. Many of them runaways who got sucked into drugs, county lines, knife crime. They were the kids who joined gangs for some form of identity, who truanted from school, who often ended up producing children themselves who rolled out all the same characteristics that had blighted their own lives. Breaking the mould was too hard a hill to climb. Few did.

Manning disappeared for a couple of minutes, returning with a photocopy of the girl's picture. She and King stood up.

'Thanks for this. We'll keep in touch and let you know whether this is Dodie.'

Stuart Manning gave an awkward smile. 'Hope I've been of help.'

'Remains to be seen,' Joanna responded, 'but thank you anyway.'

And they left.

On the way home, feeling she should keep the psychiatrist in the picture, Joanna tried to call Claire at Greatbach. It took some time for the staff to track her down. They were almost back in the Potteries by the time she was connected and the psychiatrist was instantly apologetic.

'Joanna, how long have you been waiting? I'm so sorry. I should have given you my mobile. Not my office landline. You'd have a better chance of speaking to me within twenty minutes.' She sounded gay, happy – surprising when you considered her job, the responsibility that rested on those thin shoulders and the stress it must generate.

'How are you getting on with our young lady?' Joanna asked the question without much optimism, an emotion which was soon proved correct.

'I told you it would be a long job.' She sounded vaguely defensive. 'We've started her on medication, sent off blood tests and she's having daily sessions with our psychologist and some psychotherapy. We don't have any results back for you yet and no, she's not talking.'

'We should get the DNA back soon so at least we'll know if they are mother and son.'

'It'll be a start.' The brightness remained in the psychiatrist's voice.

'Yes, it's a start. I have a photograph and a possible identity for her. Is there any chance I could come in?'

Claire was quick to respond. 'Not just yet. She's just beginning to trust me.'

'Shall I email an image over then?'

'That could be helpful.'

Putting the phone down, Joanna was resentful. If the girl still wasn't responding how the hell could Claire Roget believe that she was 'beginning to trust' her?

But she had no better plan.

THIRTEEN

Joanna pinned the picture of Dodie MacFarlane next to the picture of their girl on the board and spent some time comparing them, trying to figure out whether they were the same girl. Maybe, she thought. The same thin face, stringy hair and above all that desperate face staring into the camera. But maybe not. Desperation was a common factor in the vulnerable. DC King was running the picture through a facial recognition programme but the photo Stuart Manning had given them was poor and he wasn't optimistic. Dodie's eye colour was indeterminate and a quick phone call didn't fill in that detail. Stuart Manning couldn't remember.

In the meantime a few results were starting to trickle in from the lab. A test for alcohol on their girl was negative, as was the test they'd run for drugs. Now they awaited the DNA results from both to see if there was a match as well as analysis of the bloodstains on the dress and cardigan. And there was always the possibility that they would find a match from a sample on the database.

They had emailed over a copy of their picture but the psychiatrist hadn't responded yet.

The samples from the pushchair wheels showed nothing but the dark, peaty moorland soil. Other than that they were clean. But the examination of the little boy's anorak was a bit more informative. Some long dark hairs had been found, which did not match with their silent girl's, together with cigarette ash and some staining that looked like dark furniture polish.

Joanna realized they were relying, more than ever, on some member of the public coming forward. But so far the calls that had now reduced to a trickle had not helped. And, unsurprisingly, even though they might have a name for their girl, they could not track down one single relative or even anyone who knew her apart from the warden. Some folk live beneath the normal range of radar and it seemed that Dodie MacFarlane was one of these.

And then, late on Friday, just as they were contemplating packing up for the weekend, they had a phone call from Stuart Manning that turned out to be unwelcome. 'I feel really bad about this,' he began and the next few words were enough to make Joanna's heart sink. 'I didn't think at the time.'

She could guess what was coming next.

'Dodie had tattoos on her knuckles.' He paused. 'You didn't mention them.'

'Don't tell me,' she said, inwardly groaning. 'Love and Hate?'

'Worse. F-U-C-K on the left and O-F-F on the right middle fingers. As you didn't mention them . . .' He left the sentence to hang in the air while Joanna pictured the girl's hands. White, clean. No tattoos. No swear words.

'There's something else.'

Go on, hit me with it.

'Dodie self-harmed.' He paused. 'I don't know whether this helps.'

'I'll check,' Joanna said, suddenly weary, 'but it looks as though *our* girl isn't *your* girl. I don't think it's Dodie, Mr Manning. But thank you for your help. It might have been . . .' She let the sentence trail away into nothing, just like the lead which had started out so promising.

'Shame. I would have loved to help you.' And then, naturally, Manning's thoughts turned back to the familiar. 'So I wonder what did happen to her.'

Her, Joanna thought, *and thousands of others supposedly 'in care'*. Sometimes it could seem like a misnomer but not through the fault of those who, like Manning, tried to help.

'We'll keep Dodie on our books,' she said, 'and let you know if she turns up.' Then she said her goodbye and put the phone down, sitting still at her desk while she chewed over the unwelcome news.

Even though she was certain that their girl's knuckles were undecorated, and neither did she have self-harming scars, she rang Greatbach just in case, feeling her mouth twist in anticipation of disappointment.

She was lucky enough to catch the psychiatrist, probably also preparing for the weekend. Claire laughed when Joanna asked her about the tattoos and signs of self-harming. But of course the girl's identity was not *her* primary concern.

'Absolutely not,' was her predictable response, adding an admonishment. 'I think I would have noticed those.' But she injected some sympathy when she added, 'So your girl isn't the one from Market Drayton.'

'Apparently not.'

'We-ell, to counter your disappointment I do have some good news.'

'She's talking?'

'Not exactly. Not yet. I did warn you this would be a long job.'

'So – the good news?'

'She is nodding and shaking her head so we are getting a yes or no response to our questions.'

Great, Joanna thought sourly. *Just great*.

But she'd learnt to be cautious rather than optimistic. And polite. 'Does that mean we can interview her provided the questions we ask anticipate' – she couldn't quite edit out the mockery – 'yes or no answers?'

Obviously she hadn't been quite subtle enough. The psychiatrist had picked up on her tone. 'Now, now, Inspector,' she reproved,

'I think an interview at this point would be unwise, don't you? It might set her right back.'

So what real use is this 'breakthrough'? Joanna couldn't help thinking. And if I can't question her under caution what's the point.

She schooled herself to calm down and moderated her enquiry. 'What sort of questions is she responding to?'

'Simple ones, so far.'

'As in?'

'Responses to whether she wants something to eat or a drink or to use the bathroom, stuff like that.'

Joanna was beginning to realize that *her* end result and the psychiatrist's were poles apart.

'We've time.'

'We do have a potential crime scene,' Joanna reminded her. 'Unexplained bloodstains.'

'But nothing concrete on your radar yet.' The psychiatrist's voice was calm and very controlled. A contrast to her emotion.

In Joanna's opinion this was far too casual an attitude. But she kept silent.

'Thanks. Anything else?'

'Not so far. I'll get back to you if I have any further news. In the meantime we'll keep her here.' Claire paused and Joanna sensed she was about to make a point. 'Detective . . .'

Joanna waited.

'You have no proof that a crime has actually been committed, have you? She didn't *actually* harm the child, did she? You can only surmise at her intent.'

'She was stopped,' Joanna said bullishly. 'And we have no explanation for the bloodstaining on her dress or her cardigan. It didn't come from her and is evidence of, at the very least, injury.' She couldn't help adding, 'Which she is refusing to explain.'

'But it's not necessarily the result of an assault *by* the girl. She could have been a witness which would account for her traumatized muteness.' The psychiatrist had a very precise way of speaking, enunciating her words in a way which sounded, to Joanna, as though she was scoring points. 'So in the end you have nothing.'

Joanna could feel her temper rising. *And I need* you *to tell me that?*

But she satisfied herself with a curt: 'No.'

'OK.' The psychiatrist might as well have said, *So I win.*

But Joanna wasn't quite ready to let go. Not yet. 'So you'll continue trying to get her to speak and extract some information from her. Her name and address would be a good place to start,' Joanna said sourly and put the phone down. Hard.

It rang again almost instantly. And this time it was the lab.

'Thought you'd like the result of the DNA run-through.'

'Go on.'

'The girl is not the child's mother. There is no DNA match. They aren't related. We'll email you a copy of the results.'

It was a step forward. She thanked the technician and put the phone down, sat back in her chair and thought, reading through the report in her email.

The progress of their investigation might be slow but she now knew two things. One was that their girl was *not* Dodie MacFarlane and there was no blood link between the child and their silent woman, which sort of pointed the way towards her being the little boy's nanny.

She was about to go and report to the team when another result pinged in from the lab. The blood found on the girl's dress, cardigan and the child's dungarees was all from the same source – his father.

She immediately rang the sender, Sophie Grayling.

'Hello, Inspector.' It was a light, breezy, feminine voice on the other end with a pleasing hint of Scots. 'So you got my email.'

'Yeah. Thanks. I wonder if you could tell me any more?'

'Caucasian male. Not sure of the age. The blood comes from the child's father.' Knowing the inspector's dislike of conjecture Sophie paused awkwardly before plunging in. 'Here at the lab we've been trying to put two and two together. The girl is unrelated and we have no reports of a toddler being abducted. So we wondered. Was she his nanny, maybe, or an au pair?'

Joanna smiled, feeling some optimism and good humour. 'You want my job?'

'No.' Sophie sounded flustered. 'I do not. But, you know, somehow, it's hard just to trot out results without wondering what significance they have.'

Joanna thanked her. They were taking baby steps forward but even baby steps can cover some distance.

In time.

FOURTEEN

A t least during the next briefing she had some facts to hand out. She'd come in on the Saturday, to Matthew's annoyance, but she'd needed the time to put her thoughts in order, with the result that she was well prepared for Monday morning's briefing, relaxed, swinging her legs from a table at the front, the officers either sitting around her or lounging against the wall, listening hard. All knew she would welcome relevant interruptions, the vital point being 'relevant'.

She'd begun by bringing the team up to date with the recent developments before directing them. 'What I want you to focus on now, guys, is this: why hasn't this little boy's absence been reported? As it appears his father is injured, where is his mother? Particularly worrying when it appears the little boy's life was possibly in danger. Our mute girl might be the little boy's nanny, so you can interview agencies who supply them.'

She frowned as she recalled the apparent lack of familiarity between girl and child when she had carried the little boy into the interview room. While this aloofness seemed likely with their mute girl, it seemed odd in the child, who had, in fact, formed more of a connection with George Alderley than with the girl. Could that mean they were complete strangers?

She picked up her thread. 'Another alternative is has she abducted the child? Is this a kidnapping gone wrong? No crime scene has, as yet, turned up, which may be a good thing or it could be the opposite. Undiscovered. I think,' she continued, 'that the answers to all this will be found when we can identify our girl, so that is top of our list. The little boy is safe – for now – but I want him returned to his family ASAP.'

PC Jason Spark butted in. 'I take it our girl remains silent?'

She nodded, unable to suppress her cynicism. 'According to the psychiatrist she's "nodding and shaking her head" in response to simple questions like "do you want some lunch?" or "do you need to go to the toilet?".'

That resulted in titters and a few glum faces mirroring her own disdain.

'Anyone got anything else to report? Paul?' She turned to PC Paul Ruthin, a shy local lad hampered by a lack of height and still living with his mother in a terraced house in the town, his father having died when Paul was young. 'Over the weekend I revisited most of the homesteads in an eight-mile circumference to The Roaches,' he said, his findings trudging out in a marked moorlands accent. 'Obviously with some there was no answer.'

Mindful of the bloodstains, Joanna interrupted. 'Which properties were empty?'

PC Ruthin moved (self-consciously) to the map pinned up and pointed out a couple of farms and smallholdings. 'Some of these are second homes,' he said. 'Notably two cottages in Upper Hulme and some of the more isolated places.'

'Did any of them look currently occupied?'

'Three of them had four-wheel drives outside but no answer. I could only think they leave those vehicles up there for use in foul weather.'

'Have you checked the vehicle registrations against the owners?'

'I'm in the process of doing that now, Joanna.'

'Good. Keep at it.' She was aware they all needed encouragement as well as direction. 'I know we don't have much to go on but remember the bloodstains suggest significant injury to the little boy's father. When you add the failure of either of the child's parents to come forward I feel increasingly concerned.

'Dawn.' She turned to PC Dawn Critchlow, another workaholic but out of necessity since she and her husband were divorced and she had four children. 'You and Gilbert have rechecked local hospitals, accident reports?'

Dawn nodded. 'Nothing there, Jo. No reports of unexplained injuries treated or accident reports.' She gave a lopsided smile. 'Nothing but the usual Saturday night rumpus.'

'OK.' Joanna was thoughtful. 'So we're slowly narrowing down various scenarios. What about missing persons, DC Salvi?'

Salvi was nothing if not a showman. He strode to the front, puffing his chest out and managing to look important. 'I've checked the records of four thousand mispers,' he said as though he'd thumbed through the lot of them rather than setting the computer to work. 'Nothing that matches our girl and certainly no reports of a little boy aged around two going AWOL.' Joanna didn't suppress her smile. Trust DC Gino Salvi to make a drama out of nothing.

But she couldn't avoid heaving a great big sigh. Another blind alley.

'Anyone got anything else to add?'

She waited but no.

As she watched them disperse, talking amongst themselves, she faced the fact that at some point, probably sooner rather than later, she was going to have to try to 'interview' the wretched girl again.

2 p.m.

Another press briefing now they had a few more facts. She placed emphasis on the fact that the girl and the little boy were unrelated, that neither his mother nor his father had, so far, come forward and that they had evidence that the father might be injured. She also emphasized the fact that although they had followed a promising lead regarding the girl's identity, it had ultimately gone nowhere and they were still very anxious to know who she was. Again, she underlined, they needed the public's help.

The cameras clicked and rolled, microphones were held up and mobile phones recorded her statement.

There were fewer questions this time around, most relating to the well-being of the little boy. The fact was public interest would wane. News is very transient.

She spent the afternoon alongside DC King running through reports of accidents. They checked the missing persons' files again and spoke to contacts. Some of the officers trickled back from their house-to-house searches and enquiries with nothing significant to report. At eight o'clock Joanna logged off the computer. Time to go home. Another fruitless day. 'Hopefully,' she said to DC Alan King as they left the station together, 'something will turn up, maybe tomorrow.'

He grinned but failed to match her optimism. 'Night, Jo. See you in the morning.'

FIFTEEN

Reaching home and opening the front door, she stepped into another world. It was as though she inhabited two parallel universes the moment she stepped over the threshold of Briarswood. She left behind a world where all seemed out of kilter, damaged, wrong and puzzling too, and entered a world of happy, comfortable, predictable domesticity. Matthew and his parents were sitting in the lounge, drinking mugs of tea while they watched Jakob kicking around on the floor, surveying his own tiny hands and flinging a rattle across the room to be retrieved by any one of them. She stood in the doorway for a moment, not quite ready to cross that barrier. It would take a moment to absorb the scene and adjust.

Matthew rose to greet her with a kiss on her cheek before holding her at arms' length and making his observation. 'Gosh, Jo,' he said, 'you look all in.'

She kissed him back on his mouth. 'Thanks,' she said. 'I am.' She sank into the blissfully soft, down-filled cushion of their wide, long sofa and kicked her shoes off.

'This case,' she explained, stretching her arms behind her, 'is baffling. I have so many questions and so few answers.'

Charlotte, her mother-in-law, chipped in with a cold voice lacking in sympathy. 'It isn't all on *your* shoulders, Joanna? Surely you have a team of officers?'

'I'm SIO,' Joanna responded wearily, not bothering to explain the term. It was hard trying to explain to members of the public, even one's mother-in-law, just how complex a situation like this was. She sat forward. 'It's up to me to take the lead, direct their areas of investigation. The buck stops with me. And that's not even considering balancing the budget.'

Matthew eyed her with some sympathy then reached out and picked Jakob up, cradling him to his chest. 'Look at it this way, Jo. No harm was done. The child's safe.'

'Thanks to Mr Western's morning walk. And some harm *has* been done. We just don't know what, where, or to whom.'

Peter chipped in, horrified. 'It said on the news that the girl isn't even his mother?'

Joanna shook her head.

'So whose child is he?' Charlotte this time.

Joanna simply shrugged. 'We don't know.'

'So where *is* his mother?' Peter looked even more concerned than she would have expected as the gravity of the situation sank in.

'That's what we're worried about.'

That drew a momentary silence from all of them until Peter responded, 'Oh, that's awful. Now I see why you're so worried.'

Matthew was still holding Jakob close to him, stroking his son's hair, already curling and honey blond. They were, unmistakably, father and son. Joanna drank in the scene. This little boy was so safe with his dad – and grandparents. She felt her face crinkle up with concern. Not even grandparents had come forward to claim him. And the image that haunted her was that so far undiscovered crime scene which her mind was picturing with increasingly gory graphics.

Perhaps sensing that Joanna wanted be alone with her husband and son, Peter and Charlotte rose to leave. They kissed Matthew and Jakob warmly but the embrace they gave Joanna didn't quite break through the permafrost. Maybe, she thought wearily, whatever she did, they never would quite accept her. As she let them out of the front door to return to their bungalow not ten minutes away, Joanna wondered whether they would ever forgive and forget that her and Matthew's relationship had been born out of an extra-marital affair. She took Jakob from his dad, perhaps a little roughly. Immediately he started to howl. She might be his mother but it was his father he preferred, holding his arms out to him while kicking Joanna's chest. It was a stark contrast to the passivity of the little boy now lodged with foster parents.

When Jakob had finally settled, Matthew poured her a glass of wine and caught her eye with a smile. 'I know what's troubling you,' he said. 'You think that somewhere someone, probably your child's father, is lying either dead or injured.'

She took a mouthful of wine before responding. 'You know me too well.'

Tuesday 23 March, 7.50 a.m.

She'd had a restless night. Matthew voicing her worries had given her strange dreams, of someone suffering and calling out. But she could not hear the words. It was a mouth grimacing and twisting in silent appeal. She'd woken Jakob at six, fed and changed him, showered, dressed and headed in for work.

The morning brought not only an early start but also two pieces of good news. The first was a telephone call from a bemused lorry driver who worked for a dairy company based in Leek who had apparently just returned from a cross-Channel trip. PC Gilbert Young took the call at ten to nine and immediately knew it was the one they had been waiting for. He flicked the call to speaker and held his hand up. Joanna was by his side inside a second.

In a strong moorlands accent the caller began with an apology. 'I'm really sorry,' he said, his voice husky with weariness, 'I just got back from a bloody awful trip abroad and since then I've been in bed with a touch of the flu. One of the guys at work said something about a girl roaming around The Roaches with a young 'un in a pushchair.'

PC Gilbert Young kept his voice neutral. 'That's correct, sir. Can I have your name please?'

'Toft. Declan Toft.'

'Do you have some information that might help us?'

'Aye . . .' He qualified that. 'I might do. See, I didn't know anything about it. I didn't know the police had any interest in her though I thought it strange at the time. I picked her up, you see. Gave her and the little 'un a lift out to Ramshaw Rocks. They was walking along the road in Blackshaw Moor.'

Gilbert Young kept his cool. 'Are you able to come in and be interviewed?'

'Yeah. Yeah. Only too anxious to help, mate. I've got a kid of my own. She seemed a bit upset, said she was going for a walk.' He paused before adding, 'Though she weren't dressed for a walk exactly.'

Joanna butted in. 'It's Detective Inspector Joanna Piercy here, Mr Toft. I'm the senior investigating officer in this case. We need you to come in and make a statement as soon as possible. Can you manage today? We can send a car for you.'

'No need for that, Inspector.' He sounded startled and vaguely worried. 'I'll be up directly.'

'Thank you. And please ask for me.' She couldn't resist a fist bump with first Gilbert and then Alan King. It was the first bit of luck they'd had so far.

Declan Toft lumbered in almost an hour later, apologetic for the delay. He was a large man with thinning brown hair, a faintly worried expression and big hands which grasped hers. 'Sorry, I had to take my kid to school. And then my wife wanted me to pick up some—'

'That's quite all right, Mr Toft. No problem.'

Joanna led the lorry driver into an interview room and together she and Alan King went through the formalities, explaining their interest, giving out little more than the bare bones of the case, before moving on to the detail.

'In your own words, Mr Toft.'

'It were the Tuesday morning, quite early.'

Joanna interrupted. 'Are we talking about March the sixteenth?'

'Aye – that'd be it. I had to take some stuff over to Chesterfield and decided to drive through Buxton and then take the A6 and so on over there.' He seemed to feel the need to justify his route across the moors.

'The weather was cool with an early-morning mist that weren't shifting and the lorry's a big one – over thirty ton – so it weren't suitable for minor roads.' He spoke carefully and was surprisingly and gratifyingly precise in his explanation and justification.

Joanna glanced at Alan King. He was thoughtful and she knew he was thinking the same as she. A good witness.

'She were walking out of Leek along the road at Blackshaw Moor out towards The Roaches pushing a child in a pushchair. I couldn't see where she'd be going. She'd passed the turn for The Three Horseshoes and to be honest there ain't a lot round there and she were just wearing a thin dress which was flapping around her legs like sails in a storm. Just that, a brown cardigan that was way too big for her and a pair of wellies.' He nodded. 'The kid was well wrapped up, though.'

'What sort of time?'

'I dunno exactly. I didn't make a note but I can check my records back at the depot. Sometime after seven. Anyway, I pulled over and asked if I could give her and the kid a lift somewhere.'

'Go on.'

'She said she was heading up towards The Roaches.'

She said. He had no idea how significant those two words were. *She said.* He had heard their silent girl speak.

'What did her voice sound like?'

He looked astonished at the question and looked from one to the other. 'I thought you had her in custody somewhere?'

'Since we picked her up she hasn't spoken a word.'

He took a moment to absorb this statement before responding slowly. 'She sounded all right.'

'Accent?' Alan King put in.

Declan Toft looked confused by the question. 'Ordinary.'

'Did she have a local accent?'

'Umm. Not as you'd notice.' For the first time he was uncertain.

'Could you detect any accent that might have told you where she was from?'

Toft shook his head, frowning. 'Sorry. Not sure really.'

'Did she tell you her name?'

'No. I never asked. She seemed a bit dazed. Spaced out.'

'Did she address the little boy by name?'

Again, Toft shook his head.

'Did she say where she was from?'

Another negative. Toft's focus turned on DC King and his expression was guarded. 'If I had to swear by it she didn't have much of an accent. She didn't talk posh,' he added hastily, 'but she didn't sound local. I don't think I could say where she were from.'

'What did you think?'

He looked bothered by this. 'I don't know what I thought. I suppose I thought it was odd. But that's what she said and I just accepted it. There was no reason not to. Even though . . .' He looked thoughtful. 'She wasn't exactly dressed for climbing or hiking. Not with the little kid and a pushchair. I mean, it's not that sort of place, is it?' Now he looked even more thoughtful, his face screwed up. 'I thought mebbe she had a mate staying in one of the cottages up there.'

'What did she say?'

'Oh, she was kind of quiet but said she was headin' for The Roaches. That's all she said.' There was a hint of bluster now in his voice, desperation, something defiant. 'I just accepted it. I never questioned it. I didn't know there were anything the police would be interested in.'

'Tell me about the child.'

'He seemed asleep – or very sleepy. He looked cold and very pale. I asked if he was all right.'

'What did she say to that?'

'She said he was just tired.'

'Did the girl also look cold?'

'Not so much considering she weren't wearing a coat.'

'Was she carrying a bag?'

'Not as I noticed.'

'Did she explain how she'd arrived at Blackshaw Moor?'

'No. She was . . .' he chuckled, '. . . what you might call the silent type.'

That was an understatement.

'Not volunteering anything really. I felt a bit uncomfortable with her.'

Anticipating the answer, Joanna nevertheless asked the question. 'Did she say anything else?'

Toft shook his head.

'Did she say anything about the child?'

This time Toft started to shake his head but he pulled up short. 'Said she was minding him for a friend.'

'She didn't give the friend's name?'

'No.'

Joanna and DC King exchanged glances. *Who was this 'friend'?*

'Did you see any other vehicles on the road that morning?'

'A few. I can't remember anything in particular. Just the odd car, a van or two. No other HGVs. Nothing that stood out.'

'Did you comment on the fact that she was inappropriately dressed for such an exposed area?'

'I did.' Now Declan Toft looked uncomfortable. 'I think I said she'd catch her death up there.'

'And her response?'

'She just sort of stared at the windscreen.'

'And?'

'She said she'd be all right.' A sudden flush bloomed across his face. 'I took it to mean that I should mind my own business. So I did.' He thought for a moment before adding, 'To be honest I was glad when she bundled the pushchair out, kid with it. She made me feel like anything I asked was because I was a dirty old man. Or as if I was just being too nosey.' He looked even more embarrassed and looked around him as though for an escape route.

'Did you notice any marks on her dress?' He obviously hadn't made the association with a uniform.

He shook his head. 'I weren't looking.'

'Did she give you her name?'

He shook his head. Then frowned. 'I think she mumbled something. Sounded like Tommy?'

'You're sure?'

'No.' This time round he sounded angry. 'I can't be sure. I didn't realize it was going to be so important.'

Joanna didn't even begin to explain why they were so interested in this girl but ploughed on with her questions. 'Did she seem fond of the little boy?'

The question appeared to confuse him. 'Fond? Well, I suppose so. I mean she wasn't kissing him all the time and stuff but she – well – she was looking after him, wasn't she?'

'That doesn't quite answer my question. Did she show the little chap any affection?'

'As I said she wasn't smothering him with kisses and stuff but she did seem to like him.'

He narrowed his eyes. 'What's she done? Has she hurt him?'

DC King answered for her. 'The little boy is fine.'

Joanna showed him the picture on her tablet and Toft nodded. 'Aye – that's her all right. She's his mother?'

Joanna shook her head. 'No, she isn't. We haven't found his mother yet. When we do we hope they will be reunited.' She didn't add that in spite of countrywide appeals the mother hadn't come forward. Neither did she add that she was worried that the mother might not be able to come forward. DC King gave her a shallow grin and more than ever she wished Korpanski was sitting at her side. She could have done with his bulky, reassuring presence. He would have caught her eye with a mirroring of her own exasperation and frustration. She uttered a silent prayer.

Come back soon, Mike.

And now? She sensed they had all Declan Toft had to offer. She got him to sign his statement. Once he'd given them all his contact details they let him go.

SIXTEEN

She'd waited until lunchtime when she could close the door and have some privacy.

Recognizing her mobile number, Korpanski responded at once. 'Hey, Jo.' He sounded genuinely pleased to hear from her. 'How's things going?'

Korpanski was the one officer she trusted one hundred per cent. He was reliable and trustworthy.

'At a glacial pace,' she said, 'but . . .' And she relayed their latest.

'So we know she *can* speak. Anything else?'

Korpanski's mind was following the same trajectory hers had. 'He didn't get her name or where she'd come from? No accent?'

'No. So what's bothering me is . . .'

He finished the sentence for her.

'Where's the little chap's mother?' He paused to think, put his thoughts in order. 'Well, Jo, there's a couple of possibilities. She could be on holiday, thinking he's being looked after by someone she trusts so even if she's heard the news she doesn't connect the child found on The Roaches as being hers.'

'That doesn't wash,' she said sharply. 'If a child is with a friend – or a nanny – the natural thing is to keep in touch and make sure there are no problems and the friend's managing OK. And the pictures have been widely distributed.'

'Unless Mummy is abroad.'

'Abroad too. There's still mobile phones. Texts.' Her voice trailed away. But she could be honest with Korpanski. There was never any need to sanitize or hide her fears. 'Mike, my concern is that she's injured. Or even dead. The father too. That's my worry.'

Never one to hide from the truth, however ugly, he agreed. 'She could be dead.' But then he produced another suggestion. 'Mum and Dad could be separated. The blood on her clothes was the boy's father. It could be that the mother believes he is being looked after by his father.'

'But, Mike, even if Matthew was looking after Jakob, I'd still be ringing every day, just to check.'

'I know. So would most,' he agreed. 'Fran definitely would but not all mums are so watchful. Uhh, Jo,' he continued, 'is your girl talking yet?'

'No. But there's a silver lining.' Her voice was sharp. Her irritation was growing with the girl who, in her eyes at least, was deliberately obstructing their enquiry. 'She's currently nodding and shaking her head in response to simple questions, like does she want to use the lavatory. She's playing a game with us, I'm convinced, but the psychiatrist . . .'

'Oh yeah. What does she say?'

'She's very tolerant and understanding, bordering on patronizing, wouldn't you know. But then she won't have to deal with the fallout of an undiscovered crime scene.'

Korpanski huffed out a laugh. 'You're going to have to have some patience, Jo.'

She sighed. 'Not my strong point.'

'No. But neither the little boy nor your dumb girl is going to come to any harm. Not for now.'

'And the mother – or father?'

And that even Detective Sergeant Korpanski couldn't answer.

But Declan Toft's evidence meant they had traced the girl back. It was a small step forward but it was forward. They knew now she had come from the direction of Leek, not Buxton, wearing only a dress, a cardigan and the wellies. Not carrying a handbag or a visible purse. She had been able to speak – then. Now they needed to trace her movements back from there. How had she arrived in Leek? Why had she gone there?

She set a team of officers to search through public transport on the early morning of March the sixteenth and a check on any cars left abandoned in side streets in or around Leek. The girl had arrived there somehow, from somewhere. She wasn't local. They would focus on this geographical area.

While they worked on that aspect she'd decided it was time to approach the girl again so was heading towards Greatbach, where she had a fight on her hands.

Joanna found the psychiatrist sitting in her office. Claire didn't look at all pleased to see her. Her response to Joanna's request was cool. 'I'm sorry,' she said. 'We're progressing with her treatment. It wouldn't be appropriate. And it won't help you, you know. It might even set her back.'

Joanna fought back. 'I have concerns. I really need to speak to her.'

'It won't do any good. You won't get anything out of her. She isn't vocalizing.'

Joanna's frustration was threatening to boil over. 'Well, she was speaking perfectly all right until she was found.'

'How do you know that?'

'A lorry driver has come forward who picked her up just outside Leek and dropped her off near to where she was found.'

Claire absorbed this new information while Joanna ploughed on. 'You said she is giving nods and shakes of her head so she is communicating – at least to indicate yes or no.'

'I'm sorry.' The psychiatrist was still cool and bent on preventing her interviewing their girl.

Joanna tried again to convince her. 'It won't help us clashing over this woman, Claire,' she said. 'I need answers.'

'I know,' Claire soothed in a voice Joanna suspected she often used with her more disturbed patients. 'I do understand but it won't do any good. Police questioning can be fairly aggressive. It will traumatize her. I really don't want you to upset her.'

'I'm sorry,' Joanna said, though she wasn't, 'but we suspect she is at the very least involved in a serious enquiry.'

'Where do you get that from?'

'From the fact that the *heavy* bloodstaining on her cardigan came from the child's father. Put that with the fact that neither parent nor grandparent has come forward to ask after him and he has not been reported missing – a child of around two years old – you must understand we have serious concerns as to the boy's family's safety.'

That provoked silence. Even the psychiatrist couldn't think up a suitable rebuff to this. But eventually the doctor capitulated. 'Very well,' she said, practically through gritted teeth. 'As it's an investigation of a potentially serious crime. But please don't undo the work we've done with her. This is a delicate situation. She is a *very* damaged woman.'

Damaged or damaging?

'I need to sit in with you both. She is my patient.'

A fact Joanna bitterly regretted. She had the victory but it didn't feel like it. And she still wished she had Korpanski at her side. DC Alan King might be a competent and intelligent officer but he wasn't Korpanski.

The psychiatrist drew in a long breath. 'Can I just ask you to avoid being aggressive in your questioning?'

Joanna managed a warm and genuine-looking smile. 'Of course,' she conceded, with some condescension. Then relented. 'I'll confide in you, Claire. I'm worried about what we'll find at the end of this story.'

Give the psychiatrist her due, she responded to this coolly. 'Well, I realize that but, Inspector Piercy' – all pretence of friendship swiftly evaporating – 'I have the last word here. This is *my* hospital and the girl is *my* patient. If *I* consider that your intervention is harming her then I do have the authority to stop it. The girl's mental condition is of prime consideration.'

'And the child's?'

'He's out of harm's way.'

Joanna put her face close to Dr Roget's. 'Somewhere, out there, is this child's mother and father. What about *their* rights?'

By her side DC Alan King, who'd accompanied her, was maintaining a dignified silence. Impassive, standing stiffly, expression neutral, eyes focussed on a small mark on the wall.

Claire Roget's face displayed stubbornness. 'My patient is my prime consideration.'

'And mine,' Joanna shot back, 'is the protection of the public at large. And specifically the little boy and his family – wherever they are.'

Claire's response was an expression Joanna guessed her friends would have recognized as extreme stubbornness. She was not going to budge an inch.

Joanna gave up at that. She appeared to have met her match. And she had the awful feeling that if she turned her head just a fraction of an inch she would recognize DC King's apparently bland expression as a smirk.

So she focussed ahead and held out her arm. 'Lead on,' she said, as graciously as a duchess at a ball, and after a moment's hesitation Dr Roget did just that, stopping at a door and reminding her. 'Fifteen minutes, Inspector. And less than that if you're stepping over the mark.'

Joanna didn't even indicate she'd heard, let alone that she would comply. Her chin was jutting forward in an expression her friends would also have recognized.

SEVENTEEN

They had changed the girl into a pair of loose-fitting grey jogging bottoms and a navy T-shirt. They were too big for her and made her look even thinner, more vulnerable. She had a pair of backless clogs on bare feet and was sitting in a room on her own in a high-backed chair, staring out of the window at the people clustered in the quadrangle below. Her hair was pulled back loosely in an elastic band which displayed her angular bones and pale complexion. As Joanna entered she turned around and met her eyes and there was recognition in her face combined with a tightening of the lips, wariness in the tawny eyes. As Joanna approached her shoulders slumped forwards as though she realized here came her nemesis, someone who would not be as understanding or gentle as the psychiatrist. The tension in her face was preparation for battle.

Joanna pulled up a chair. 'Hello,' she said. 'Remember me?'

There was no response except a flicker in her eyes and a movement of the hands resting on her lap.

'I'm Detective Inspector Joanna Piercy, Leek Police. We have met before on the morning that you were brought into us having been found with a little boy on The Roaches. Do you remember that?'

She could have sworn the girl was about to smile. Her lips twitched.

But her face remained resolutely impassive, the eyes still trained on her.

'Do you understand where you are?'

Her eyes narrowed, now unmistakably hostile.

Joanna repeated the question. 'Do you understand why you're here?'

There was the tiniest frown as though she was puzzling this out.

Joanna moved closer. 'You're here because of your refusal' – the flame returned to the girl's eyes – 'or inability to speak and explain certain things.' She wasn't going to spell it out for her. Not yet. Little by little she would let out the facts.

The girl folded her arms and settled back into her chair. She looked like a stubborn teenager.

'But we know now from a lorry driver who picked you up, that before you were found, you were speaking perfectly normally.'

No response.

'Do you remember what led up to this?'

The girl was watchful, wary, but remaining silent.

'OK, then I'll explain. Last Tuesday a gentleman was going on his morning jog. He does this every day. Or should I say most days.'

Alan King, standing by the door, shifted his weight. Unused to her methods, he was getting restless.

Joanna's smile broadened. 'I suspect he doesn't go in really heavy rain or a snowstorm.'

Something flickered in the girl's eyes. Guarded. She too was waiting for the detective to get to the point.

'Anyway, on this morning the weather wasn't bad. A bit damp and cold but then it nearly always is up there.'

The girl blinked, her eyes signifying agreement but her neck remained rigid, sinews and muscles clearly defined.

'He saw you standing on the edge of the drop with the little boy in the pushchair,' Joanna continued smoothly. 'It looked as though you were going to push him over the edge. Why?'

At this question the girl's eyes drooped and Joanna continued with hardly a pause. 'Let me tell you what we already know. And then what I think. We know he isn't your child because we've checked his DNA against yours.'

The girl's lips twitched.

'And now I'll tell you what *I* think. You wanted to get rid of him, didn't you? He was in the way, wasn't he?'

The girl's eyes filled with tears. A couple rolled down her face and she gasped. It was the first real emotion she'd displayed.

'And then we realized your clothes were bloodstained. Which made me think something else. What have you done to that little boy's parents?'

The girl's lips moved as her eyes locked into Joanna's.

'I'll tell you what led me to this conclusion. The blood on your clothes belonged to the little boy's dad.'

The girl dropped her face into her hands. Joanna sensed a movement of air as Claire moved forward, but she continued speaking brutally. 'Is he hurt?'

The girl's eyes dropped, hiding her response to this.

'It was a significant amount of blood which could indicate serious injury.'

That drew no response.

'We will find out, you know, who you are. We will find out what has happened. Your silence and refusal to cooperate will be noted . . .' Behind her Joanna heard Claire clear her throat.

'It is just delaying what is and will continue to be a major police investigation.'

The sound that came now from the girl was a soft groan.

The girl's head jerked from side to side in a violent negative. Joanna gave a swift glance at Claire who had taken a step forward.

In response, Joanna softened her voice. 'Why has no one reported you or the toddler missing? Is there no one who cares about either of you?'

The girl's eyes flew up to Joanna's. Her mouth opened and she gave a soft gasp.

'You might want to know about the little boy's welfare.' Joanna's tone was conversational but unmistakably ironic. 'We have him with foster parents. He will stay there until we can reunite him with his family.'

The girl frowned again, taking up the pose of a sulky teenager.

'Why don't you tell us who you are?' Joanna said, her voice coaxing. 'Help yourself. Maybe help someone else? The little boy's mother? We don't even know his name,' she added.

The girl squeezed her eyes tight shut as though she was in pain and Joanna shifted, preparing to go. 'If you have committed a crime we will bring you to justice whoever you are, whatever your name.'

The girl's head drooped lower.

'And until we know *all* the circumstances you *will* stay here.'

She put her face close to the girl's and spoke softly, almost out of the psychiatrist's hearing. 'You will talk, you know, in the end. It won't be through therapy, nor drugs or simply talking but through an intense police investigation. We will find out your backstory,

Miss Whoever-you-are. And if a crime has been committed we *will* charge you.' She waved her hand around her, encompassing the room, the view, the psychiatrist, the TV on the wall and the bed in the centre. She moderated her voice even softer. 'You won't be able to hide behind this psychiatric mumbo jumbo . . .'

'H-hum.' Behind her Claire Roget cleared her throat, expressing her fury.

Joanna stood up and walked to the door.

Outside the psychiatrist spoke, a note of coldness as well as malice in her voice. 'Well, did you get what you wanted?'

But Joanna was ready for her. The lorry driver's testimony had altered something. Rather than seeing the girl as a victim, dumb nymph or a dryad, Joanna knew she was an ordinary girl with a child whom she said she was minding for a 'friend'. A child she had been prepared to discard over the cliff, like a piece of litter.

As they walked away from the girl's room she questioned the psychiatrist. 'Exactly what methods are you using to try and persuade our girl to talk?'

The psychiatrist looked at her and Joanna pressed her question.

'Hypnosis? Abreaction?'

Claire turned to face her, almost indignant. 'What do *you* know about abreaction?'

'I have a psychology degree. Before I went into policing.' She waited while Claire absorbed this, then pressed again. 'Well?'

Her response was brief and uncompromising. 'Neither.'

'So what *are* you doing?'

Claire was defensive. 'Psychotherapy. We give her the *opportunity* to speak and she's on a mild anxiolytic.'

'Which isn't helping much.'

Joanna's retort didn't affect the psychiatrist's cool. 'They take a while to kick in. These things can't be hurried.' Her voice was calm, placid, unruffled.

While Joanna's was the exact opposite. 'And in the meantime . . .?'

Her irritation wasn't helped by the psychiatrist hiding behind the cliché. 'My responsibility is to my patient.'

And mine to just about everyone else. But Joanna swallowed the comment. Instead she voiced her disapproval with a loud sigh.

EIGHTEEN

In the car heading back along the A53 to Leek, DC Alan King was silent which Joanna interpreted as disapproval and made her resent him more. Korpanski would have vocalized, challenged her methods. If he'd disapproved of something she'd said or done they would have argued all the way back to Leek. And by the time they'd reached the station they would have ironed out their differences and be laughing at something, taking the mickey out of each other. She heaved out a long sigh. She missed Mike's humour, that great noisy guffaw of his when something struck him as funny. She wanted to get some response out of King who was driving, his long bony frame folded almost in half, filling the space between steering wheel and seat. As they passed the Moorcroft bottle kiln and the Port Vale football club on their left she tried to evince some honest reaction out of him.

'So what did you think of my methods, King?'

His hands, she noticed, gripped the steering wheel even harder, knuckle bones whitening, so she anticipated his disapproval. 'You don't know what's true and what's not.' He risked a swift look at her. 'Our witness.'

'Jeremy Western?'

'Yeah. The hiker who first saw her. It was his interpretation. You don't know she was about to hurt the little boy.' He was warming to his subject now. 'She could have been protecting him.'

But she shook her head. 'From whom? From what?'

King had no answer so she continued. 'Why take him up there? Why not hand him in to a police station or a hospital if he needed protection?' The ice crystals in her voice should have warned him. But DC King was, bravely, not about to let his theory go.

'Maybe it was because the rendezvous went wrong,' he ventured. 'Maybe she was just going somewhere she felt safe.'

'On the edge of a ninety-foot drop?'

'Well . . .'

She could feel his discomfort. 'And the blood on her dress as well as on the child's clothes? How do you explain that?'

King's shoulders hunched and he risked a glance at her. 'You know how much blood you can lose before it means something serious. It doesn't necessarily mean someone's dead or badly hurt, does it?' Those last two words displayed a sudden loss of confidence in his theory.

'King,' she said, in a voice as tight as a headmistress's, 'I simply thread the facts together, putting them into a narrative and testing the waters. I didn't accuse her of anything. I just gave her the opportunity to explain. And she continues to refuse to help us.'

King was on the verge of giving up. 'She's obviously—'

She jumped in. 'Disturbed? Yes. I grant you that. And it's possible that her refusal to speak, as the psychiatrist believes, is due to some trauma, recent or long ago. Or it could be a simple refusal to answer our questions because there isn't an answer that doesn't implicate her right up to her scrawny little neck. Have you thought of that?'

As she spoke she was realizing other things about this case. She was angry with the girl. Rather than pitying her she was beginning to dislike her. Partly because of the way she had treated the child which was coloured by her own motherhood, but also because of the waste of resources. Had the girl spoken up she could have saved the Force an awful lot of blind alleys, like the Stuart Manning/ Dodie trip to Market Drayton. Someone, somewhere was hurt, at the least, and she was anxious to find them.

'And where are the little boy's parents?'

When King didn't respond to that, except to bite his lip, she continued, 'It could be that she hasn't managed to cook up a reasonable story to explain why the hell she was about to hurt the child.'

King gave in then. 'I guess so,' he said grumpily and she smothered a smile. Mike would never have backed down so easily.

But underneath Joanna knew there was a grain of truth in King's words. The only facts they really had were the blood samples and Western's story. Even though now they knew *how* she'd reached her location from Leek to The Roaches, they were still far from understanding how she had travelled to Leek in the first place or where she was from.

4 p.m.

It was time for another press briefing and she had little to give them. Also she couldn't help noticing there were fewer attendees this time round. Media quickly dries up. She glossed over the fact that the girl was still 'acting dumb' before going into detail with the statement from the lorry driver emphasizing the details they knew against the many questions they still had.

'The girl was first seen wearing only a dress and a cardigan, walking out towards Blackshaw Moor at approximately seven a.m. on Tuesday the sixteenth of March. To jog your memory it was a cold, misty morning so she was inappropriately dressed.' She scanned the room. 'What we need to know is how did she get to Leek? Bus, car, taxi? Or did someone give her a lift. From where? Is a coat hidden somewhere along with her personal belongings, mobile phone, bag? The lorry driver who picked her up has given us a little more detail. She claimed she was looking after the child for a friend. No friend has turned up to claim the little boy. So now we want to trace her steps *before* he picked her up, which probably puts her in Leek before seven o'clock in the morning.' She indicated the picture of both girl and child and also described the girl's outfit in detail, speaking directly to camera. 'A dark red dress, brown cardigan, with wellington boots. An unusual outfit. Does someone remember seeing a girl, with a child, dressed like this? So far we have not recovered a bag, a coat, or a mobile phone. Nothing with which to identify her. No one from the little boy's family has, so far, come forward, which is worrying in itself.' She paused. She couldn't and wouldn't hide this from them. 'We are desperate to find this little boy's family and are concerned they might be hurt or injured. Has any member of the public missed a toddler, his parents? Not seen them for a couple of weeks? What *is* this girl's connection to them? We're currently working on the assumption that she is the boy's nanny as there is no blood link according to DNA.'

She had the reporters' undivided attention. They were already penning headlines in their minds.

After a pause she continued, 'The indications are that the girl, if not local, at least has some local knowledge because of the location in which she was first seen. This is an ongoing police investigation. Finding the girl's identity is vital in the search for this little boy's family and to reunite them.' She repeated the telephone numbers, speaking directly into the cameras and finished with a polite, 'Thank you.'

She dealt with the few questions but she'd covered the important aspects of the case. And now it was time to continue with their checks and wait for the public to provide an explanation. The appeals would begin as soon as the local radio stations and media outlets had updated their information.

The rest of the afternoon was spent with dealing with a plethora of phone calls, each one followed up.

The case was about to turn.

It was PC Jason Spark who took the call just before six o'clock.

It began, as usual, with an apology.

'I hope I'm not wasting your time.' It was a male voice with a local accent.

In spite of the fact that he'd heard the same phrase at least twenty times this afternoon Jason was still smiling as he reassured the caller. 'We can be the judge of that, sir.' He took the caller's name before listening.

'I think I might have seen your girl.'

'Go on.' Jason smiled. 'Let's start with your name.'

'My name's Karl Jordan. I'm a bus driver. I live up Bentilee.'

'Yes,' PC Spark prompted gently. 'And?'

'It were around a week ago. I were on the early shift.'

'Can you tell me the exact date?'

'My wife tells me it were a Tuesday . . .'

Spark heard a voice but from a distance.

'Sixteenth. Tell him it were the sixteenth. The day our Mandy . . .' Jason was not about to find out what Mandy had been up to on that day because Karl Jordan recovered his memory.

'Aye. The sixteenth.'

'Go on.'

'I were on the early shift on the buses. I think it were the same girl. The one on the telly. I remember her wellies.' Jason put his hand up and the phone on speaker phone. The room went quiet and Joanna was behind him, listening in.

'She were struggling with the pushchair and the little one being

so quiet like. Not like most of the kids on the buses. Scream like
hell they do.'

'Where did she get on?'

'Up Hanley way. At the station.'

'And off?'

'Went right through to Leek as far as I remember. To the station
there. One of the other passengers helped her get the pushchair off
t'bus.' His thought processes, like his speech, were slow and pedantic.

'Times?'

'She were on the first bus. The six fifteen. My first of the day.
Beginnin' of the shift, like.'

'Is there CCTV on the buses?'

'Aye.' He thought for a moment, perhaps thinking he needed to
justify this. 'They have it in case of vandalism or punch-ups. You
know?' He stopped to think. 'I hope it's been hung on to and not
scrubbed off.'

Jason Spark didn't want to suggest anything to the driver, whose
deliberate and precise speech suggested he was an honest man,
but he wanted more information. 'Did you notice anything unusual
about the girl's appearance?'

'Not as I remember. Oh – she'd spilt something on her dress.
Coffee or tea or something but she was wearing a coat over it so
I didn't rightly see.'

A coat? Joanna's skin prickled.

'Did she say anything?'

'No – not apart from asking for a ticket for Leek. That was all.'
And then curiosity took over. 'She's all right, is she?'

'I'm not really at liberty to share that detail with you.'

By his side Joanna nodded. Jason spoke again. 'Ye-es. She's
all right but we still don't know who she is.'

'Oh.' Jordan was obviously struggling with this. 'And the little
one?'

Spark could answer this more honestly. 'Oh yes. *He's* fine.'

Jason had the attention of the entire room now. Barely
concealing his grin, he took down the driver's contact details,
failing to suppress his excitement at what he knew would be a
breakthrough.

'Let's not get our hopes up,' Joanna said, even as a flood of
optimism disobeyed her own simple instruction.

Note to self: wait until you know where this leads.

She clapped him on the back. Jason's face was red with pride, almost matching the tinge of his hair and his grin stretched right across his face. He was an endearing young PC whom Joanna had marked for his buoyant enthusiasm when he had been a cadet. That very enthusiasm would take him far. His fellow officers ragged him for it but secretly some of them envied this happy commitment.

'Well, Sparks,' she said. 'You've just earned yourself a little trip to Hanley bus station and an evening's TV watching with an officer of your choice.'

She already knew who he'd choose. It was an ill-concealed secret that PC Jason Spark of the bouncy enthusiasm was prisoner to the smooth skin and big eyes of the station's glamour girl, PC Kitty Sandworth. Somehow Jason always seemed to find himself near her during the briefings and when, as now, it was suggested that he take another officer on an investigation, it was invariably Kitty. Not that Kitty minded.

They were soon out of the door and Joanna felt a wave of sudden frustration. She needed to get out of the station, move away from the whiteboard with its paucity of information and lists of questions. And, in a burst of frustration, she told DC King she was going to see the child. She could read the puzzlement in his face. He may as well have asked the question out loud. *What do you expect to glean from a two-year-old?* And she could have answered, *No more or less than from his silent companion.*

Ignoring the futility of her trip, she went anyway.

NINETEEN

6.30 p.m.

Sandra and Michael Clowes were well known to social services as foster parents who seemed unable to deny a child a safe haven at any time of the day or night. They lived in a chaotic ex-council house on an estate just off Ball Haye Road at the top of the town. The atmosphere in the house was one of happy chaos which Joanna recognized the minute she arrived at the property, entering through a low wicket gate with peeling paintwork into a garden where two boys, around ten years old, were kicking a ball around. They moved respectfully back as she approached the front door along a concrete path, giving her a tentative smile as she passed and a friendly 'hi'. After a brief pause the boys were soon back to kicking the ball around.

While she waited for the door to be opened she found herself picturing Jakob in years to come, kicking a ball around with her and Matthew. What would he be like? she wondered. What sort of child would he be? At the moment he was simply cute, big blue eyes, blond curls and a stare that seemed to commit your face to memory.

The door opened and Sandra Clowes stood there, the little boy clinging to her, his arms around her neck.

Sandra was a big woman with a large, floppy bust and a sturdy pair of legs encased in black jeggings. Over these floated a top in a thin, blue/green, watery material. She gave Joanna a wide grin and spoke to the child.

'See here, little one, here's the nice inspector come to see you.'

She and Joanna had met on numerous occasions when a child had needed to be removed from its environment. Somehow the foster mother soothed a troubled soul whether that soul be six months or nearly sixteen years old.

'Come in, Joanna,' she said, standing back while the child watched her through big, round eyes. Sandra stroked his head. 'I call him Little Man,' she said, 'so he doesn't get confused when we find out his real name. Blimey . . .' She hoisted him up her hip. 'He's a lump. Too heavy for me to be picking him up all the time. Does my back in. But what can you do? Cup of tea, Joanna?'

'Yes, if it's not too much trouble.' Knowing it wouldn't be Joanna sat down on the sofa whose bright pink throw did not quite hide the numerous stains: tea, orange juice, milk, coffee and 'unidentifiable'.

Sandra handed her the child with an explanation. 'He's a bit insecure,' she said. 'Likes to be cuddled a lot.'

So now the still nameless little boy clung to *her*, arms tight around *her* neck. He smelt of soap and chips and did feel heavy. Much heavier than Jakob. They studied one another while Joanna wondered aloud, 'Who are you, hey? Where's your mummy and daddy?'

The little boy simply stared at her while Joanna wished he, at least, could and would talk. Had their silent girl been employed as this little boy's nanny? Joanna gazed down at his face. 'Even your name would be a help.' But rather than respond the little boy continued staring at her, his eyes now ever so slightly curious. She wondered when Jakob would start to talk. What would his voice sound like? She did not, however, need to wonder what his first word would be. It would, inevitably, be 'Daddy'. One day she would remind him that *she* had been the one who had carted him around for nine long months inside her womb.

The child continued to stare at her, his face expressionless. And then he reached out a hand and touched her hair, winding it around his finger and looking at it with intensity.

Sandra bustled back in with two steaming mugs and a Tommy Tippee cup for the child.

'Here you are,' she said, handing it to him. Obediently the little boy lifted the cup to his lips, still not taking his eyes off Joanna. She accepted the mug of weak, milky tea while Sandra lifted the boy off her lap.

'Is he saying *anything*?'

'Starting to,' Sandra said with some pride. 'I told him my name's Sandra and he has a go, don't you, my little man?'

'Saaa sa,' the child said.

Joanna asked the next question in a low voice. 'Have you asked him where his mummy is?'

Sandra shook her head. 'I thought it might upset him.'

Joanna drew out a picture of their silent girl and showed it to the boy, pointing with her finger. He stared at it.

'Do you know who that is?' Joanna had tried to jolly the question along but it did little good. The boy's face screwed up and his colour turned puce. Sandra looked at Joanna accusingly.

'Are you getting anywhere with her?' she asked in a low voice.

Joanna shook her head. 'Still not speaking.'

If only, she was thinking, this child was a year or two older. Then she could have asked him questions and maybe pieced together at least some facts. A name, a place, a car, something.

It was in desperation that she put the photograph close to the little boy's face and asked, 'Who is this?'

The little boy's body went rigid before starting to shake, almost as though he was having a fit.

'No,' Sandra said firmly. 'I can't allow you to try and question him. It's not kind. And . . .' She eyed Joanna. 'I'm not sure it's legal. He's just a little boy,' she said, kinder now. 'He can't answer anything anyway. It's pointless. Whatever happened to him I'm here to look after him now.' She stroked the child's hair. 'Now don't you worry, Little Man. Nothing's going to happen while Saa saa's here.'

The little boy moved in closer to the ample bosom and started to suck his thumb.

'I know. I know it's a bad habit,' Sandra said, eyes flashing out a warning, 'but we can sort out these things at a time when he's not so troubled.' Her focus returned to the child. 'Can't we, my darling?'

The little boy sucked his thumb even harder, eyes screwed shut in concentration.

Which gave Joanna an idea. 'Sandra, is he a habitual thumb-sucker?'

'What?'

'Does he have the signs on his teeth as well as his thumb pads that this is a habit he's had for a long time?'

'No,' she said wonderingly. 'There weren't no sign he's always done this.'

It wasn't much but it was something that indicated . . . what? Stress? Trauma? Would whatever events he'd witnessed stay in his memory, leave a scar? Joanna finished her tea and left. Little more would be gleaned from the child.

She should have returned to the station, tidied up the day's loose ends, but that feeling of restlessness hadn't left her so she called at Mike's.

At first she thought he was out. One of the cars was missing from the drive and no one answered the door for a minute or two. She was about to leave when she heard a noise inside and then Mike, using elbow crutches, stood before her. 'Jo,' he said, with obvious delight. 'Great. Come on in. Fran's out. She had to go back to work. I said I'd manage.'

She tried to disguise the joy she felt at seeing him back on his feet. 'I haven't brought you a bunch of grapes.'

'No worries. I'll forgive you. Come on in. Tell me how your investigation's going?' As he hobbled back towards the sitting room he threw back, 'Saw you on the TV. Quite the film star.'

'Yeah, except it wasn't acting.'

'So how is it going?'

'Painfully slow.'

Korpanski grimaced. 'Like my leg.'

She felt a pang. 'I'm sorry, Mike.'

'It wasn't your fault, Jo.'

'Indirectly?'

He smiled. 'Not even indirectly.'

'It was.'

This time his response was to shake his head.

'I know this isn't fair to ask but . . .' She hardly dared ask.

He pre-empted her. 'When will I be back at work? Three months minimum, Jo.'

Then his face changed. '*Never* is maximum. I saw the doctor yesterday and he sounded pretty glum. Apparently I've been too optimistic. And I've spoken to HR. I'll have to pass fitness tests before they'll let me back. They're not convinced I'll ever be back to front-line policing, Jo. They'll probably stick me behind a desk and let me get smothered in dust.'

Her heart sank. 'I hope not. I'm missing your—'

'Wit?' They looked at one another. Korpanski had been off for just over three months. It would have seemed longer to her had she not been on maternity leave. But now she was back and the full force of life without Korpanski was hitting her hard.

'Now give me something else to focus on. Bring me up to date with your case.'

She related everything that had happened so far including the lines of enquiry they were hoping to take.

'You'll get there, Jo.'

Without him she was not so sure.

TWENTY

Wednesday 24 March, 8 a.m.

PC Jason Spark had got his dearest wish and been granted PC Kitty Sandworth to work with him to follow up on Karl Jordan's statement, so the next morning they found themselves in a squad car heading towards the offices of the revamped Hanley bus station.

Trouble was that though Jason was normally chatty, almost garrulous, in social situations, whenever he was within six feet of PC Kitty Sandworth, he was, like their silent girl, struck dumb and could never think of anything remotely interesting or clever to say.

Kitty, however, with acute feminine awareness of Jason's feelings for her, tried to put him at his ease.

'Gosh, Jase,' she said, 'just think of it. We might be the ones to break the case. Find out who she is and from there track back to – whatever.'

He risked a glance away from the road, flipping his heart into a somersault. 'We'll be lucky to do that.'

'I have a feeling.' She giggled and touched his arm which set off a tingling as though he'd been brushed with a live wire. Kitty watched the colour rise in his cheeks. She was perfectly aware that Jason Spark fancied the pants off her. And, truth be told, she really liked him. She liked his clumsiness and his awkward boyish enthusiasm, but most of all she loved the fact that he was devoted to her. Months ago she'd noticed how he coloured every time he addressed her. How his eyes brightened when he looked at her. PC Jason Spark might not be the handsomest cop in the shop, but if they ever got it together (which if he didn't get his finger out and ask her for a date might never happen) she believed she would be sure of him all her life. He had the devotion of a Labrador.

Jason was smiling as he turned into the main building of Hanley bus station, revamped from the ugly 1970s concrete version. They parked up and made their way to the main office where the manager was waiting for them, a diminutive woman almost as wide as she was tall, whose name badge detailed *Lorna*. She boasted a pronounced Potteries accent. 'I 'ave the stuff ready for you,' she said, without introduction. 'Stuart told me the dates and times you'd be interested in. We have CCTV on all the buses,' she finished proudly before giving them a severe look. 'We've had such a load of trouble on the late night ones. Lucky for you we 'adn't scrubbed them.'

Kitty managed a wide smile. 'That's great, Lorna,' she said. 'Where can we watch them?'

'You can use my office. You shan't be disturbed there.' Lorna gave them a big, confident grin. 'No one would dare disturb me.' And she puffed her ample chest out.

After pointing them in the direction of the coffee machine she ushered them into a small office with a panoramic view over the lines of buses which headed out like the spokes on a wheel, to serve the whole of Staffordshire and beyond.

Lorna flicked on a screen and inserted a memory stick. 'That's the one you'll be interested in.'

Then she left them. With times and dates on the top right-hand corner they were soon watching people boarding a bus. Sleepy and slow, a column of early-morning workers.

Six fifteen a.m. Tuesday, March the sixteenth.

At first glance, early on a dull, damp March morning all the people looked similar, the colours grey, their attitude subdued. Heads were down, bodies bundled up in fleeces or padded jackets. And then they spotted her, initially because of the pushchair. They froze the picture down and zoomed in to see her wellies and complete the identification. They peered closer to get a better view. It was their girl.

'She's wearing a coat,' Kitty observed.

'And carrying a shoulder bag.' They turned back to the screen and shifted the picture frame by frame. They saw the girl speak to the driver, hand over some money, awkwardly trying to hold the child with one arm while folding up the pushchair with the other. A woman in a bulky jacket held out her hand and took the pushchair from her, folded it up neatly and stacked it in the luggage area. There was a hint of irritation in the action, as though the girl was holding things up. The woman walked to the back of the bus while their girl took a seat near the front, the child on her lap.

They tagged the sequence.

What seemed like hours later, people getting on and off, robotic and with no sound, the girl was getting to her feet. The stop on the bus VDU was named as Leek town centre, the time six fifty. The child was tucked under her arm, seemingly placid and compliant. There was no sign of a struggle as their girl pulled the pushchair from the luggage rack. No sign of the woman who had originally helped her. Their girl was on her own this time. She descended from the bus. Through the window they saw her thread towards the pelican crossing by Barclays Bank and then she vanished from sight.

She was still wearing her coat.

And carrying a bag.

They stood up, took the memory stick and found Lorna. 'We have what we want,' Jason said. 'Thank you.'

'We'll take this' – Kitty wafted the memory stick – 'if it's OK with you?'

Lorna acknowledged the thanks with a smug smile and a dip of her head. 'I 'ave helped then?' she asked, adding saucily, wiggling her wide hips and with a hint of mockery, 'with your enquiries?'

Kitty's response was warm. 'You have,' she said, shaking her hand. 'Thank you so much. You've given us some new lines of enquiry to follow. We're really grateful, Lorna.'

Lorna's pale face was beaming now. 'I never thought I'd get involved like this with a real live case.'

'Oh, but you have.'

Jason was tempted to shove Kitty towards the door. For the first time ever he realized that, beautiful though she was, there was the vaguest chance that Kitty Sandworth could possibly become annoying. Then he caught the sparkle in her eyes and realized she was winding him up.

Maybe not.

He couldn't wait to get back to Leek and relate his findings.

TWENTY-ONE

10.30 a.m.

'Brilliant,' was Joanna's response when she'd taken a look at the images herself and got DC Alan King to enlarge and enhance them until the pictures were clean sharp.

'Fantastic. Now we can go viral, get these on social media and release the details to the press. Not only that but if people come forward we might learn something about her. Her accent, whether she's local. Let's see if we can track down the woman who helped with the pushchair. More importantly' – she peered into the screen – 'somewhere in Leek is that coat and her bag. Now maybe we'll even find out who the mother of the little chap is. Well done, you two.' She could have bottled the look Jason and Kitty gave each other and sold it in a jar for sheer pride, love and happiness.

Young love, she thought longingly as she prepared the pictures for public display. What a long time ago it seemed that she and Matthew were white hot for each other. Now Matthew's love appeared centred around his son. Her son too, she reminded herself. So why should she feel jealous? Because she felt she had been displaced, as though her role had been a mere vehicle for his heart's desire? And what if Jakob didn't live up to his father's and grandparents' expectations: clever, sporty, compliant? Baby perfect.

She brushed the thought aside. There was work to do. And this introspection wouldn't achieve anything.

Before she faced the press to present these new findings she spent some time reflecting. The relationship between the police and the media was a complicated one. This case, almost more than any, indicated that they needed each other, the police for providing stories and the press to involve the general public and glean any information. But there was a downside. The number of calls rose exponentially following any airing on the networks. And sometimes it encouraged those who simply thirsted for notoriety, their three minutes of fame.

Their new information had the girl boarding an early morning bus in Hanley. So they had tracked her back to the city centre. But they still didn't know how she had reached there. She could have driven there herself and left the car in one of the side streets lined with terraced houses. Equally someone could have taken her. Or she might have caught a bus to the city centre. The alternative was that she lived in Hanley. So they had a piece of information. But it wasn't enough. They needed more.

She detailed a couple of uniforms to search the streets of Hanley for a car that had been left there for over a week. It is surprising how a car neglected for even a few days gathers dust and leaves, a dry patch beneath when it has been raining. And if her hunch, that the girl had driven there herself and abandoned the car, was correct, finding it would provide the ANPR with the owner's name and address. From there it should be plain sailing to unearth the backstory.

Then she sat back and pondered. The backstory. What had led to this stubborn refusal to speak, bloodstained clothes and an apparent attempt to hurt a child? Why? Joanna's degree in psychology frequently led her to ask this question and for all it was just three letters long it could be one of the most difficult questions to answer. The depressing fact was that in most cases there was no why. Nothing logical. Perhaps drink, a temper, morbid jealousy, sometimes delusions. Fear? A desperate attempt to escape? Panic? And at its heart? According to Sophie at the forensic lab the amount of blood on the dress and cardigan as well as the splashes on the little boy's dungarees didn't necessarily translate to a homicide. But the fact that the little boy's parents had still not come forward gave Joanna a dark feeling.

She pictured the location of the drama and their initial involvement. The Roaches was a high, remote location and from the top one had a 360-degree view. You could see anyone coming. Was it possible their girl had sequestered the little boy not to hurt him but to protect him? Had she been escaping a crime scene? Joanna thought back to the CCTV footage of the girl boarding the bus. Had she been fleeing? Where were her coat and bag? Dumped somewhere to keep her identity a secret? But she'd had officers searching bins through the town and anywhere else they might have been left. So far they had not found them.

Focussing on the area where the girl had first been sighted made her wonder. Why there? What was her connection with The Roaches? And Leek? It wasn't a particularly well-known spot even to folk from the city of Stoke-on-Trent. Had it been suggested by this 'friend' who, so far, had failed to come forward? Had the area some significance in her mind? The Roaches was memorable, the rock profile of the winking man watching over a remote road, the A53, which threaded over the moors linking Leek to Buxton. Once seen it would stick in the memory.

Had she gone there to kill the child or abandon him?

She found herself rejecting this theory. That wasn't it.

There were easier and more certain ways of disposing of a two-year-old than tipping him over the edge of a cliff. He could have survived the fall and drawn more attention to the situation – as would she, if she had followed him over the drop.

And lastly the greatest puzzle of all. Why had she clammed up so completely? Evasion? Concealment? Guilt? Was the psychiatrist correct, that it was the result of trauma? She had spoken enough to tell the bus driver where she wanted to go. And to Declan Toft, the lorry driver who had picked her up. She hadn't been dumb then.

She picked up the phone, already aware it would lead to a confrontation.

Dr Roget was guarded in her response. 'I don't see what you hope to achieve by another pointless interview. Apart from nodding and shaking her head she is still hardly communicating.'

'And you continue to believe this is involuntary rather than deliberate?' Joanna finished the question with scepticism bordering on mockery.

But Claire Roget was her equal. 'I don't *think* it, Inspector,' she said, acid in her response. 'I *know* it.'

Joanna was defeated. In her heart of hearts she knew the psychiatrist was probably right. But she had to find out what had happened to the girl. And that meant continuing to put pressure on her, whatever Claire Roget had to say about it.

TWENTY-TWO

Midday

She released the CCTV from the bus to the press hoping it would lead to them finding the missing items.

She homed in on the bag before moving on to show the girl struggling with the pushchair, appealing for the lady who had helped her stow the item in the luggage compartment to come forward. They had re-checked with the lorry driver who had later picked them up and confirmed. 'She was wearing just a dress and wellingtons.'

'She didn't leave anything in your lorry?'

'No.' He sounded slightly miffed. 'If she had I would have brought them in for you.'

Sensing his defence Joanna had thanked him. But it was always as well to check and re-check statements. Simple facts misheard or misunderstood hampered many an enquiry.

One of the hacks shouted out his question. 'Is she still not talking?'

'No.'

There was a smirk from a couple of reporters who had picked up on her mood.

To try and hide it she turned back to the screen and again flicked up the close-ups of both the coat and the handbag. 'As neither the coat nor the bag has yet been found we are working on the assumption that they were discarded either in Leek or somewhere on the way out to The Roaches.'

While the reporters' cameras flashed gratifyingly on the two images, she faced the possibility that someone had found one or both items and decided to keep them. Not everyone is honest.

Then she turned back to the image they had taken on the screen. The girl looked pale and hunched. Apprehensive. More a victim than a killer.

The questions came thick and fast but she was aware that the questions the media were posing were a depressing echo of her own.

'The bloodstains could have been a result of a domestic fracas,' she agreed with one of the local reporters. She felt suddenly exhausted with all the questioning.

Richard Corby, the *Sentinel* reporter, put his head on one side and looked at her thoughtfully as though he could read her mind. She liked the guy, had worked with him over a number of major cases and she knew he was fair and honest. His stories were largely factually correct. 'So what's next Inspector Piercy?'

She was tempted to respond, *I wish I knew*, but she elected to play the safe line.

'We're continuing with our enquiries.' She left it at that and turned to leave.

She tried to smile at Corby as she walked out, but it was hard. Every time she thought of the little boy clinging to Sandra Clowes she felt guilty, as though his prolonged predicament was solely down to her failure.

She left the contact number on the screen and left.

Almost instantly the phones began to ring and ring and ring.

TWENTY-THREE

2 p.m.

Joanna headed over to Greatbach once again, one of the most depressing places she'd ever visited. Claire Roget was in her office; Joanna now knew the way only too well.

If Dr Roget could have prevented her from seeing her patient, Joanna sensed, she would have. As it was Claire satisfied herself with folding her arms and beaming out her negative vibes, an air of resentment souring her words.

'You'll get nothing from her. You're wasting your time, Inspector.'

'I have to try and keep trying.'

'It's pointless.'

This made Joanna flare up. 'We don't know she's a victim. You think it's pointless to search for the child's parents when there is a distinct possibility that the reason your *patient*' – her voice was laden with sarcasm – 'is struck "dumb" is because she has assaulted them?'

'You don't know that either,' Claire said quietly.

'Blood spatter analysis is a pretty precise way of reconstructing a crime scene and quite apart from splashing on the girl's dress and a pretty big stain on her cardigan, there is the issue of the little boy's dungarees. Whatever happened he was there. A witness.' She was reduced to pleading. 'Think of it from my perspective, please. It's been well over a week now and not a peep out of either parent wondering where their little boy is. Do you have children, Doctor?'

'No, I don't.' Claire's voice was very clipped and defensive.

Joanna regarded her thoughtfully, aware that she had just stepped on the doctor's corns.

She tried to make her point. 'I do, Doctor, I know where my son is and who is caring for him every single moment of every single day. Why hasn't at least one of the parents come forward?'

Claire pressed her lips together and heaved yet another of her great big sighs. This time, judging by the slope of her shoulders, in surrender. 'I'll take you to her.'

As though to emphasize that this was her patch she stalked ahead of Joanna who was beginning to boil over with resentment at the psychiatrist's attitude. It was OK for her. No one asked her on a daily basis why she hadn't persuaded her patient to talk. There was no public scrutiny of her slow or even wasted perform-ance. No newspaper headlines screaming at her incompetence. She was protected and shielded by 'patient confidentiality'. She could hide behind this smokescreen for ever and would get kudos simply by writing up this unusual case. She wasn't judged, as the police were, by swift results.

It didn't help that, once they had been key-padded into the locked ward and were stood outside the door of their girl's room, Claire entered first to explain to her patient that the inspector was here and had requested *another* interview.

If it was possible the girl looked even paler and thinner than when she had last seen her. As though she was vanishing inside her dumb self. Her eyes were tired but watchful, but this time her gaze locked into Joanna's eyes, whether to suck out information or to convey something was unclear. She was taking in every single word that was said. Joanna thanked the psychiatrist, hoping she'd realize this was a tacit dismissal, and waited until she'd left before sitting down in the chair and speaking in a calm, controlled voice. This time she was going to play the game differently.

She opened with a smile which was not returned.

'I don't know your name; neither do we know where you came from on that' – another smile – 'rather chilly morning.'

The girl's eyes remained fixed on her face.

'I don't know why you were going to tip that little boy out of his pushchair.' After a pause Joanna continued, 'Perhaps that was never your intention?'

Joanna kept her eyes trained on the girl's.

'So, we know that the child isn't yours.'

The girl's eyes flickered but she pressed her lips together.

'Just as we know that the blood on your frock and cardigan wasn't yours either but his father's.'

The girl's colour drained. For a moment Joanna thought she might even faint. But after a pause of a few seconds the girl's colour returned, though she now kept her eyes trained on the floor as though worried Joanna might read something in them.

'We also know that you caught the early morning bus from Hanley bus station out to Leek.' This comment elicited a jerk of the girl's thin shoulders. 'We have CCTV footage of you climbing onto the bus and struggling with the pushchair. A woman helped you with it.' Joanna caught the slight start the girl made. It encouraged her. 'We also know that you were wearing a camel-coloured coat and carrying a bag when you climbed onto that bus and when you left it. It's all recorded.'

The girl's eyes lifted to Joanna's mouth, watching her form the words.

'Is the little boy's father dead?'

There was no mistaking the terror in the girl's eyes now. Or her gasp.

Joanna ignored it. 'We don't know yet who your young charge is so we can't call him by his name. That's a shame, isn't it?'

This provoked a slow, tired blink.

'And we can't contact his parents.' She waited but now there was no response. 'We don't know your relationship to him. Were you employed as his nanny? Paid to look after him? That doesn't include dropping him over a cliff, does it?'

The girl's head dropped. In shame?

Joanna leaned in. 'Whatever it looked like I'm not convinced that you meant to hurt him. So why did you go there? Why there?'

The girl's eyes flew up. Instinctively Joanna knew that the girl was wondering whether she could trust her.

She tried out another smile. 'There are patches in our knowledge which you would easily be able to fill.'

No response. 'We've made appeals to the general public and I'm confident that before long someone will find those missing items, the ones you discarded in Leek. The lorry driver who was kind enough to pick you up said that you weren't wearing a coat; neither did you have a bag. We *will* get our answers however hard you're trying to suppress them.'

Joanna rose from her chair. 'What I'm saying is we don't *need* you to talk. It's OK. It would save us time but at some point a member of the public *will* come forward and identify you and or the little boy and we will follow the trail back to his home. Either that or we'll find that coat and bag which, I am sure, will have some ID in it. After all, you paid the bus driver, didn't you? And then we will be working backwards and searching the place and the mess you have left behind you.' She aimed her gaze at the ceiling. 'What will we find there, I wonder?'

She had thought the girl's face couldn't be paler. But now her skin was ghost white. Her hands shimmered with a fine tremor. The girl was terrified.

She worked on the assumption that the girl's terror was not for her but someone else.

'You can't hide here for ever, you know?'

The girl slumped down in the chair.

'When we have found the place you left we can start to piece together the story. And we will charge you with any crimes you might have committed including wasting police time.'

Fingers crossed Dr Roget was not listening at the door.

'I am sure you understand me perfectly, don't you? So you can give up the pretence of being dumb and believing that you can obstruct our enquiries by appearing damaged.' She put her face close to the girl's. 'I want you to know, it's not washing with me.'

The girl sank back in her chair, eyes half closed, legs extended straight out in front of her, in an attitude of hopelessness. Her breath was coming in short, sharp gasps.

Joanna leaned in. 'I know you're perfectly able to talk and at some point you will. But I want you to know that this silence of yours, this affectation of dumbness, will be considered an obstruction to the police enquiry when we do finally unravel your story.'

The girl put her hands over her face. Like the old game: if I can't see you, you can't see me. Joanna felt a strange twist in her heart. What on earth had driven this young woman to such a place? To hide behind being mute?

She waited but there was no further response. The girl had shut down.

Claire walked in without knocking. She gave a fake smile which failed to disguise her triumph. 'Any luck?'

Joanna scowled. 'I didn't think she'd talk,' she said, closing the door behind her. 'That wasn't the point of this interview. It was to tell her things, warn her that we were unravelling her story. But I wanted her to know that hiding behind being *struck dumb*' – she managed to inject the words with the scepticism she was feeling – 'was going to cost her in the end. I think if anything loosens her tongue it will be that . . .' She avoided adding, 'Rather than your drugs or psychotherapy'.

Claire moved as though to remonstrate with her on this point but let her hand drop. 'OK,' she said in a carefully controlled voice. 'You've made your point.'

But despite having made her point – as forcefully as she dared – Joanna was forced to acknowledge that the psychiatrist had won the toss.

TWENTY-FOUR

Thursday 25 March, midday

For twenty-four hours the police were inundated with calls. False sightings, reports of neighbours missing, a whole host of grandparents who had not seen their grandchildren for weeks, months, sometimes years. Missing couples had separated or were on holiday, staying with friends or abroad. A few of the leads were even easier to disprove. They simply picked up the phone and told police, sometimes quite haughtily, that everything was fine in 'their' household. All had, so far, checked out. A few callers claimed to recognize the girl but didn't lead anywhere. It seemed as though the girl and her young charge had sprung out of nowhere.

The police waited patiently and optimistically, manning their dedicated lines, but there was nothing of substance and their optimism was beginning to shrink.

Joanna had detailed a couple of uniforms plus DC Hesketh-Brown to make a search of anywhere in Leek the girl might have dumped the coat and bag. They'd raided bins and searched wasteland but so far had turned up nothing. Which was a puzzle. The images of both had been well publicised. The coat had looked expensive. Well-cut and distinctive, camel wool, and the bag had been large – big enough for a mobile phone, purse and make-up as well as the usual mummy-clutter – spare nappy, a drink, baby wipes and a plastic bag to put a soiled nappy in. No one in charge of a young child moves an inch without one. So where was it? Why hadn't it turned up? Another puzzle. The bus had dropped their girl off in Leek at six fifty a.m. The lorry driver had picked her up 'quite early' a mile out of Leek at Blackshaw Moor. Pushing a child in a pushchair, progress would have been slow. So maybe around seven fifteen. She hadn't had much time to dispose of the two items, neither had she had time for much of a detour. The area between the two points had been scoured and they'd turned up plenty: litter from takeaways, plastic water bottles, discarded fag packets and more. But these two distinctive items remained stubbornly concealed.

Spurred on by an increasingly despondent SIO, the officers persevered, sticking doggedly to their remit. One of those phone calls would surely provide them with a lead.

On the Friday morning Joanna spent an uncomfortable half hour explaining to Chief Superintendent Gabriel Rush exactly where they were up to and had to confess that from where he was sitting they hadn't really left the starting blocks. He looked suitably unimpressed. 'Well, Piercy,' he said, voice sharp as flint, 'you don't appear to have made much headway here. Hmm?'

'No, sir.' Trying to avoid looking at his ginger eyelashes and thin scar of a mouth was a challenge. When you are determined to avoid looking at something it always seems to find your central vision. Her eyes constantly returned to CS Gabriel Rush's face as though magnetized. Once – maybe twice – in the years since he had taken over from Arthur Colclough she had seen that tight scar of a mouth bend into an imitation smile. Most of the time it remained humourless. And CS Rush had a talent for spotting weak points in her narrative.

'You don't actually know her intention towards the child. So no charge.'

'No, sir.'

'Neither do you know that a crime has been committed.'

They were always statements, never questions.

'No, sir.'

Next, rather surprisingly, instead of bleating out something about resources or deployment of officers, he gave her a searching look. 'You have a bad feeling about this, don't you, Piercy?'

Well, that was unexpected. She felt her mouth drop open. But the question presented her with a quandary. Feelings weren't exactly *de rigueur* in the police. All the same she nodded. 'Yes, sir, I do.'

'You believe the girl is deliberately not speaking.'

She nodded.

'But the psychiatrist believes this mute condition is the result of trauma.'

'Yes, sir.'

His mouth then did bend in his imitation smile. 'I wonder who is right.' And without waiting for a response he dismissed her, only speaking again when she had reached the door. 'How is DS Korpanski?'

'Healing slowly, sir. I visit him most weeks.'

'Hmm. When will he be back at work?'

'He mentioned three months, sir.'

His pale blue eyes warmed. 'I expect you miss him.'

She nodded and left.

TWENTY-FIVE

In the end it took three days, during which time Joanna lost heart and started to believe they would never find an explanation for this bizarre set of circumstances. She heard nothing from the psychiatrist and started to wonder whether she should be redeploying the officers.

Monday 29 March, 10 a.m.

The call came in on the Monday morning.

It came from the charity shop at the far end of the High Street. A tentative voice calling the helpline with the usual bleat: 'I hope I'm not wasting your time.'

PC Paul Ruthin reassured her with a stolid, 'Let us be the judge of that, madam.'

The voice was still timid. 'I think I *might* have found something you're looking for.'

'What exactly?'

'A coat?' the voice said tentatively. 'Looks good quality. Beige. Wool. And a big handbag too.'

When PC Ruthin's hand shot up Joanna crossed the room and was at the officer's side in a millisecond.

Their caller gave out her name and address and minutes later Joanna and Alan King were in a car screaming down Stockwell Street heading to the animal charity shop, to be met by a harassed-looking woman in her early fifties who stood outside, waiting for them. She held out her hand and introduced herself as Doreen Spencer, one of the voluntary helpers. Joanna took in salt-and-pepper gingery hair, a thin frame and an anxious expression which straight-away launched into an apology. 'I'm so sorry. You see, we get left so much stuff we don't always get to unpack it straight away, or even' – her face flushed – 'for weeks sometimes.'

They followed her into the shop as Doreen Spencer continued with her breathless apology. 'You see, people just leave stuff outside in bin liners and we . . .'

'That's OK.' Joanna responded to halt the woman's protestations because she wanted to focus on the contents of the bag. Before slipping on a pair of latex examination gloves she looked around her. The shop was small and deep, with a narrow bay window onto the street. Inside was a chaotic jumble: jigsaws and dresses; shoes and books; plates and ornaments; children's toys; and a stack of DVDs that had almost toppled to the floor.

Doreen Spencer handed her a bag. Ironically Joanna noted it was a Co-op 'bag for life'. Hopefully, she reflected, that was what it would be. A bag for life. Not death. She knew straight away that this was what they had been searching for. She could feel the weight of the coat through the plastic.

And underneath was a large brown leather bag, a cross between a rucksack and a handbag. Big enough for the spare nappy and drink. There was other stuff below the two items of interest. At a guess, Joanna thought, their girl had done a clever thing. She had stuffed her expensive coat and the bag in with someone else's contribution left outside the shop.

Rather than pull it out and perhaps lose some material evidence she placed the lot in a larger bag. While DC King sealed and labelled it she spoke to Ms Spencer whose eyes now were round with excitement. At a guess her connection with the case in the news would be spread around Leek by the end of the afternoon.

Without any hope of a precise answer, Joanna asked the question anyway. 'Do you know when this bag was left?'

Ms Spencer's face flushed with embarrassment. 'I'm not sure. I can't be . . . We don't really log the stuff in. And quite often bags are . . .' She gulped. 'We have a small area behind the gates which are locked when we leave. Quite often people drop bags over when we're closed so we don't even see . . .' Her voice was trailing away until she took up her story again. 'We don't even see who left the stuff.'

'I take it you don't have CCTV?'

That resulted in a regretful shake of Doreen's head.

DC King vanished outside and he too shook his head. 'None in this particular part of the street.'

'It was already in the Co-op bag?'

Doreen looked even more embarrassed. 'Sometimes things are left and the staff bag them up. For neatness,' she added, with more inspiration than credibility.

'Can you get me a list of the people who work here? And if you could get some idea of when the bag was dropped off.'

'I'll try.'

Even Joanna could hear the doubt in her voice.

She couldn't wait to see what the forensic lab made of the Co-op bag and its contents. And whether their girl's identity would now be revealed.

She almost gave a whoop as they left the shop. 'Bet you a bottle of wine we know who she is once we've had this bag unpacked.'

For the first time DC King sported a hint of Korpanski's sense of humour. 'What sort of wine?'

She responded with a flourish and a grin. 'Nectar of the Gods,' she said. 'Rioja.'

DC King laughed, throwing his thin face back and guffawing loud enough to wake a donkey. She looked at him in surprise. This was a first. Perhaps they were getting used to each other.

Because of the nature of the case and her fears for where this new evidence might lead them she decided to take the Co-op bag straight to the lab herself. Everything then could be neatly tagged and analysed. The trouble was the forensic lab was in the south side of the Potteries, forty-five minutes away. They needed to get there ASAP so they used the blue light to get through the lunchtime traffic, arriving in record time. Joanna and DC King donned forensic suits and gloves. The last thing they needed was any risk of contamination. They hardly dared breathe as they handed over the bag to the lab assistant, putting the coat to one side for now.

Joanna pressed her palms together in an attitude of prayer.

Sophie Grayling met Joanna's eyes and gave a broad smile. 'Success?'

'Let's see.'

They all turned their attention to the expensive-looking handbag. Soft leather, big enough to hold most requirements, with a long, buckled shoulder strap. And expensive enough to twin with the coat. A Mulberry label. It looked almost new.

With the delicacy of a neurosurgeon Sophie dusted the outside with fingerprint powder and photographed the results, taping a few of the clearer examples. 'Be interesting to see if your girl has a track record.'

'Not so far,' Joanna responded. 'We've already run her prints through the database. She didn't come up.'

'Well, here goes.' Sophie tipped the contents out onto a plastic tray. Lipstick, purse, mobile phone. Joanna felt exultation.

Now I have you, she thought. *I'll know who you are. I'll know your name. I'll know everyone you've spoken to. I'll see your pictures. I'll know your contacts and I'll have an address. Only a matter of minutes now.*

Sophie pulled out a plastic bag containing baby wipes and a spare nappy. 'All there.' Her smile was broad. There was nothing she liked better than making significant finds.

Joanna reached out and took the purse. Opened it and pulled out a debit card in the name of Louisa C. Newton. Heaven. They would soon know everything there was to know about Mrs Louisa C. Newton. They'd even know her shopping habits. 'I'll take this if that's OK.'

Had she been with Mike they might have slapped a high five or a fist bump, but she and King merely exchanged a faint smile. And that was it.

So was Louise C. Newton their girl or was she the mother of the little boy?

She picked up the mobile phone, an expensive 5G Apple iPhone which King was eyeing with the greedy eye of a starving man. He could squeeze the data out of an iPhone easier than juice out of a lemon. Unless the phone was locked. She handed it to him.

Next they turned their attention to the coat, spreading it out, arms outstretched, Jaeger label exposed. King was already searching his own mobile phone.

'Over three hundred quid,' he said.

The outside of the coat was relatively clean. But when they held the flap back, the lining inside was a different story. In the right armpit was the same bloodstain that had marked the girl's cardigan. Sophie Grayling put her hands over her mouth.

Joanna touched the stain with her gloved index finger. It felt stiff. Would this bloodstain be mixed with a second one? Maybe the child's mother? Something puzzled her. Their silent girl was maybe a size eight or ten, five foot two. The label inside the coat identified it as size fourteen. Their girl would have drowned in it. Ergo it wasn't her coat. 'OK,' she said to Sophie who was already laying out the rest of the contents ready for examination. 'I think we're done here. Best to leave this to you.'

Sophie looked positively bright at the prospect. 'My pleasure, Inspector,' she said with a grin and a mock curtsey.

TWENTY-SIX

Back at the station half an hour later they were laying out all they knew about Mrs Louisa C. Newton. The 'C' stood for Caroline. She lived in a rural area, a remote lane just north of Congleton, in an isolated, detached house incongruously named 'The Cottage'.

Why did people do this? Joanna wondered. Downgrade their homes by naming them cottages when they were mansions as though it was an 'in' joke? They Google Earthed it and Joanna whistled. 'It must be worth a couple million,' she said as they zoomed in. It looked as though it had been built sometime in the last ten years, as big as a Tesco hypermarket, surrounded by mature trees and reached by a long drive which was sealed off by high, electric gates. There was a garage big enough for a couple of Rolls-Royces as well as a cottage on the edge of the estate. The bag and coat had suggested money. This confirmed it.

The address was registered to a Louisa and Anthony Newton and a child, Steven. Without any hope of response Joanna dialled the phone number. As expected, no one picked up and they were through to an automated answerphone. A man's voice, curt and dismissive, said, 'We're not here at the moment. Leave a message and we *may* get back to you.' There was a hint of dry humour. She wondered if he was still alive.

King was downloading information from the mobile phone. 'Leave that with someone else,' she said. 'Let's go call.'

Common sense was already telling her their girl was not the

woman who owned this house, neither was she married to the man who had left that confident message. She was, as she had surmised, probably their nanny.

However much she dreaded the scene she would unearth, she was anxious to get out there and quickly. But first she made time for two phone calls. The first was to Sandra Clowes. 'We believe we have a name for your little boy,' she said before giving her a potted version of their findings.

Her response was warm and typical. 'So he's a little Stevie,' she said. 'Well, it'll be nice to be able to call him by his name.'

Joanna's second call was to Dr Claire Roget to share the facts they knew so far. It came with a warning. 'We don't think your girl is the Mrs Newton whose identity we have just discovered. It's more likely that she was Steven's nanny. She made a clever effort to conceal her identity. You might try facing her with the fact that we have found the coat and bag she was so anxious to conceal.'

'I understand.' For once the psychiatrist was relatively amenable and her response sounded subdued.

'We're just heading out to the address now.'

'Let me know what you find.'

Joanna put the phone down with a wry smile. The psychiatrist was, at last, 'getting it'.

It was late afternoon by the time they set out for The Cottage.

The road between Leek and Congleton includes a stretch of the A54 beloved by motorbikers who find the steep decline and sharp bends a challenge. The result is that there were warning signs displaying the numbers of deaths on this short stretch of highway – less than six miles – which had claimed the lives of too many adventurers. It made it a sobering trip even apart from her apprehension for what they would find at journey's end.

Joanna had let King drive with a warning not to be in too much of a hurry. He'd accepted the advice and kept a steady speed all the way there while Joanna tried to suppress her worst fears.

She might have a clue to the girl's identity but there were still some pretty big holes in the narrative. The concealment of the coat and handbag suggested intelligent planning. Much better to dump the coat and bag outside a charity shop where such items were left all the time. Hide a tree in a forest. Hay in a haystack.

Clothes and a handbag – even an expensive one – outside a charity shop where people leave bin liners of such items all the time. Had their girl dropped the coat and bag into a litter bin it would have been picked up and brought to their notice that much sooner. Unless someone had pilfered it. But the action with the child pointed in the opposite direction, of someone who didn't know what to do. It suggested confusion and indecision. Blind panic? Was there a plan which had gone wrong?

King pulled up in front of a set of gates. Tall, electrified and standing open. They could see the house at the end of the drive. Large, white, square. It looked deserted. There were no cars outside, but there was a large garage. All was quiet, peaceful even. Joanna glanced at DC King's set face as he too surveyed the scene and wondered if he was feeling the same cold, creeping sensation coming over her – that, as the gates stood open, inviting them in, the house had been waiting for them all this time. The stage had been set almost two weeks ago and now, as anticipated, they had walked – or rather driven – right in. Maybe, Joanna thought uncomfortably, they should have come with backup. She spoke into the car radio. 'We've just arrived at . . .'

This was no cottage. She struggled with the attempt at mockery, a sort of reverse pretention.

King drove slowly up the drive, both of them fixing their gaze ahead, willing a door to open, someone coming out to greet them or ask what the hell they were doing.

Nothing.

No one.

Even though built in the last ten years, the house had made a feeble attempt at Georgian style. It sported long sash windows to the front and a stone portico. The drive was long, straight, tree-lined and ended in a little roundabout, its centre a grass circle with a huge dolphin spitting water into a fishpond. They were plainly visible from the house. But still no one came out to challenge them.

As they drew closer Joanna realized The Cottage was an imitation of many smart country properties, but the architecture was all wrong. Like the name. UPVC windows imitating Georgian sashes. A portico at the front, plaster pillars to the side. King pulled up at the front door, tugged at the handbrake and they sat, reluctant to leave the safety of the car. While they observed the house, all was quiet and peaceful, but Joanna felt anything but relaxed. They stepped outside the car and rang the mechanical bell pull which jangled loudly, echoing through an empty hall. Then waited. No one came and all was silent.

Joanna was having trouble connecting their bedraggled, blood-stained girl to this place. She could not picture her here. Where did she fit in to all this? And who, she wondered, as they waited beneath the portico, with its fake plaster pillars, would open the door?

TWENTY-SEVEN

N o one, it seemed.
They stood there for a few minutes, eyeing one another before moving to the side, crunching over gravel, peering through tall, ground-floor windows. The house was furnished with huge gilded mirrors, plaster statues, silk flower arrangements and cream-coloured sofas big enough to sleep on. There was a TV (also huge) in every room. But all was neat and tidy. Nothing that suggested a crime scene. They walked through a stone archway around to the back, a paved area more utilitarian with a washing line and a pile of logs in a store, peering in at the windows, this time into a space-age kitchen, all stainless steel, granite and gadgets. Again, nothing looked amiss. No sign of a battle here, an assault or a break-in. All was in order. In spite of her fears it did not look like a crime scene.

Adjoining the back of the house was a large glass conservatory, resplendent with orange trees, more plaster statuettes and cane furniture.

Joanna tried the door and this time it opened. Slipping on gloves and calling out to warn anyone present that the police were entering, she and DC King walked inside.

They were soon confronted with the space-age kitchen. Overhead lights blazed down onto polished granite work surfaces. Joanna scanned the room. Nothing. Not a spot of blood, nothing out of place. It was as tidy as a film set waiting for the actors to enter.

And she felt a growing sense of unease. Access had been too

easy, the house almost waiting for them to walk in. It all felt strange. She scanned the set, pivoting round the entire room. No expense had been spared in the kitchen. Everything was of the highest specifications: enormous cream units; grey granite work surfaces with a central island; huge American-style fridge. The equipment along the granite surface implied a skilled cook or someone who wanted to appear a gourmet chef. There was an impressive collection of copper pans, numerous implements hanging from a rack. A knife block. One missing. But for all the hints at a foodie there was no scent of food. The only smell that lingered was one Joanna was familiar with, a Jo Malone candle, which was burnt right down to its wick on the central island.

The silence of the house, like the silence of the girl, seemed at once oppressive and at the same time designed to exclude them. The chill in the kitchen, reflected from the granite surfaces in spite of its luxuriousness, felt more like a morgue.

Joanna glanced at King whose face was pale – whether from excitement or apprehension she couldn't even have guessed. She still didn't know him well enough.

They called out again and their voices bounced off the gleaming surfaces, seeming to mock their obtuseness.

Seek and ye shall find.

Joanna frowned. 'Where's the burglar alarm? Why isn't it set?' Her voice echoed over the tiled floor and marbled surfaces.

They looked at each other. Because . . .

Because they *shouldn't* have been able to enter. The doors *should* have been locked, the burglar alarm set. Someone *should* have seen them. But there was no one here. The emptiness was absolute.

They left the kitchen and walked through the hall into the sitting room they had observed through the window. It was so large, and the carpet pile deep enough to absorb all sound, one would have to shout to be heard by someone at the far end. In here, as in the kitchen, all appeared in order. It was a room furnished entirely in cream, pale enough and plain enough to expose the smallest bloodstain. They returned to the hall and entered a room on the right which was almost filled by a huge snooker table with large green lamps beaming down. Switched off.

Beyond that was another room kitted out like a cinema complete with wide plush red seats and a far wall white enough to act as a screen. Together with the designer bag and expensive coat the house had all the hallmarks of a wealthy family who wanted everyone to know it. There was self-consciousness in this parade of wealth. Someone had been pleased with themselves.

They returned to the hall and opened another door. This time they were hit by the smell of chlorine as they faced an indoor swimming pool, the water smooth as blue silk. Bifold doors overlooked a paved area and beyond that hedges and a garden.

Everything looked perfect and yet they both felt somewhere in this vast property was the source of the bloodstain on their girl's dress.

King nudged her arm. Through the windows and beyond another archway they saw a man digging manure into a rose bed. He was dressed in baggy blue trousers and a grey/blue fleece. A hoodie hid his hair. Joanna pulled back one of the doors. 'Police,' she shouted, startling the man.

He stared at them for a moment before responding. 'Gardener,' he replied, grinning, and straightened up. 'What are *you* doing here?'

Where to start, Joanna thought.

'Where are the people who live here?'

'On holidays, I think.'

King butted in. 'How come the house is unlocked? Left wide open? Gates too.'

'Shouldn't be,' the man said. 'Should have been proper locked up.'

'Well, it wasn't,' Joanna said crisply. 'We've just walked right in. Which way did *you* enter?'

The gardener pulled his hoodie down exposing a ginger beard and a mop of curling hair which he scratched, puzzled. 'My cottage is the other way. I come from over there . . .' He pointed to the fields at the back of the house. 'Along the footpath. I don't come in by the big gates so I wouldn't have noticed if they were open or shut unless I was working at the front of the house.' He was somewhere in his forties with a sunburnt face, eyebrows bleached by his outdoor life.

He regarded them for a moment before asking the obvious. 'Why are you here? Not just because of the gates, surely?' His accent was West Country, perhaps Bristolian.

'Have you read the news lately?'

The man's face cracked into a smile. 'Hardly bother,' he said, shrugging. 'Doesn't affect me.'

'So you haven't read about a girl and a little boy who've been found on The Roaches?'

The gardener shook his head and glanced back at the rose bed he'd been digging.

'Who lives here?'

The gardener put his head on one side and grinned. 'You're the police,' he said cheekily. 'You should know.'

Joanna waited.

'Mr and Mrs Newton and their little boy.'

'And?'

'Well, the nanny, of course.'

The nanny. 'Did the little boy go on holiday with his parents?'

The gardener shook his head. 'They likes to have a good time,' he said. 'Little boy would cramp their style. Leave him with the nanny, they do.'

'Where have they gone on holiday?'

The gardener shrugged. 'I don't know,' he said. 'They wouldn't tell me. They have a lot of holidays.' His attention was still on the rose bed, his interest in his employers barely registering.

'So the nanny is supposed to be here?'

He nodded, perhaps at last realizing something was wrong. 'Isn't she there then?'

Joanna shook her head. She pulled up the picture of their girl on her phone. 'Is this the girl?'

The gardener looked for a moment then nodded, smiling. 'That's her all right. Little Miss Welshie, I calls her. Very hoity toity. Don't have much to do with a humble gardener.' He moved his head back and fore, making a face.

'And this is the little boy?'

The gardener's face softened. 'Aye, that's little Stevie all right. Right little chap he is. Toddles around after me.' The gardener laughed. 'Tries to pull a big brush along and he can't manage it. Nothing he likes more than a ride in me wheelbarrow.' His expression altered. 'He is safe, is he?'

No need to go into detail. 'Yeah. He's fine.'

'Good.' The gardener pulled his hood back over his hair and picked up his spade, angling his body ready to continue forking in the barrow load of manure.

'We're going to want you to make a statement.'

'About what?'

'About the fact that your little Miss Welshie has turned up in Leek with the little boy.'

The gardener looked astonished. 'Leek?' He was as shocked as if they had said Timbuktu. 'Leek,' he said again. 'What she go there for?'

'That's what we're hoping you can tell us.'

The gardener shook his head vigorously. 'Not a clue.' He paused, thinking. 'What was she doin' up there? With Stevie, you say?'

'Yes.' She let that sink in before asking, 'What is Little Miss Welshie's name?'

'Bethany. She's surely told you that.'

'Bethany?'

'Rees. Bethany Rees.'

DC King stepped forward. 'And your name?'

The gardener switched his focus to the DC. 'Adam,' he said, with another grin. 'Good name for a gardener, eh?'

King's face didn't crack. 'Adam . . .?'

'Judd. Adam Judd.'

Joanna took over. 'And how long have you been a gardener here?'

'Nearly two years.'

He asked the next question. 'So do Mr and Mrs Newton know Little Miss Welshie had taken Stevie up there?'

'We don't know. We haven't spoken to them yet. You say they're probably on holiday?'

'Probably.' He switched that to, 'I dunno. They's always off somewhere or other, somewhere where it's hot and sunny and don't rain all the time. Funny, isn't it?' He glanced over their shoulders towards the swimming pool. 'They have this great big mansion of a place with every mod con going and they spend all their time escaping from it. Don't make no sense to me. If I had a place like this I'd never leave it.'

Maybe, Joanna was thinking as she too looked back at the swimming pool, *this time, they didn't.*

She drew in a deep sigh. They still had no explanation why 'Little Miss Welshie' had suddenly decided to take a bus out to the Staffordshire Moorlands and apparently make a clumsy attempt to dispose of her young charge.

'What is she like,' she asked curiously, 'this nanny?'

The gardener didn't answer straight away but took some time to choose his words. 'Strange,' he finally came out with. 'Very strange sort of girl. Keeps herself to herself. Full of herself. Like she's got anything to be snobbish about.'

'How did she get on with her employers?'

'All right, I suppose. I don't really know.' The frown was back.

'How many cars do they have?'

'Two or three. They have a Range Rover, a Tesla and a lovely old Jag. Like the one Inspector Morse drove.'

'Which one did Bethany drive?'

'Usually the Range Rover. I think that's missing now. It might be in the garage. I can check for you if you like.'

'Thank you. We'll do that. Is it usually locked?'

The gardener shook his head. 'But the Newtons would have taken one car,' he pointed out reflectively, 'if they drove themselves to the airport. Though sometimes they took a taxi or got me to give them a lift if they were going away for a long time. Airport parking,' he said sagely, nodding his head. 'Expensive.'

'We'll run a check. And we're going to need a statement from you, Mr Judd. You live . . .?'

'Over there, in that cottage.' He indicated across the field where a slate roof was just visible. Without smiling DC King took a note of his details while the gardener grinned and put on a mock American accent, speaking out of the corner of his mouth. 'So you're tellin' me, don't leave town?'

Joanna responded drily. 'That's about it.'

Both were aware that the gardener's explanation still didn't explain what their girl had been doing on the morning of the sixteenth.

'Well, at least we now know the girl's name,' Joanna said as they returned to the house. 'And the little boy's. And we have an explanation of sorts. If the Newtons *are* on holiday, thinking their son is safe with his nanny, it would explain why they haven't raised an alert about him being missing. It sounds as though they were casual parents and would have assumed that Bethany was caring for him as normal.'

But she was still uneasy. 'I suppose we'd better take a quick look upstairs.'

TWENTY-EIGHT

The upstairs was as lavishly furnished as the ground floor. They moved from room to room. Bedrooms with four poster beds, bathrooms all with stylish showers and sinks. They found Stevie's bedroom, all Fisher-Price toys and Winnie the Pooh wallpaper, and the bathroom he shared with Bethany, who had a suite of rooms all to herself. In here there were the first signs that all was not well. They had left in haste. Her bed was unmade, the duvet flung back, the wardrobe door hanging open. In Stevie's room the door to his wardrobe was also open and in their bathroom a tap was dripping.

Finally they reached the master bedroom and a door which was locked from the outside. Joanna turned the key and opened the door inwards. And now her worst nightmare had a form and a scent. Putrefaction is unmistakable.

The whole house was a film set, but a horror film in this room. He was in the bath, slumped forwards, almost doubled up, wounds in his back and Joanna knew he'd been here all this time. All the time the girl had been sitting with her mouth clamped shut she must have known he was here decomposing, his body degrading into this. As the bathroom had been fitted out as a wet room the smell had been effectively sealed and not permeated through the rest of the house. But the moment they'd opened the door they smelt the stink as well as hearing the buzzing of the inevitable flies who told their own story. Joanna had seen decomposed bodies before. The stench is unmistakeable and never quite leaves you. It stays in your memory, reawakening any time you smell even a hint of it again.

The bath was in an alcove at the side of the room, mirrors at its back, so she glimpsed her own pale face. As she swept her eyes around the room, absorbing every detail, she feared she would disgrace herself by being sick.

'You all right there, Joanna?'

That was what stopped her. She couldn't – wouldn't – puke up in front of DC Alan King, who looked a bit green around the gills himself.

'Call it in,' she managed.

Mr Newton (presumably) had been taking a bath. He was naked, his back to the doorway. She reached out a hand. His hair was still damp to the touch. The knife was still sticking out of one of his wounds. She counted six. Blood had dripped into the water, which was stained pink, in static swirls. A navy towelling dressing gown had been dropped over a chair. There was still a faint underlying scent of soap and bath oils. It was the nightmare scene Joanna had been recreating in many shapes and forms for the last two weeks. But even her imagination had not pictured such a starkly cruel image.

She could hear King speaking over the phone, his voice urgent but far away.

Well, she thought, starting to find clear thoughts again. It was undoubtedly a murder scene. Newton hadn't stuck the knife in his own back.

Bethany might have managed to preserve her secret for a short time but they all shared it now.

Her next question would be where was Mrs Newton? Was she a part of this? Victim or villain?

They descended the stairs and waited.

DC King went outside and spoke to the gardener. Joanna watched from the kitchen window and saw Adam shake his head, read his shock and disbelief. Then incredulity.

He'd been happily tending the garden while a man lay dead and decomposing in the house? His hands flew out. *No way!*

Joanna glanced at her watch.

If you have ever waited for an ambulance you will know that time stretches. A moment seems like minutes. Then an hour while teams are scrambled together. They waited for things to happen and people to arrive. For the blues and twos, the forensic teams, the equipment. And the pathologist.

It might be obvious that the man was dead, but this was a crime scene and Matthew was a Home Office pathologist with vast experience. Sometimes he could be as invaluable as another police officer. So she called him on her own mobile phone.

He responded straight away. 'Jo?'

'Matt.' Suddenly she wished that she had called to tell him that she loved him, not to report this and request his professional services. But he must have picked up on something in her tone because he pre-empted her message with a: 'What is it, Jo?', soft and full of concern.

'We've got a body, Matt. There's a knife sticking out of his back. He's been dead a while.' She kept her voice low.

'Is this connected with your silent girl?'

'I think so.'

'Where are you?'

She gave him the postcode and directions.

'I'll be with you in forty-five minutes.'

Relief flooded through her. 'Thank you.'

But he didn't hang up straight away. 'You all right, Jo?'

She drew in a deep, nauseated breath but managed a jaunty, 'Yeah. 'Course.'

To which her husband chuckled. 'Really?'

Which, in spite of the circumstances, made her smile. He knew her so well.

Her next call was to Karen Murphy. This situation would alter the social worker's role. Far from being reunited with one or both parents imminently it looked likely that little Stevie Newton's stay with the Clowes would be prolonged.

'We think we might have found his dad.'

'Oh.' Karen's voice started off bright. And then she must have started to put two and two together. Her second, 'Oh' was much more subdued. 'I take it they won't be reunited any time soon?'

'No.' It was all Joanna could give her. For now. But her hands were itching to dig her fingernails into their silent girl. AKA Bethany Rees. AKA Little Miss Hoity Toity. AKA Little Miss Welshie. She could hardly wait to get back to her and squeeze the truth out of her stubborn little mouth. Force her to talk. And then she pulled herself up short. Louisa Newton, the dead man's wife, was missing. There was a possibility that Bethany had snatched Stevie to protect him from a vengeful woman. Mr Newton had, after all, been sitting in the bath. Possibly unaware of the person who had entered. And who was more likely to enter a bathroom than the man's wife?

Had Bethany watched Louisa Newton kill her husband? Was she refusing to talk to protect Stevie's mother?

It didn't make sense that Bethany had rescued the child only to throw him off the edge of The Roaches. So why did she go there?

She heard the cars approaching almost in the exact same moment that she saw blue lights strobing up the drive, followed by the crunch of heavy boots striding over gravel and voices sharp with instructions.

Her first job as SIO was to direct proceedings. Approaches to a crime scene have to be preserved as carefully as an egg in aspic, beginning with sealing it off and personnel who had business to be there being allowed in. There is endless collecting of samples, examination for bloodstains, fingerprinting, photographs, videos. The house and grounds might be extensive but every inch needed to be covered using grid references. It was possible that Louisa Newton had fled the scene, but her body could also be here too. There was much to scour – garages, cars, attics, outhouses. The work would take days. Weeks even. Like squeezing juice from an orange they would need to extract everything. Even the pips.

She wondered whether the Newtons had CCTV at the property. That could make their job a lot easier. And it was possible that they had their prime suspect in custody already. But she didn't contact the psychiatrist. Not just yet. That could wait.

Matthew turned up an hour later and entered, protected by his paper suit, mask, overshoes and gloves. A lock of his hair had escaped his paper hat. She was tempted to tuck it back but kept her hands away. If it turned up as evidence she would soon be able to identify it. The slight curl as well as the colour and length was unmistakable to her. Through the mask she could read his smiled greeting and the sympathetic warmth lighting his eyes. He raised a hand in greeting. 'Hi.' And moved close enough to speak in a low voice. 'Jakob's with Mum and Dad so no pressure.'

She mouthed a 'thank you' and led him upstairs where he focussed all his attention on the body, photographing it from all angles and checking for lividity. At one point she saw him frown before focussing on the wounds, particularly the wound in his back.

Matthew had his own methods, almost like a mental tick list. She'd watched him a few times before and realized he read a body, its surrounds and the various physical signs, as she might read a crime scene. He did it almost instinctively without forming a conscious plan. But it was all there, stored in his brain, ready to produce in his report. After as thorough an examination as he could perform while Anthony Newton (presumed) remained in the bath, he straightened up. 'He's been dead around two weeks. And it looks as though he was killed here.' He checked and recorded the ambient temperature of the room before scraping some of the blowfly larvae into a specimen pot and holding it up. 'Our friends have been busy.'

Joanna contented herself with a brief nod. She felt sick.

When Matthew had finished he approached her, pulling his mask down so she could read his smile. 'Your man?'

'I think so.'

'And the mother?'

She shook her head. 'Not so far.'

He frowned. 'So where does your silent girl fit in to all this?'

She spoke in a low voice, not wanting the others to hear. 'Going through the rooms it looks like she left in a hurry. She's the little boy's nanny.'

He pursed his lips and blew out his opinion. 'Not exactly Mary Poppins.'

'No.'

Matthew's gaze drifted back to the naked man in the bath. He shook his head. 'So what on earth . . .? The wife?'

She shrugged. 'Who knows.'

'OK, well I'm done here,' he said. 'Unless you've another body?'

'No – at least not so far. We'll carry out a more thorough check over the next few days.'

He nodded. 'Well – you can send Mr . . .'

'Newton, I think,' she supplied.

'Send Mr Newton down to the morgue when you're ready.' He glanced back. 'There's not exactly any great hurry about the PM. I think he can wait a bit longer.'

She nodded.

'I guess this means you'll be pretty much tied up for the foreseeable?'

'Looks like it.'

He gave her an encouraging smile and patted her shoulder. 'My fault for marrying a copper.'

But she knew that pat. It expressed a whole host of messages. Sympathy for the job ahead, yes. Understanding that her work hours would now prove even more erratic, yes. But it was also an expression of his love. That pat on her shoulder broke through the hard shell she habitually wore at work. She turned her face towards him and read the gleam in his green eyes. 'Thanks, Matt,' she managed and he nodded.

The rest of the evening and much of the night ahead would be spent checking the property. It was a little after two a.m. by the time she headed home.

TWENTY-NINE

Tuesday 30 March, 8 a.m.

S he'd fallen into bed and thankfully slept deeply next to Matthew.

They'd both stirred a little after six. After feeding Jakob and changing his nappy, she dressed him in a pair of red dungarees and button through T-shirt, marvelling at his eyes turning the same green as Matthew's as she handed him over to his father so she could quickly dress herself, grab breakfast and a much-needed coffee before rushing out of the door.

Now her home life, Matthew, his parents and Jakob faded into the background. The case soaked up her entire conscious thought as she drove to the office.

PC Paul Ruthin updated her when she walked in. 'No sign of Mrs Newton,' he said, yawning.

'What about the cars?'

'Tesla and vintage Jag in the garage. The Range Rover's gone.'

'Do we have the reg?'

'Yep. I've put out a Search and Stop on it.'

'So either our dumb nanny took it or else Mrs Newton – and my money's on Bethany. She had to get to Hanley to get the bus somehow.'

Mr Newton's body had been removed to the mortuary where it would await a post-mortem. Matthew had texted her that he would perform it the following morning.

She texted back. 'Fine.' Then added, 'Thanks.'

She tried to get hold of Dr Roget to update her on the case, give her patient a name at least, but staff at Greatbach told her the psychiatrist was not in today. So she spoke to her registrar, a lady called Dr Salena Urbi, reinforcing the fact that their patient, Bethany, was now officially a murder suspect and that she would be over to interview her again in the next couple of days. She released the information to the media that a man's body had been found at the address together with the usual appeal for anyone who had information to come forward. She arranged a press conference for after the post-mortem.

Then it was time to gather the information in, direct operations, keep a check on the forensic team and leave a message for CS Rush who was also 'unavailable'.

Wednesday 31 March, 8 a.m.

She rode in with Matthew. She'd meet up with DC King and PC Bridget Anderton at the mortuary and hitch a lift back with them.

Their talk in was peppered with domesticity and the work that awaited them both.

Now Matthew was involved she spent some time bringing him up to speed.

'So you think your nanny murdered her boss?' He turned to look at her.

'Not necessarily. She could have been a witness.'

'Her clothes were bloodstained?'

'Yeah. Would you take a look at them?'

'Of course. I'd be glad to. You want some sort of analysis?'

'Well, now we have a body . . .'

They were almost at the mortuary. 'You must have some theories?'

She smothered a smile. 'I'm working on them.'

'I take it you'll "surprise" Bethany with your latest findings?'

'You read my mind. I want to see her reaction. She took enough trouble hiding her identity.'

'You think when she realizes you know who she is her tongue will magically unlock?'

'Don't mock me, Matt. Of course I'm hoping that'll happen.'

He glanced across and noted her frown and tense look. 'Hey,' he said, smiling now, though there was nothing to smile about. 'Once Little Miss Welshie starts talking she'll probably never stop.'

'Yeah, but then we'll have our next conundrum. When she

speaks will it be the truth? Or has she a head start thinking up various scenarios? Maybe she needed to buy herself time.'

'You think that's why she's keeping schtum?'

'It's a possibility.'

'Surely *anything* she says will be better than nothing?'

She turned to look at him. 'One would think so. Sometimes I'm not so sure. I'll reserve judgement, Matt.'

'And the missing wife?'

'Still missing.'

'So will your next stop be Greatbach?'

'Later. I'll wait for the results of the post-mortem before I hit her with it.'

He looked pleased with himself. 'Well, at least there I can help.'

'Thanks, Matt.'

He gave a cocky nod and a crooked smile. 'Just doin' my job, ma'am.'

'I think I can guess what your findings will be.'

'Now, now,' he said reprovingly. 'Don't do me out of a job.'

'As if . . .'

They'd reached the mortuary. A squad car was already in the parking lot. Matthew key-padded them in and held out a gown. 'Take over?'

She slipped the gown on. 'No, thanks.'

Bridget and Alan were already gowned up and waiting for them. The post-mortem room was all hard surfaces, white marble mainly. With the fans on full it was like walking into a fridge. They were noisy but necessary to clear the air of any scent apart from disinfectant and formaldehyde. Mr Newton had spent the night zipped in a body bag along with some fly spray. Garbed up and ready for action, Matthew unzipped the bag and began by taking photographs, measurements and samples as Joanna and the two officers stood back and watched. Her husband was in his own little world, eyes taking it all in, frowning as he gathered specimens and handed them to the officers. It wasn't the first time she'd observed this metamorphosis. He was utterly absorbed in this body, unaware of everyone else in the room. She watched his mask move as he started to construct a narrative around the injuries he observed, the state of the tissues surrounding each knife wound, taking samples for toxicology, examining stomach contents, fingerprinting, weighing organs, measuring the depth of what looked like the fatal injury.

Each sample was meticulously labelled; the chain of evidence stored. Like the police Matthew had his own boxes to tick and his own reasons for each statement, qualified by hard evidence, not conjecture. Who knew what might be challenged in a court room? She had watched him give evidence before. Matthew was careful not to overstep his mark, to steer clear of supposition, acknowledge when he had no evidence to support a theory and stick to certainty within the facts he knew and the evidence of the tissues. He was honest about anything he had doubts about.

Even before the first incision he'd measured the depth and width of the knife wounds with a probe, comparing them with the knife they'd found still in Newton's back, which in turn fitted into the gap in the knife block they'd brought to the mortuary. There were six wounds, all inflicted from behind – three on the left side of the chest, two on the right but nearer the spine and one high up, in the neck. All had maggot infestation. Matthew was frowning as he bent over them and once or twice crossed the room to study the photographs of the crime scene. Then he looked up and she caught the flash of green in his eyes.

'Jo,' he said, 'do you have any pictures of the blood pattern on the girl's clothes?'

'I can do better.' DC Alan King stepped forward, an A4 envelope in his hands. He pulled out a few photographs of the clothes they had removed from the girl they now knew was Bethany. King clipped them up on a board and Matthew crossed over to study them before returning to the body.

Apart from Matthew's quiet mutterings into the audio recorder and the whirr of the extractor fan the ambience now was soft and quiet, the pace unhurried. No one spoke. She experienced the usual feeling – nausea and intrigue in equal parts – but at least this time she wasn't sick. Neither did she feel faint. Her emotions were under better control these days.

At the end he peeled off his gloves and ripped off his mask, looking at her intently. 'Well, Inspector Piercy.'

'Matthew?'

'A healthy man somewhere in his forties, well-nourished, cause of death multiple knife wounds to the back which punctured a lung and severed a major blood vessel, not to mention one which severed the spinal cord. They were all inflicted within minutes. I suspect, but we'll have to wait for confirmation, that he'd had a few whiskies.

'Your assailant,' he was frowning now, 'began by incapacitating Mr Newton with a penetrating knife wound to the neck. There are five puncture wounds in the back, some of which indicate that our victim tried to turn but was ultimately unsuccessful.'

'So he died within minutes?'

Matthew nodded. 'I've taken samples just in case he was drugged but my feeling is that he'd just had whisky.' He paused. 'The marks on the man's chest and elbows indicate he was scalded.'

'Tortured?'

He nodded. 'Hot tap. I'd advise your forensic team to take a good look there.'

'Any idea *when* he died?'

'A little over two weeks ago. Got enough to go on for now?'

'Cause of death?'

'Shock due to blood loss consistent with traumatic knife wounds.'

'Would it have taken a very strong person to have stabbed him?'

'No-o. Not particularly.' He smiled thoughtfully. 'What you're asking is could your girl have inflicted them?'

She waited.

'Possibly,' he said. 'How tall is she?'

'Five feet two.'

'And the wife?'

She shrugged. 'We don't know.'

'It's more likely his wife was in the bathroom, rather than the nanny unless . . .'

She could read between the lines. 'Could it have been a man?'

He thought about that for a minute before nodding. 'He would have had his back to the door. I guess the mirrors would have been steamed up. You need to find out what relations were like between husband and wife, whether there was any . . .' He paused and gave a mischievous smile. 'Hanky panky between employer and your nanny.'

He crossed to the pictures of the corpse. 'On balance,' he said, 'it's more likely to have been a woman. And my money's on his wife.'

'Who scalded him when he was incapacitated?'

He nodded.

'Identification? Do you want me to locate a family member?'

They both glanced at Newton's face. 'I think we'll stick to DNA and dental records. Anyone who was close to him would . . .'

He didn't need to say more. Except: 'You'll get my report tomorrow morning.'

'Thank you, Matt. One more question. The blood spatter on the little boy's dungarees?'

She could tell he didn't want to say this but . . .

'He was there, Jo. In the bathroom when his father was murdered. It's possible the nanny picked him up and that was how her clothes were bloodstained. I'll need to get an expert's opinion.'

They both processed this horror until he touched her lightly on the shoulder, leaving his hand there for a moment. 'I guess I'll see you when I see you.'

She nodded.

He took a step closer and his face softened. He spoke in a quiet voice so only she could hear. 'I'm clocking up the hours,' he said, disrobing from the long apron and green gown, stripping down to his scrubs. 'And when you get your overtime back, Mrs Levin, might I suggest we have a little . . . couple time?'

Her face felt warm as she nodded.

THIRTY

A lan and Bridget were waiting for her in the car.

They were halfway up the A53, threading through Stockton Brook, when Joanna's phone rang. It was DC Danny Hesketh-Brown and he could hardly suppress his exuberance. 'We've found the car,' he said. 'The Range Rover. It was picking up parking tickets in a residents' only parking space in Hanley just around the corner from the bus station. It's been there a couple of weeks. The traffic warden first saw it on the morning of the sixteenth but obviously didn't connect it with our girl.'

'So it looks as though she left the house sometime very early on the morning of the sixteenth or even on the Monday night, parked up and caught a bus out to Leek.'

'Looks like it, Jo.'

'Well done, Danny. Thanks. Anyone gone out to it?'

'A couple of uniforms are giving it a once-over. They'll give us a call.'

'As it's now a murder investigation we'll bring it in for forensic examination. Get it on a low-loader.' She asked the next question with a degree of trepidation. 'No bodies in there?'

'Not so far.'

'Thanks. Keep me informed.'

Back at the station Bridget was logging in the samples taken from the post-mortem while Alan returned to his beloved computer. Joanna watched his bony fingers for a while as he searched through the car's history as well as anything else he could pick up on either the Newtons or Bethany. Then she turned away. King was best left to himself. He would make a report to her later. Behind the scenes the initial search of house and grounds of The Cottage was ongoing but so far they had not found the dead man's wife. They had widened their search and checked airlines and ferries. As two cars remained in the garage they had spoken to local taxi firms, again with no result. Some of the officers were trawling through contacts, starting with neighbours, family and friends, but so far they were no nearer finding out what, exactly, had happened to Mrs Newton.

She decided to leave Alan King there and return to Greatbach just in case Bethany, faced now with the fact that they knew who she was, decided to talk. Would being addressed by her own name be the arrow that finally pierced the armour of self-defence the girl had surrounded herself with by remaining mute? Had she killed Anthony Newton while he lay in the bath? Was there a backstory of jealousy, illicit love? Did she know where her employer's wife was? Had Louisa killed her husband in a rage before fleeing? So many questions.

But she needed someone with her when she interviewed the nanny, someone who would come over as empathetic, sympathetic and understanding rather than impatient and angry. She smiled to herself. Maybe *interviewed* was being a little optimistic. The likelihood was that yet again it would be a one-sided conversation, with her doing all the talking, asking all the questions, while Bethany stared back with that glassy-eyed, blank response. Joanna wandered into the briefing room and collared PC Dawn Critchlow. Perfect.

Dawn was a Trojan of an officer. Mother to four children, caring and supportive to her husband, Craig, who had a beltload of failed businesses behind him and suffered from chronic, incapacitating depression. Luckily for him he was married to an eternal optimist who, unusually for a police officer, rarely saw harm in anyone. She would make the perfect companion to this difficult interview. Joanna had no doubt that Bethany held answers. Maybe not quite all of them but she knew at least part of what had happened. But would she tell? Joanna consoled herself with thinking, if anyone might induce their dumb nanny to tell all Dawn was the one. Joanna clapped her on the shoulder. 'Come on, Dawn,' she said. 'We've got a job to do.'

While Dawn was driving towards Greatbach the call came in that the Range Rover had been searched. There was no body in it but there were bloodstains on the driver's seat and on the restraints on the toddler's seat. It had now been sealed in plastic and removed to the police pound where it would be microscopically examined. Nice.

But although their investigation was progressing Joanna still felt an overwhelming sense of gloom as they parked in the hospital car park, walked through the archway and looked up at the heavy, depressing walls of the institution with their blind windows.

She'd already spent a tense few minutes on the phone bringing Dr Roget up to speed, resisting the impulse to say I told you so, and before the psychiatrist could make any objection said that she would need to interview her patient again, making it plain this was a statement, not a request. The psychiatrist's response had been cool and unemotional. 'If you wouldn't mind calling in at my office before you start interviewing *my* patient.'

Which made Joanna feel confrontational. 'She may be your patient, Doctor,' she snapped, perhaps with a little more heat than usual, 'but she is now a prime suspect in a murder case. At the very least a witness if not the perpetrator.' She couldn't resist adding, 'Pretending to be struck dumb won't negate that.'

The psychiatrist's response was a long, drawn-out sigh of acceptance. 'I realize that, Inspector, but she is still traumatized, *unable* to speak and *my* patient.'

Joanna had ended the call still fuming.

So now as she and Dawn strode through the archway towards the main entrance she could feel her tension mounting. Anthony Newton was dead. He'd lain in that bath for almost two weeks, naked, decomposing. It was an ugly thought and had been an ugly sight. She couldn't rid her mind of the flies buzzing around his body and the writhing of maggots in the wounds. Bethany had fled from the sight, apparently intent on injuring the dead man's son. But she knew it didn't make sense. One a cold-blooded murder, concealed, the other a bungling attempt of – what? – right out in the open. Added to that the dead man's wife had vanished. There was no sign of her. So now it was paramount to discover whether Bethany's actions had been directed at protecting the child and she was somehow responsible for the grisly scene, or was she a victim in this scenario?

She pushed open the door to Dr Roget's office and the psychiatrist looked up without a smile. Joanna extended her hand. 'Good afternoon.'

Claire gave her a cautious smile as Joanna related the post-mortem findings. She listened without comment but her mouth was tightening and her eyes were wary.

Inspector and psychiatrist were skirting around each other, wary as a pair of boxers in the ring.

Claire was defensive. 'You really think Bethany has killed them both before running off with the child?'

Joanna tried to diffuse the hostility between them by putting the question differently. 'Is it possible Bethany had some sort of tragic, violent meltdown and this dumb act is a way of avoiding or blanking out what happened?'

She was aware from the twitching around Claire's mouth that she was blundering into a field she knew nothing about.

Claire put a hand on her shoulder. 'Inspector,' she said, 'I very much doubt it. The types of characters who erupt into violent assault usually show a previous lack of restraint. You might learn more about her if you spoke to a previous employer. Bethany does not display this characteristic. If anything she is wholly, totally, tightly in control. But I grant you this. She does display signs of a very disturbed personality. If she were responsible for Mr Newton's murder, the fact that *Mrs* Newton has not been found speaks more of planning rather than a random eruption. The more you can unearth about Bethany's prior character the easier it will be for us – and her – to unravel the truth. I do have one thing to add. I've done a thorough physical examination. There is no physical reason for her muteness. It is psychological.' She stopped speaking and waited for Joanna's response.

Joanna, for her part, regarded the psychiatrist for a moment. Her gaze was steady, intelligent, reassuring.

Then Claire stood up. 'Shall we?'

Joanna nodded. Claire opened the door and led them towards the ward.

'Have you told her we know who she is?'

The psychiatrist shook her head and for the first time there was a feeling of complicity. Dawn Critchlow trailed behind them.

On the way over, in the car as they'd crossed the city, Joanna had briefed her. 'Get her on your side, Dawn. Make her believe you are her friend. Convince her that you can help her.'

'And you?' Dawn had asked.

'I'll do what I do best,' Joanna had replied. 'Bad cop.'

And they had both laughed.

Now, as they went up in the lift towards the locked ward, Joanna was planning. They would start by peeling back the Newtons' lives and that of their nanny. She smiled to herself. Every time she was faced with a difficult investigation she recalled retired Chief Superintendent Arthur Colclough's words. 'Everything you learn about both a murder victim and the suspects is important. Buried in there is a reason. Even if it was accidental or the result of alcohol or drugs there is always a backstory, events that led up to that moment.' He'd given that paternal smile. 'Think of it as method policing.'

She had taken the advice to heart. Every time she recalled his words she missed him. And Chief Superintendent Gabriel Rush was a poor substitute.

As they walked along the corridor, accompanied by the scent of Pine disinfectant, the sun streaming in through tall windows and glancing off the sepia photographs of Greatbach patients and staff through the ages, she relished the thought of confronting the girl with her real name. Producing it with a flourish – and watching for her reaction.

Claire only turned back to her once. 'So you really believe, Inspector, that my patient is a killer?' Her grey eyes rested on Joanna, steady and unblinking, uncompromising as she waited for Joanna's response.

Joanna wished the psychiatrist would stop calling Bethany Rees 'her patient'. It made her angry, sanitizing the scene she had witnessed, a man murdered while naked, defenceless in his bath, the scene undiscovered for so long while the only two witnesses kept the secret, one deliberately and the other because he was too young.

Her response was acid, her tone equally cold and distant. 'Whatever you might think, Claire, we don't make assumptions. We acknowledge possibilities. But I've seen the state of Anthony Newton. And I will find out the truth. With or without "your patient's" help.' She didn't even try to disguise the irony in her tone.

Claire Roget was silent in answer to this and then, unexpectedly, she turned and smiled. Warm and generous, feminine and at the same time vulnerable. 'I'm so sorry,' she apologized. 'I think we've got off on the wrong foot, haven't we? I've assumed that you just want a conviction, whereas I have only one goal – and that is to find out why this girl is so traumatized that she can't' – a faint smile touched her lips – 'or won't,' she acknowledged, 'speak.'

Joanna felt her irritation melt. There is nothing like an olive branch to soften resentment. She found herself smiling back. 'Yes,' she said. 'I think we've probably both been misjudged and misunderstood. But we're on the same side. We want to find out the truth. This isn't some projection of a crime that might or might not be committed. A man *has* been murdered. His blood *was* on Bethany's clothes. I'm not Sherlock Holmes but it is fairly easy to make some sort of connection between the crime and this girl who is currently under your protection. It's in all our interests for us to find out what her part was, what she saw, what she knows. The quickest way to find this is, surely, for her to tell us.'

Dawn Critchlow was watching the interchange between the two women with interest, her mouth open, her eyes flicking from one to the other while smothering a smile. Not many people neutralized the inspector quite so efficiently.

Claire Roget led them up to the ward and then held back outside the door of Bethany's room. 'I'll watch through the window,' she said. 'I can hear from out here.' In spite of the thawing in their relations she couldn't resist tacking on a soft admonishment, 'I take it you'll be kind . . .' Her voice trailed away as again she smiled.

But Joanna hadn't quite finished. 'In deference to you, Doctor,' she said, also smiling, 'we're not bringing Bethany in and I'm not charging her with being an accessory or withholding information, but whether she understands or not, I will be interviewing her under caution. Under the law I have to offer her a lawyer. If she doesn't respond I can take that as a negative and PC

Critchlow and I can proceed to question her. Whether or not she chooses to respond is out of our hands. Obviously my hope now is that she will offer an explanation.' She stopped for a moment. 'That's a little optimistic, I know. If she doesn't assist us in our investigations and nothing in our current enquiries suggests otherwise we will, at some point, be arresting her and taking her down to the station. At each point we will explain her rights but if she doesn't speak – at all – we'll treat her as though it was a "no comment" interview and rely on any supportive evidence.'

The psychiatrist nodded. 'That seems fair. In the meantime we will be keeping her here – under lock and key,' she added.

THIRTY-ONE

There was a heightened awareness, antennae alert in the girl as they entered. She looked wary, a cornered animal. Perhaps it was the presence of Dawn in her uniform, clanking with handcuffs, radios, baton, body cam blinking on her jacket, that gave the interview a sense of seriousness. Or maybe it was the simple fact that as Joanna entered she spoke the girl's name.

'Hello, Bethany.'

Bethany's head whipped round, her eyes wide and startled. At the same time her shoulders dropped. She'd been rumbled.

Joanna watched her as she sat down in the chair with her back to the window, so pale daylight bleached Bethany's face. Joanna leaned forward. 'Bethany Rees,' she began, only too conscious of the irony of the well-worn words, 'you are being questioned in connection with the murder of Anthony Newton. You don't have to say anything . . .'

And when the girl did not respond, she added, 'Yes. We've found him.'

Bethany sat, frozen.

'Once we found out the identity of the owner of the clothes and bag you dumped, we went to the Newtons' house.'

Dawn watched from the doorway, blocking the exit. Bethany's

eyes flickered from one to the other. Joanna could sense her panic
and crossed her legs, leaning back in the chair, relaxed.

'So,' she continued briskly, her tone businesslike. 'We know
who you are. We've found Mr Newton's body and we know who
the little boy is. His name is Stevie, isn't it? This is an opportunity
for you to explain what happened. Set the record straight and
maybe tell us where we can find Mrs Newton.'

There was not a sound out of the girl, so Joanna continued.
'We will be charging you either with being an accessory or,
possibly, of the crime itself.'

Bethany's eyes widened.

'For the time being, Bethany, you will remain here, at Greatbach,
under lock and key. Until you decide to talk.'

The girl's eyes flickered when Joanna spoke her name but she
continued to stare straight into the room, her breathing sharp and
shallow, her breaths blowing out as though she was trying to steady
herself, control the rate.

'Unless, of course, you can give us some alternative
explanation.'

Still the girl said nothing. Through the Judas window Joanna
saw Claire watching. Though her face was expressionless
Joanna felt the psychiatrist knew she was winning here.

Dawn stepped forward, face warm, open, smiling. 'Come on,
Bethany,' she encouraged, 'it'd be really helpful if you could fill
in the blanks.' But apart from a quick once-over Bethany gave no
sign that she had heard and Dawn stepped back, giving Joanna a
shallow shrug.

Joanna continued. 'You have the right to a solicitor.'

Nothing.

'Or someone to act as your advocate.'

Still nothing except a long, slow, almost insolent blink and that
abstracted stare.

Which pulled Joanna up short. Was she still missing something?
She ran over events in her mind, searching for a chink in the
scenario, something that would help her see the background as
clearly as the facts in front of her. But she failed. Maybe, she
thought, she could shock the girl into giving herself away.

'A post-mortem has been performed on Mr Newton although,
to be honest, the knife sticking out of his back was a bit of a
giveaway.'

Bethany bowed her head. An act of submission, but her face was still set into that tense but neutral expression.

'What was the relationship between you and Mr Newton?'

Nothing.

'Were you fond of him?'

It was the almost smile that told Joanna she was barking up the wrong tree. 'Was it Mrs Newton that you had trouble with?'

Still nothing.

Joanna revised her line of questioning. 'Do you have any idea what a body looks like after two weeks?'

A shudder.

'No one would want that to happen to someone they knew, would they?'

The girl's eyes lifted to hers, met them with what could have been a faint 'no', then dropped again.

'At least not to someone they knew and liked.' Joanna stood up. 'At some point, Bethany, we will remove you from here and take you to the station for further questioning.' The irony of her threat was not lost to her. Further questioning? When they'd not had one bloody word out of her? This was testing what little patience she had.

'*I* believe you don't *want* to speak.'

She could have sworn there was mockery in the girl's face now. A challenge.

'Dr Roget has examined your tongue, throat and larynx. There is no good reason why you cannot speak, is there?'

Still no response.

'Dr Roget is convinced your muteness is involuntary, the result of anxiety or trauma. But I am not so sure.'

The girl met her eyes and pressed her lips together, one eyebrow lifting just a touch in an attitude of irony, a tossing back of the challenge. *Well, there's a surprise.* And: *Prove it.*

'Maybe it's that you haven't yet learnt your lines?'

Bethany's eyes dropped to the floor. Joanna gave Dawn a swift glance. She'd hit home with this missile. So she pursued it.

'I think you haven't worked out what story to tell. Once in the cells, Bethany, your reluctance or inability to talk might prove problematic when you want food or the bathroom or a shower.'

The girl's shoulders drooped further now and she looked weary. But Joanna wasn't through yet. 'We know that you used the car to drive to Hanley because we've found it. What we don't know – yet – is why you took Stevie to such a remote, potentially dangerous place or where *Mrs* Newton is.'

Without much hope of an answer, she pressed on. 'Do *you* know where she is, Bethany?'

Bethany closed her eyes and her breath whistled in like an asthmatic's.

'Where is she?'

After another silent pause Joanna moved towards the door where she waited, giving the girl a last chance to speak before she left. Something changed in Bethany's face. It crumpled. There was more than a hint of despair. Which worried Joanna. Were they about to find a second body? Bethany's head bowed. She had shut down again.

THIRTY-TWO

Over the following couple of frantic days, as the police worked through the crime scene, waited for results and started the mammoth task of interviewing anyone who had a connection, however tenuous, with the Newtons, the press played around with various headlines. From Dumb Girl Witness to Mute Murder with the fairly factual details, that the girl was currently detained under lock and key in a psychiatric unit refusing to give her side of the story.

The police were now focussed on finding Louisa Newton, or any sign of her, and in delving into Anthony Newton's past life. Which turned out to be interesting and varied.

He was loosely described as a businessman which, in Joanna's slightly tainted view, could cover a whole host of possibilities. He was listed as a classic car dealer amongst other things: property owner, dabbler in the stock market and speculator. Unearthing Newton's life uncovered a whole pile of anomalies. For a start, his tax returns didn't cover the cost of his luxury home and lifestyle.

To be on the safe side they had also run background checks on the gardener which had turned up nothing. He was clean.

As promised Matthew's report had come through on Thursday morning and confirmed what he had already shared at the post-mortem. Anthony Newton had died from shock and blood loss due to multiple stab wounds to the back, the first of which had severed the spinal cord at C6 and would have paralysed him. Time of death estimated at somewhere between two and three weeks ago. It was logical and formal and would pass the 'court test' but at home that night, Matthew confided two points to her. They were having a rare, quiet dinner at home, spaghetti bolognaise, with a bottle of Rioja. Jakob had crashed out early after a trip to Rudyard Lake with his equally exhausted grandparents which had included an exciting ride on the miniature train and Joanna had snuck off work on time – for once.

'You know I sent pictures of the girl's dress as well as the little boy's dungarees to a blood spatter analyst.'

She looked up. 'Something's bothering you?'

'I think the boy was present for at least one or two of the stab wounds and that the blood on the girl's dress is consistent with her having picked him up.'

She nodded. 'And the blood on the cardigan?'

'I think she reached over to the tap.'

'To switch it on? Off?'

'My guess is off. Had the tap been left running,' his green eyes were serious now, 'water would have overflowed and at some point might have either leaked through the ceiling or caused enough damage for the gardener or someone else to investigate.'

Matt shrugged and wound another forkful of spaghetti round his fork. 'How tall is your girl?'

'Five two – if that. Matt, what on earth are you getting at?'

'I did some measurements,' he said. 'Just stand up a minute, Jo.'

She did just that.

'The side of the bath,' he said, 'is just under two feet. I measured it. You're five eight. The spray of blood was on the lower part of the skirt of the dress.'

'So what are you saying?'

'She didn't do it. If she'd inflicted those wounds the blood spray would have been higher up the dress and the bottom of the skirt would have been behind the side of the bath. Someone taller than five feet two inflicted those wounds.'

'If she was wearing the dress at the time.'

'Well, the little boy's dungarees matching the blood on her dress indicates that the events happened in quick succession. My expert'll get her report to you as soon as possible.' He was smiling as he watched her. 'Do you think you can be patient, Jo . . . just this once?'

She responded to the mockery in his tone. 'If I must.'

'There's something else,' he said. 'I couldn't put this in the formal report. It's too vague, too much conjecture.' His forehead now was screwed up in a deep frown.

'But,' she prompted.

'Newton was quite wiry. Strong. He could have fought anyone off. There was soap on his back. Even through the scent of putrefaction I could still smell it.'

It connected. 'There was a bar of soap in the bottom of the bath. Or what *had* been a bar of soap. It was completely melted. Where are you going with this, Matt?'

'Who soaps a man's back?'

'Are you fishing?'

He was grinning. 'I wish. But no, I'm not. Most likely his wife. You really think he would have sat there, naked, in a bath, while the *nanny* soaped his back before stabbing him?'

She wasn't quite willing to let go of the girl. Not – just – yet. Not after the prolonged playacting. 'You said he'd had a few drinks.'

The look he gave her now was of amusement, his face soft and indulgent and he paused before continuing with his narrative, speaking in a gentle voice. 'Newton had had the equivalent of half a bottle of whisky. Around twenty units of alcohol.'

'You put that in your report.'

'Jo,' he said.

She put her wine glass down. 'What?'

'From the state of his belly and fatty liver, this state of intoxication was not exactly a one-off. My money,' he said quietly, 'is on the wife – if she's tall.'

'I can ask the gardener.'

'Whoever soaped his back was someone he trusted.' He continued, 'My guess is Bethany left in a desperate hurry because she'd seen the body and was afraid she might be blamed for it. She panicked and ran.'

But Matthew's theory didn't *quite* complete the picture. She couldn't put her finger on it but something didn't fit. It was like a pair of shoes you really like but they pinch. The shoe and the foot are not comfortable together. When a theory did not fit it was the wrong theory.

She forked in another mouthful of spaghetti but she hardly tasted it. Matthew's words had set her thinking. She'd instinctively felt that the money trail was an important one. Why? Because in Newton's life and maybe his death there would have been some very nasty people. Just the sort of people who did stab their foes while they sang in the bath. Matthew had a point. It was time to move the spotlight away from Bethany.

For now.

Friday 2 April, 8 a.m.

She found DC Alan King on his usual perch, gazing into a computer screen in exactly the same position as he'd been when she'd left the previous night. 'Have you been here all night?'

He didn't answer her question but leaned back, dragging his fingers through his hair. 'This has taken some unravelling.'

She drew up a chair and peered into the screen alongside him. 'Newton shifted money around as though he was playing marbles,' he said. 'Multiple bank accounts, in different countries. Investing in his own businesses using different identities. I wouldn't be surprised if some money laundering is involved. Buying stuff from the Far East.'

'What stuff?'

'Car parts, mostly. But . . .' He clicked on an icon. 'Looks like a bona fide clothes manufacturer, doesn't it?'

She moved in.

'Except there are no clothes. People order online and the company dissolves. That's not all. Some money has been diverted from UK accounts, solicitors, estate agents, banks.'

She looked at him. 'I thought banks were relatively safe.'

Alan grinned. 'They are. It's the people who get misled who aren't. They believe some wise guy who persuades them to invest in fraudulent companies or companies that are vastly overvalued. They're duped into thinking they'll make a quick buck on the edge of legality, a legal loophole. So when they realize they'll lose money instead of making it, they don't complain. Another little string to Newton's bow were emails intercepting perfectly legal transactions, a simple message advising them to settle their bills to a different bank account. The money then is whisked away here there and bloody everywhere. Really difficult to follow the trail.'

'Crooks like this,' she said, observing the screen, 'leave behind them a trail of enemies.'

'Quite.' He swivelled around in his chair. 'A trail of very nasty enemies.'

'Anyone in particular?'

'I'm working my way through that.'

He swung around in his chair to face her. King was long and skinny with big white teeth that seemed hardly to fit in his mouth. He was one of those officers whose thoughts followed logic. Given direction he would hang on, working through suggestions with all the pedantry and tenacity of a British bulldog. He spoke fluent French and Spanish and had a pair of perceptive grey eyes. The one attribute he didn't have was an imagination. His answers would always be straight, factual and lack embellishment. In the years since Joanna had worked with him he had never proffered one original idea. She knew he had a long-term partner, Kylie, but little else.

As his fingers danced over the keys he suddenly stiffened. 'I've traced some of the money to a Spanish bank,' he said, fingers manipulating the keys exposing money transfers. 'Banque de Bilbao.'

'Does Mrs Newton have any connection with Spain?'

'Parents,' King said. 'They retired to the north of Spain. We haven't been able to make contact with them yet.'

'She hasn't left the country, has she?'

King shook his head. 'We've checked airlines, ferries and the channel ports. She's not been through.'

'So where is she?' Joanna fell silent as she peered into the screen, reading figures, details, times, dates all verifying King's statements. Something was staring back at her but, like a long-sighted person in the wrong glasses, she couldn't focus on it. It was under her nose. Too close.

'No activity on her mobile phone?'

Again King shook his head but Joanna knew that wasn't the question she should have asked. It was something else.

THIRTY-THREE

Saturday 3 April, 7.30 a.m.

Every time she looked at her small son Joanna was aware that Stevie Newton remained with Sandra and Michael Clowes, perfectly safe but so far unclaimed. So her focus during the morning's briefing was to locate the little boy's grandparents, either side.

At some point she would have to try and speak again to Bethany Rees, but maybe the best strategy for now was to leave her alone to think and wonder. She couldn't face another one-sided interview.

She decided to focus attention on the Newtons and returned to The Cottage with DC Danny Hesketh-Brown.

The Newtons had kept the tall gates firmly locked against their neighbours, making The Cottage in reality a castle with a drawbridge permanently raised. And they were a private couple whose circle of intimates was small.

Joanna and Danny arrived early and found Adam Judd working in the garden. It was a fine morning, still cool. But the birds were singing loudly and the sun was just starting to warm the ground. Judd was in his shirtsleeves, mulching around the rose bushes pruned close to the ground. He straightened as she approached and greeted her with a grin. 'Morning. Lovely, isn't it?'

'Yes. Beautiful.'

The gardener looked around him. 'Always something to do in a garden.'

'Indeed.'

He paused, head on one side, waiting for her to speak.

'What was the relationship like between Mr and Mrs Newton?'

'I don't really know. My work is outside. I didn't have much to do with them.' He followed that up with: 'You don't think she killed him? Why? Why would she? She had all she could want round here.' He looked around him. 'I don't follow your thinking, Inspector. I can't see her killing Mr Newton. No. Doesn't seem likely.'

He was an attractive man, mid-forties, with an engaging grin and an open manner. He was watching her quizzically.

'How did you come to work here?'

'I was at a loose end. I was friends with Tony's brother-in-law and he suggested I come and live in the cottage rent-free in return for a spot of gardening, see how it went.'

'And you've stayed here nearly two years?'

He scratched the side of his mouth. 'Yes. Longer than I'd expected. It's been a quiet life but it's suited.'

'Many people come here?'

'No.'

'What about Mr and Mrs Newton's friends, visitors, people who came to the house. Family?'

'Not family and they didn't have many visitors. Kept themselves to themselves.'

She pursued the point. 'Did they have *any* visitors?'

The gardener thought for a moment, wiping his hands on a pair of jeans stiff with mud. 'Only one really regular. I think she was a mate more of Mrs Newton. Very close they were. She was here quite often. Two, three times a week sometimes.'

'On her own?'

'Yeah, usually. She'd come late morning. I'd hear the pair of them clinking glasses and laughing. Sounds like they had a bit of fun together. Glamorous sort.' Adam Judd winked lasciviously. 'Flirty, if you know what I mean.' Another wink, accompanied this time with a leer.

Hesketh-Brown grinned in empathy although a more uxorious person could hardly have existed. DC Danny Hesketh-Brown was married to Betsy, who was a teacher at a special school in Tunstall. He had two children, Tom and Tanya, to whom he was devoted. His desk was festooned with pictures of the two grinning faces.

Joanna interrupted the tacit boy-talk. 'What was her name, this glamorous sort?'

'You going to chase her up?'

Joanna pursed her lips and he supplied the answer.

'Cindy. I think her surname was Mellor as far as I remember. I have the feeling her husband and Mr Newton were in business together.'

Joanna's ears pricked up. 'But not any more?'

'I don't think so. She drove a really nice old 1990s Mazda

Roadster convertible.' Wink, wink to Danny. 'Don't know her address though. Sorry. But she is a corker. The car too.'

'Thanks.'

It didn't take long to track her down.

Cindy Mellor lived in Newcastle-under-Lyme in a large detached house behind similarly tall, locked electric gates. Opposite the house was a green area with a gang of youngsters, mostly in red-and-white Stoke City football strips, booting a ball around. Joanna watched them for a moment, enjoying their noisy enthusiasm in the Bet 365 logo. The Potters. She felt an affection for them.

The response to her request into the intercom was a clipped accent trying too hard to disguise her Potteries origins. 'Hello?'

Joanna's reply was equally clipped.

Cindy was standing on the doorstep, waiting to greet them, a tall, smartly dressed, buxom woman in her forties, well preserved in tight white jeans and a flowing scarlet top. Her hair was long and silky.

She flicked it back behind her shoulders and gave them both a theatrical smile.

Joanna began with formality. 'Thank you for agreeing to see us.'

Very much in control, Cindy Mellor pushed her shoulders back, smiled and acknowledged the thanks with a gracious tilt of her head. She was clearly high maintenance, wafting an expensive scent which clung to the air around her. Carefully coiffured hair, expertly applied make-up, a little too heavy to quite convince. But the effect was of unnatural glamour and a woman who cared about her appearance. Very like her friend, Louisa, Joanna suspected.

Without offering them tea or coffee Cindy ushered them into a conservatory with potted palms which gave the interview a surreal, continental effect. Joanna sat gingerly on a cane two-seater while Danny stood in the doorway, observing and following the conversation.

Joanna went straight in. 'You've heard on the news that Mr Anthony Newton has been found dead.'

Cindy Mellor's response was cool and unemotional considering her friendship with his wife. 'Yes. I did hear. I do read the paper.' She was audibly on the defence.

'But you didn't come forward.' Joanna wished it hadn't sounded quite so confrontational.

Mrs Mellor shrugged. 'What would be the point? I don't know anything about it.'

Colclough's words were ringing in Joanna's head. *Get to know the victims, their friends, their family, their acquaintances. Their life. Drill down into it. It's there, Piercy, waiting for you to unearth it.*

She took up the challenge. 'Louisa Newton is missing. I understand she is a close friend of yours.'

'Understand? From whom?'

'The gardener.'

'Adam?'

Joanna tucked the response away. Perhaps it was a clue?

Cindy was thoughtful, leaving Joanna to wonder. This 'close' friend could also be dead. On the other hand, she could have murdered her husband and done a runner. So what was with the sphinx-face?

She pressed on. 'When did you last hear from her?'

'More than two weeks ago.' Her answer was casual.

'You realize she is a potential suspect in her husband's murder?'

Cindy shook her head, smiling now. 'No way,' she said. 'They were . . .' She stumbled over the cliché 'devoted', substituting a probably more honest: 'good together'.

'If this is so we're concerned that she might have come to harm.' Joanna was watching Cindy very carefully to see what reaction this would elicit but she looked unconcerned.

'No one would have wanted to hurt Louisa. She was a little . . . lamb.'

Joanna scrutinized her face trying to trace any irony but it was impassive.

'Did she have anything to do with her husband's business?'

'God, no.' Cindy looked appalled at the thought. 'We let the guys get on with it. Our job is to run the home – perfectly, look good – and spend the money.'

'Is it usual to hear nothing from her for nearly three weeks?'

'Oh yes.' Cindy Mellor studied her long, painted fingernails. 'Her mum and dad live in the north of Spain. She often pops over there for a week or so. Nothing unusual in that. We're not joined at the hip, you know. We do have our own lives.'

She looked wary now.

Joanna continued smoothly. 'Do you have any idea who might have wanted to kill Mr Newton?'

Cindy's response surprised her. 'Take your pick,' she said casually. 'He had a few skeletons in his cupboard. Anthony was a crook. It was all going to catch up with him sooner or later.'

Joanna tucked the blunt comment away.

She waited for a split second before pressing on. 'The nanny was found at a remote spot with the little boy, Stevie, apparently with the intent to harm him.' Joanna flipped a photograph of the child onto the table. Cindy took a cursory glance, displaying no emotion, before looking enquiringly at Joanna. 'So?'

'Can you explain why that might be?'

Cindy looked blank so Joanna changed tack.

'When you last saw Louisa, how did she seem?'

Cindy Mellor smiled. 'Fine. Normal. I was there for hours. We polished off a couple of bottles of wine. My husband's away quite a lot on business. I'm always glad of a bit of company.'

'What is she like?'

'Louisa? She's fun. You can always rely on her for a laugh – a good drinking companion.' She looked defiantly first at Joanna then at Danny.

Both police were having the same thought. They could run a bet that Mrs Mellor wouldn't pass a breathalyser test after one of her and her mate's get-togethers.

'And Anthony, Mr Newton? Did he mind your being there?'

'No. He was glad if his wife was happy, with friends, looking the other way. I was one of the friends he approved of.'

Joanna watched her carefully and Cindy Mellor continued, seemingly taking a ramble down memory lane.

'Anthony and my husband were in a sort of partnership.'

Joanna picked up on the phrase. 'What sort of partnership?'

'Anthony dealt in classic cars,' Cindy said. 'Damien, my *adored* husband, has contacts in the EU. Anthony wanted to import parts from the Far East but Damien thought they were substandard and didn't meet regulations.' She hesitated. 'Anthony had workshops.' Another pause. 'To be honest Damien thought they were doing a shoddy job so they parted company. Simple as that. No hard feelings, of course. We still spent a lot of time together.'

'You liked the Newtons?'

'I liked Louisa.'

'And the nanny?'

Cindy Mellor lit up a cigarette and took a deep drag before

responding. 'The nanny?' She sounded surprised. 'I didn't think about her at all. I hardly met her. She was quiet, colourless. A nothing.'

'And Stevie?'

Both officers waited while Cindy Mellor took another drag from her cigarette and let the smoke drift up towards the roof. She licked her lips – to the cost of the sticky pink lipstick. 'I can't . . .' She started again. 'I don't know much about him. Louisa considered him . . . an inconvenience.' She leaned in conspiratorially though there was no one near enough to hear anyway. 'I think he was an accident.'

Cindy Mellor saw the shocked looks on their faces and tried to qualify her comment. 'She never wanted children. Stevie. He got in the way.'

Joanna asked the next question quietly. 'Where do you think Louisa is?'

Cindy shrugged and stubbed her cigarette out in a plant pot. 'Try her parents.'

'There's no record of her having left the country.'

Cindy Mellor stubbed her cigarette out and met Joanna's eyes. 'Sure about that, are you? She can be quite . . . slippery.'

'And Stevie? Did he usually go with her?'

Cindy Mellor looked surprised that the subject had been raised. 'Not necessarily. That was the nanny's job. Anyway . . .' Her tone was indignant. 'I thought the nanny did it.'

So she had been following the case.

'If the nanny did it why has your friend disappeared?'

Cindy shrugged this off. 'She's probably abroad, slipped your net and having a good time not even aware of events at home. She's out of it.'

The phrase struck Joanna. *She's out of it.*

Joanna presented her with the ridiculous scenario. 'So you think your friend took off the moment the nanny had murdered her husband and is too busy sunning herself in Spain to bother coming home to pick up her son?'

Cindy backtracked then. 'Well, put like that I must admit it doesn't exactly sound likely.'

'No, it doesn't, does it?'

Cindy Mellor opened her mouth, thought the better of whatever she had been about to say and closed it again.

Joanna watched her. Cindy's eyes blinked slowly as she dwelt on the situation. Her eyelashes looked heavy with extra lashes glued in. They were too long, incongruous and artificial, but her response this time was genuine. 'It's what I hope,' she said quietly. 'The alternative . . .' The muscles on her face tightened. 'The alternative is just too awful to contemplate.'

Joanna recalled Matthew's comments about their killer soaping the murdered man's back and tried a different tack. 'Was there anything between Bethany and Anthony Newton?'

Cindy Mellor shot out a hoot of laughter. 'I hardly think so. She wasn't exactly his type. He doesn't go for shrinking violets.'

'So what does he go for?'

'Think pole dancers. He liked them saucy and sexy. You know. Babe sorts.'

'Not men?'

Cindy stared at her. 'You think Anthony Newton was *gay*?'

It was obvious the thought had never entered her mind.

'We're considering all possibilities.'

'Well, you're barking up the wrong tree there, I can tell you. No way. Look, I'd help you if I could but I'm as mystified as you are.'

Joanna changed tack again. 'Do you have an address for Louisa's parents?'

Cindy shook her head. 'Somewhere in the north.' She screwed her face up. 'In the Basque country, I think.'

Danny spoke up. 'What is their name?'

Cindy flashed Danny Boy a little smile, sweetly coquettish and wildly inappropriate. She was wasting her talents. 'Cardew, I think, Officer.'

'What about Anthony's parents?'

'They live somewhere up north. I didn't get the impression that he was exactly close to them. They won't be of much help. I don't think he'd had any contact with them for ages.'

Joanna diverted the conversation back to a point where she had sensed uncertainty, evasion.

'Your husband and Mr Newton parted company in . . .?'

'Last year.' Belatedly she added, 'They parted *amicably*.'

'And you and Louisa remained friends.'

'Yes.'

Joanna changed tack again. 'Their home is a real paradise.'

'Isn't it?'

Joanna pushed. 'They must have made plenty of money from the classic car parts.'

Cindy's heavily made-up eyes surveyed her with cynicism and the hint of a smile. 'Yes, they must.'

Joanna wasn't getting anywhere. She pushed again, just that little bit harder. 'In your opinion is it possible that Mrs Newton killed her husband?'

Cindy Mellor shook her head so hard her hair flipped over her face. 'I thought you had your suspect.'

Joanna didn't confirm or deny this. 'One last question. How tall is Louisa?'

'How tall? I don't know. Round about my height, I suppose.'

'Which is?'

'Five seven.'

'Thank you.'

As Joanna rose to leave Cindy must have felt she should convince them further. 'It's always the quiet ones, isn't it, Inspector? The ones you don't notice, who suppress their emotions, keep them under wraps. And then whoosh.' She flung her arms up. 'They lose it. Surely it's that quiet, sneaky little nanny who murdered him and Louisa's hiding out somewhere, frightened. It's the only logical explanation.'

But it wasn't a logical explanation at all, Joanna thought as they left. Louisa Newton's disappearance didn't make any sense.

THIRTY-FOUR

She was reflective as Danny drove back to the station, analysing what she had learned from this friend.

She had a vivid picture of the relationship between their missing woman and her son – 'an inconvenience' was the phrase that rang most true.

The portrait Cindy had painted of Bethany fitted with her own impression: colourless, someone you'd hardly notice. But she had still believed Bethany had killed her employer, that the girl's quietness was cover for a sly personality.

How significant was the bit about different ideas on sourcing parts for the classic cars?

The real gem had been the suggestion that Louisa had headed for her parents. Cindy had seemed unconcerned for her friend's safety – even taking into account Anthony's fate.

The abiding impression she'd had was Cindy Mellor was genuinely fond of her friend. They were two mates together. But their husbands? That was a little more obscure.

The relationship between husband and wife had been described in all honesty as OK. But the fact remained she didn't know where Louisa Newton was. Until she was found the question remained. Suspect or victim?

She was going to have to report in to Chief Superintendent Gabriel Rush before long. And say what? That she was keeping an open mind as far as who had killed Anthony Newton. She resisted a grim smile to herself, seeing her weakness from CS Rush's point of view. She still only had bits of the story. The bigger pieces were still missing. And the biggest bit was the intro. Where on earth did dumb Bethany and the dramatic scenario in which she had presented fit into it all?

Joanna tucked a strand of hair behind her ear and cupped her chin in her hand. Admittedly Bethany could hardly have left the little boy behind, alone in a house with the corpse of his father.

She'd fled because of the murder. She gave a deep sigh and Hesketh-Brown glanced across at her. 'All right there, Jo?'

'Yeah,' she said glumly. Then more truthfully, she added, 'No.'

The DC drove a few more miles before venturing, 'If only we could track Mrs Newton down.'

'Yeah,' she said. 'If, when and where.' Then she added more quietly, '*Dead* or *alive.*'

The next step was obvious.

Back at the station she set herself down next to DC Alan King who was still tapping away at the computer keys.

'You say there's no sign of Mrs Newton in the UK? No cash withdrawals, no mobile phone data?'

He didn't stop working, neither did he look her way. 'No.'

'We tracked the Range Rover using the satnav. It simply went to Hanley and before that just local stuff. We've had the cadaver dogs search it and there's no evidence a body has been transported in it.'

Now he looked at her. 'So?'

'She's somewhere else,' she said firmly, her mind shifting between theories. Bethany was looking more and more like a victim, a fall guy rather than a perpetrator.

She'd got King's full attention now. 'There's definitely no record of Mrs Newton having left the country?' She focussed on the screen with its myriad of data, dates and numbers, while King shook his head.

'I've been really thorough,' he said. 'Checked all exits.'

And then an idea took hold, rooted and flowered. 'Do me a favour, King,' she said, excited by her own idea. 'Rerun Mrs Newton's details as well as Bethany's. Just in case she borrowed her nanny's ID.'

He swivelled his chair around and was soon absorbed in the task. Left to herself she felt a sense of being on the verge of something. Perhaps she was beginning to see through the girl's mute state.

She could see a pattern but it still had a huge hole in the centre.

She tested various theories. Had the two women conspired against Anthony Newton and thought they'd get away with it? She shook her head. That wasn't it.

Was it a simple case of domestic abuse and a day of reckoning?

Domestic abuse was one of the crimes they were currently targeting, with special apps and algorithms on their tablets designed to identify the cases likely to result in serious assault or even murder. But there was no record of any complaint against Anthony Newton. And she still couldn't find a logical reason for the nanny's actions. If Bethany had committed or been complicit in one murder what stopped her simply killing the child? Why stand at the top of a rock, appearing to the world that she was about to tip the pushchair over the edge? The starting point of the police drama. Only it hadn't been. The starting point had been further back that morning, possibly the evening before.

At the evening briefing she shared all her misgivings and uncertainties, threw questions into the room for the assembled officers to chew over and make from them what they could. She watched as they took these thoughts on board and tried to come up with solutions of their own. Then she spent some time planning her move forward, knowing that they pivoted around finding Louisa.

*   *   *

It was almost midnight when she let herself into a silent house. No howling child, no nappy to change, no feed. Only peace and silence. And she felt guilty for the feeling of relief that engulfed her. She was mentally and physically exhausted. It was always like this when tussling with a case, trying to work it out. Her brain found it hard to switch off. Even after solving a case she was anxious about the conviction. As all police officers should be. Had she fingered the right collar? Would she be able to prove it beyond reasonable doubt?

Sometimes she wondered if Matthew felt this way too after a post-mortem. Did he worry whether he'd got it right, stepped outside his remit, stated a fact which was not? Believed something to be true when it was not?

She slipped off her shoes, climbed the stairs and tiptoed into the bathroom. Two minutes and she could be in bed. Three and she would be asleep.

THIRTY-FIVE

Sunday 4 April, 7 a.m.

As SIO she could not afford the luxury of a weekend off but she did start the day with a degree of normality by feeding and changing her baby son and taking a sleepy Matthew a cup of coffee. She left with a stab of affection for both and headed for the station.

Into her other world.

The day began well. She cycled the mile or so into Leek on quiet roads. Sunday morning Leek was a ghost town. But as she pedalled that instinct was back, uncomfortable and disturbing. That big black hole in the centre of the case was expanding, sucking the rest in. She learned details but they weren't helping to fill in the gaps.

Like every detective before or since, as she locked her bike against the railings and stepped inside the station, she was asking the perpetual question: what am I missing?

Her office was quieter than during the week and she welcomed the peace. She would have to face Rush the following morning and she wasn't relishing the fact. She was still working him out. Initially she'd considered him humourless and unsupportive, a numbers man who forgot about the people behind the crimes, both victim and villain. But lately she was not so sure. She could have sworn once or twice that she had seen his mouth twitch as though a smile hovered just at the edge.

Once she'd changed out of her cycling gear into jeans, boots and a maroon sweatshirt and entered the briefing room, she definitely sensed a ripple.

Elected to break the news, King stepped forward and in his face there was no mistaking the look of sympathy.

'The gardener's gone,' he said. 'Done a runner.'

She stared at him, processing the blunt statement, recalling the man, beanie pulled low down to his eyebrows and a scraggy, sandy beard. She couldn't remember his eyes because, she realized now, he had averted them, looking beyond her or else down at the ground. Dirty hands and mud-stained trousers tucked into wellies had completed the picture. That was it.

Knowing this was a major cock-up she stared at Alan King. 'Fill me in.'

He turned his back on the assembled officers and kept his voice low. 'A couple of uniforms went round to his cottage yesterday afternoon. They just wanted to go over some routine questions. When he'd last seen Mr and Mrs Newton together, Bethany, the little boy. If he'd noticed when the car went. Stuff like that. They thought they'd just check. You know?'

She nodded. King's normally pale face was flushed an uncomfortable pink.

'And?'

'He seemed fine.'

'But?'

'We reckon that must have spooked him.'

'Anyway they wanted to confirm some of the points again, so they went back early this morning. Thought they'd catch him in. The cottage was empty, Joanna. Doors wide open, some stuff missing. He wasn't in the garden.'

'The cars?'

'Both there but he had an old pickup and that's gone.'

'Do we have the reg?'

King looked awkward. 'It wasn't registered to him or to the Newtons.'

'So who was it registered to?'

'A Kelvin Shipley.'

'Who the . . .?'

'We don't know who he is,' King said quickly, 'or his link to the Newtons.'

The hole was deepening and she was falling into it.

'Put out a Search and Stop for him,' Joanna said automatically, adding, 'both names.'

Inside she was struggling. Adam Judd had been checked through and was clean. He did not have a police record. Something clanged at the back of her mind. Bethany. Was there a link between them?

'Phone the ward,' she said quickly to Paul Ruthin. 'Tell them that it is possible a suspect might try to gain access to her. They need to watch her in case he makes contact.'

Ruthin left the room.

Was it possible *the gardener* had killed his boss? Had she let a killer slip through her fingers? The unforgiveable crime. Had she been naive? How often did this trip you up? The invisible person who was so bloody invisible, they parked themselves right under your nose, in your line of vision. And you didn't see them.

She shared the unwelcome news with the assembled officers. 'Let's take a look at your bodycam for any images of him,' she said. 'And take another look round his cottage. See if there's any link between Judd, this Kelvin Shipley and Anthony Newton.'

'Got it,' Alan said, something happy in his response. There was nothing DC Alan King liked better than combing the police database for villains.

She wondered now. Had Judd's jeers at Little Miss Welshie been a smokescreen?

Maybe they should focus back on the nanny. 'Do me a favour,' she said to King. 'Bring up Bethany Rees's details. What have we got on her?'

'Her fingerprints didn't match anything on the computer.'

'Get her bank account up.'

DC King's fingers danced again. 'Not a lot here, Jo. Couple of hundred. Frequently overdrawn.' He smiled, recognizing a familiar pattern of ODs. 'Not a very rich girl.'

She stood back, frowning and tracking in a different direction. What about the relationship between Mrs Newton and the gardener? A sort of Lady Chatterley affair? Was, even now, Adam Judd making his way to a rendezvous? And who was Kelvin Shipley?

King had run Shipley's name through the PNC and come up with a petty criminal, burglaries, car theft. He'd done time for one minor assault up in Manchester but it didn't amount to much. It was perfectly possible that Judd and he had simply been acquaintances.

But the Spanish connection continued to trouble her. 'Let's get hold of Louisa Newton's parents. They live in the north of Spain.' She grinned at King. 'Don't suppose your Spanish stretches to Basque?'

King didn't even bother to answer.

She looked beyond him to the waiting officers. They were a good bunch, she thought, eyeing them up. They were, for the most part, intelligent, well trained and full of energy and enthusiasm. She caught sight of PC Gilbert Young struggling to stay awake, his eyelids drooping. 'Get Young some coffee, will you,' she said to no one in particular. 'I think he's been burning the candle at both ends.' She smiled. Rumour had it that PC Young had recently taken up with a teenage media student from Staffordshire University. Young was in his thirties and by the look of him the age difference was beginning to tell. A police station is a microcosm full of its own dramas and melodramas, tragedy, comedy, romance and some-times these small dramas spill out onto the floor. Poor old Gilbert Young. A more unlikely candidate for a (rumoured to be) glamorous media student could hardly be found. She shook her head. Did she really need a child when she had this lot to mother?

Dawn returned with the coffee and Joanna stood up, as always, wishing Korpanski was at her side. Soon, she thought. He'll be back soon.

'So,' she said, determined to put a positive slant on this latest development, 'the gardener appears to have done a runner. Which turns the spotlight onto him.' Even as she spoke the phrase snagged at her. He would have known that. What had he hoped to achieve by his flight? It was as intriguing a question as wondering what his part had been in all this. Aloud she said, 'Maybe if we share that information it will unlock our girl's tongue.'

She cleared her throat.

'Let's look into the relationship between Mrs Newton, Bethany, the gardener and the dead man.' She flashed up a picture they had retrieved from The Cottage and studied it closely. Louisa had a firm chin, thick dark hair. A challenging stare. Perhaps not a classic beauty but there was a hint of strength there. If someone crossed her, Joanna mused, Louisa did not look the sort of woman who would take it lying down.

She continued. 'The Newtons have been married for thirteen years and have one son, Stevie. We're tracking down her parents who live in the north of Spain. And we'll interview Anthony Newton's parents in case they can shed any light on this. We're having a bit of trouble tracing them as they appear to have moved house fairly frequently and are currently under the radar.' She paused for a while, thoughtful. 'So we don't have a current address for any of Stevie's grandparents. We have no record of Mrs Newton leaving the country.' She turned and stared again at the picture of the missing woman. 'She could be dead too. We don't know much about the Newtons' marriage. Few people knew them well. There are allegations that Anthony's business was questionable, using fake parts for his classic cars and Mrs Mellor, whose husband was in business with Mr Newton until a year ago, claims that he did a shoddy job on the cars. Cut corners.' She smiled. 'It seems a bit extreme to put this as a possible motive for murder.'

She heard muttering from DC Phil Scott. 'Share it, Phil.'

He was smiling. 'You don't know classic petrol heads,' he said. 'Talk about obsessed. My father-in-law . . .'

She brought them back into line, sharing details of Newton's injuries. 'We will be investigating Anthony Newton's business affairs. We know that Bethany used the Range Rover to get to Hanley. We don't know exactly when, probably early on the sixteenth, the Tuesday morning or Monday evening. Presumably she used it to escape but we have no idea what took her and the child out to Leek or what she meant to do there. The fact that the other two cars remain at The Cottage means that Mrs Newton had no transport to leave the house unless it was with our now missing gardener, in his pickup. A scrutiny of the cars and the grounds of the house has not found any evidence of assault. Mrs Newton may be with her parents but we have no evidence that she has left the country.

'We have no positive sightings of Mrs Newton for a number of weeks. Considering the fact that it was her husband who was found naked in the bath, and forensic analysis of the scene may suggest

Bethany and Stevie were witnesses to the murder when we get the report, she's now our prime suspect. But we still don't know how she left The Cottage. If indeed she ever did.'

Putting it like this only reinforced the knowledge that they were probably not even halfway there.

Again she turned around to study the picture on the board, and tried to divine the story behind the face. This had been a woman on her guard. But why? She scanned the watching faces before turning back again to the picture of Bethany Rees this time, the diametric opposite of her employer. A frightened mouse of a girl. She looked vulnerable, a victim. Why wasn't she speaking? Because she hadn't learned her lines? Were the psychiatrist and Matt right about her being a traumatized witness? Or was she part of a plot with Louisa Newton?

'I don't want the focus to shift entirely away from Bethany Rees. Jason, I want you and Kitty to take a car down to South Wales and speak to her parents. I've already had a brief word with them and given them sketchy details. Get a flavour of her. Find out all you can including past employers and if there was any previous contact with Leek or its surrounds. The psychiatrist is convinced that her inability to speak is the result of mental trauma. I'm sceptical. I think this is a refusal to speak because she finds herself in a pickle and doesn't know what line to give. See what you can dig out about this girl.' If only Bethany would speak. Joanna knew she had all the answers.

She tried to ignore the happy smirk which lit the young PC's face. She could read his mind. A day out at the seaside? With Kitty Sandworth? Heaven. She gave him a stern look and reminded him. 'This is an important part of the investigation, Jason. If we can persuade Bethany Rees to talk or find out something which is key to her refusal to talk we might get at the truth a whole lot quicker. Her employer is dead. Understand?'

He nodded but still couldn't quite hide that grin.

Young love, Joanna thought sentimentally. There was something so endearing about it. She shifted her glance to Kitty Sandworth who also looked pretty happy at the task ahead and the officer by her side.

So everyone was happy – except her. News would leak out and the gardener's flit would make juicy headlines indicating incompetence. Which it was. They should have watched him more closely.

THIRTY-SIX

J ason Spark and Kitty had an address for Bethany's parents. It was by the sea, although today the sea was not a place to paddle and have an ice cream but a blustery, unwelcoming grey place with a hostile wind and waves which seemed determined to splash over the promenade and soak the unwary. Maybe in summer it would be beautiful – but crowded. Today Porthcawl was like a ghost town apart from the roar of the waves which seemed to blast through the entire town. On the way down they had discussed how they would conduct the interview. 'Just fact find without giving too much away,' Joanna had advised. 'And definitely don't even think of telling her parents that she's implicated in a murder case. Just get a flavour of their daughter. Specifically whether she's ever had any mental issues, spells in hospital for anxiety – stuff like that,' she'd finished vaguely. 'If you can get a work record all the better. We need to find out if she's been in any trouble – theft, perhaps, or not quite treating her darling little charges with the respect they deserve. Get a handle on any relationships she might have had in the past.' She'd given them each a pat on the back with the parting shot: 'Try and come up with something other than the quality of the local fish and chips.'

They were determined not to let her down. But they were by the sea and it almost felt like a day off.

The address they had was halfway along a long road that stretched into the distance, at right angles to the sea front. It consisted of 1940s semi-detached houses, each with a semi-circular bay window facing the road. They were well maintained, with an air of respectable gentility about them. Ben and Lynne Rees were both retired. That was all they knew so far. The parents had been forewarned of the visit by the local constabulary.

'Here goes.' Kitty gave Jason an encouraging smile and put her hand up to knock. The door opened almost at once and Kitty assumed a friendly, enquiring expression. 'Mr and Mrs Rees?'

The man who stood there, in a frilled red pinafore, gave them a welcoming smile and held his hands out. 'Hello,' he said. 'We've been expecting you.'

His wife, a plump lady with generous thighs in flowered leggings and a voluminous T-shirt, was in the sitting room, perched on the edge of a grey sofa. The room was cluttered with ornaments and photographs and smelt equally of dogs and an underlying waft of sea air. The bay window faced the houses on the other side of the road. But by turning to the extreme right you could just glimpse the sea writhing in the wind, tossing spray into the air. It gave the room a strange sense of movement.

Without getting up Bethany's mother looked at them eagerly. 'We're hoping you're going to tell us how Bethany is. We know that she's had some sort of crisis involving that young boy she looks after and isn't talking – that's what the detective said – and she's in a psychiatric hospital so she can be properly assessed, but we've not heard from her for nearly a month. We tend to spend our days outdoors with the dog and don't watch much telly.'

Not surprising she hadn't tried to get in contact given her apparent inability to speak, Jason thought. But without giving too much away he asked innocently, 'Is that unusual?'

Mrs Rees seemed flustered by the question. 'Well yes and no. Sometimes she's never off the phone. At others she goes all quiet on us sometimes for a month or two at a time. Funny girl. Hard to know what she's thinking sometimes.'

Jason and Kitty exchanged glances.

'She's all right, is she?'

'Yes and no.'

'Hasn't she said anything to that detective yet? But I'm sure she wouldn't have hurt the little fellow.'

'We don't know because she hasn't said a word.'

For a moment mother and father were as dumbfounded as their daughter.

'You can help us,' Kitty spoke again, 'by telling us more about your daughter.'

'We-ell.' It was her mother who spoke now, frowning, as though making an effort to leave nothing out. 'What sort of things do you want to know?'

'Let's start with her childhood. Where did she go to school?'

'Here in Porthcawl. The local comp.'

'Did she do well – was she happy there?'

'As far as we know. She never complained.'

'And then?'

'She got some GCSEs.'

'And?'

'Well, you see,' her father took over, 'she wanted to travel. There was no stoppin' her. So off she went. Hardly saw her for a few years. Didn't really know where she was, not even what country sometimes. She'd just ring, you know, out of the blue.'

'She didn't want to go to college?'

'No,' her father put in. 'She wasn't an academic.'

'So she came back when?'

Lynne Rees looked embarrassed at Kitty's question. 'She didn't really come back. Except for a couple of days now and then.'

Both officers were getting a picture of a daughter whose relationship with her parents was not exactly close.

'What work was she doing?'

'Nannying, I think. Whenever we asked her that's what she'd *say*.' With the emphasis on the last word Jason wondered whether they had quite believed their daughter's story. 'But you thought . . .?' He let his voice trail away into a formless question.

'Well, she could have been doing anything, couldn't she?' Lynne Rees was showing her sceptical side now.

'What else did you think she *might* be doing?' Kitty had asked the question delicately and both parents frowned and took a minute to gather their responses. 'Why would you think she might lie? Did you suspect she was doing something illegal?'

'Oh no,' Lynne was swift to defend her daughter. 'No, it's just that her brother's done so well for himself. She might have felt, you know, inferior.'

'Is he older or younger?'

'Older. Two years.'

So it was the same old story. Clever brother outshines little sister. Instead of competing little sister drops out. And the parents cling to the favoured one.

'Are you able to give me the names of any of the people she worked for?'

Mother and father looked at each other blankly.

'No one?'

'Well, there was someone in Bournemouth.'

'What part of Bournemouth?'

'Poole.'

'Are you able to give me anything more? A name? Perhaps an address?'

Lynne Rees gave a small shrug. 'I'm sorry. I don't think we saw much of her round about then. You see Darren had just got his PhD. Doctorate.' She couldn't hide the look of pride. Her eyes drifted towards the mantelpiece where there were three pictures of a thin young man in cap and gown. In one he was wearing a blue gown trimmed with red.

Both parents were looking at them expectantly, one at a time. It was the mother who spoke. 'She is all right, isn't she?'

'Umm.' Kitty wasn't quite sure how to respond to this.

Lynne Rees filled the awkward hiatus by asking, 'You don't think we should visit her at this mental hospital, do you?'

Once, long ago, Jason had spent a term studying Latin. And if he remembered rightly through those tortuous lessons there were ways of asking questions. *Nonne* and *Num*. One anticipated the answer yes and the other no. Lynne Rees anticipated his response to her request about visiting her daughter as being 'no'. She wanted reassurance that the right thing to do was to stay away – which was exactly what she wanted to do.

Jason's mum was a homely, warm character. If he'd been in a mental hospital she would probably have insisted she have a camp bed by his side. He stared at Lynne Rees. Certain mothers produce certain children. The puzzle was that Bethany had decided to make nannying her career choice.

Kitty was watching him with a little smile on her pretty face and he returned the compliment with a goofy grin. He felt a warmth for her that he'd never felt before for anyone.

He wanted to get out of here. Go home. Back to Staffordshire where they both belonged. He wanted to whisk Kitty to a posh restaurant and drink in the other diners' jealousy for having the prettiest girl in the room. Suddenly the seaside seemed blustery and cold.

Kitty asked the next question with a delicacy he could never have achieved. 'Tell me, Mr and Mrs Rees, has Bethany ever been accused of harming any of the small children she looked after?'

They looked at one another then Lynne Rees shook her head

firmly. 'Not that we know. But as I say she didn't exactly keep us in the loop. Most of the time we didn't know where she was working or who with or even which country. So we wouldn't know.'

The questioning seemed to have stalled. Jason made to stand up. 'Well, if there's nothing you can add . . .?'

'I think the name was Washington.' It was the father who spoke, the words crumbling slowly from his mouth. He'd been frowning hard for the last couple of minutes and now he'd produced the goods. His wife might have been distracted by their son's success but he obviously felt some loyalty for his daughter too. Or was it the opposite? Was it disloyalty? Or guilt?

'The name *was* Washington,' he said curtly. 'They lived in one of those posh houses that look over the sea. I think it's somewhere opposite Brownsea Island. I'm sure she said that. I think she said she'd seen squirrels there.' He smiled, perhaps forgetting the circumstances for a moment, 'Not those horrible grey ones, the Canadian imports. The red ones.' Maybe dredging up an old memory, his face looked sad. 'She took the twins over to the island and they spotted some. Ever so excited she was. She rang us from there.' He clasped his hands together as though praying. 'She loved her little charges. She would never have hurt one of them.'

And Kitty and Jason realized he loved his daughter.

'Thank you.' Now they both stood up. Their visit had provided something at least.

Bethany's father tried to retrieve something. 'You'll keep us informed, will you?'

It was Kitty who answered warmly for both of them. 'Of course, Mr Rees. Of course we will.'

Outside Jason tried to recapture the seaside atmosphere. 'Don't suppose you'd like an ice cream?'

Kitty wrapped her jacket around her. 'No bloody fear. It's freezing.' Then she linked arms with him and smiled up into his face. 'I wouldn't mind some fish and chips though.'

And so ten minutes later they were sitting in a café overlooking the sea which looked as uninviting as an ice bath, fingers in vinegary chips and salty fish, a mug of tea in front of them and PC Jason Spark felt toasty, warmer than he'd ever felt before. He grinned at Kitty Sandworth, his toothy grin and sticky out ears looking, to her at least, endearing. He was, she decided, a really nice bloke. And they had news to share.

Both thought the fish and chips the tastiest they had ever had.

THIRTY-SEVEN

Monday 5 April, 9 a.m.

Of all the places she did not want to be Greatbach was up there, top of the list. But Joanna was obsessed with finding answers and she was sure Bethany's impenetrable demeanour was starting to crack. And so, here Joanna was, back again. This time Claire Roget had told her she'd be in a clinic and trusted her to treat her patient well.

But Joanna was struggling.

She had begun with a frosty reminder. 'You are still under caution, Bethany.'

The girl's eyes locked on to hers with a hint of a challenge.

'Bethany,' Joanna began, feeling exasperated with these silent interviews. 'Please, we only want to find out the truth. We need to hear your side of the story. We told you that we've found Mr Newton's body and we know you were somewhere near when he was attacked. So was Stevie,' she tacked on to the end.

Bethany gave a quick jerk of her head. No.

'We know you were there but you're not cooperating. If you're an innocent victim in all this, Bethany, you need to start talking.'

Bethany's eyes flickered; Joanna read panic and confusion in her tiger's eyes.

'Did Louisa kill him?'

No answer. But that was not to say there was no response. Bethany gave the slightest shake of her head.

Joanna pressed on. 'The blood on your dress was his. We've tested it. And the blood on your cardigan was also his. Did you turn the tap off?'

Bethany's shoulders stiffened; her breathing quickened and she sucked in a breath as though she was drowning. Joanna waited,

convinced she was about to speak but nothing came out except
the softest mewling, like a newborn kitten.

'Louisa Newton is missing. Do you know where she is? Why
would you protect her?'

Bethany's eyes dropped to the floor. It didn't take a psychiatrist
to read concealment behind the action. She knew.

'Where is she? Is she dead, Bethany? Who killed Stevie's parents?'

The girl's shoulders drooped. She looked defeated. Crushed.
And very unhappy. Miserable.

Joanna pressed on. 'And now,' she continued conversationally,
'on top of all that the gardener's gone AWOL.'

Bethany's head jerked up. She put her hands in front of her
mouth. Her eyes were wide, startled as she started breathing hard.
This, Joanna surmised, *was an unexpected event.*

She followed that up with a stab in the dark. 'That wasn't part
of the plan, was it?'

The girl dropped her face into her hands and bent over almost
double in a show of abject grief which was as articulate as words.

She might as well have screamed. *No, no, no.*

Bethany began to shake.

Then she lifted her eyes, the tawny brown flecked with yellow
appeared cat-like and deceitful again. Her lips moved and again
Joanna held her breath. *The girl was about to speak?* But after a
second which seemed to stretch interminably she dropped her eyes
and exhaled.

Damn. But Joanna wasn't finished yet.

'Is Louisa Newton close to her parents?'

A shrug. *Don't know. Don't care.*

Joanna studied her nails as though considering whether she needed
a manicure. 'Mr Newton had been stabbed six times,' she said
conversationally. 'Five in the back and one in the neck while he
was in the bath. But of course, you already know that, don't you?'

Bethany crouched down.

'One of them had severed his spinal cord. Nasty. It would have
rendered him paralysed while someone drove the knife in again
and again. Just think what that would have felt like.'

The slightest, softest moan forced its way through Bethany's
lips. It gave Joanna some hope.

So close now. The girl will speak.

'And then how cruel. They turned the hot tap on, scalding a

man who was naked and could not defend himself. Bethany,' she said softly, almost kindly, 'I don't know whether you realize how much trouble you're in? At the moment you're the only person we know who was at the scene – and Stevie, of course. At the very least, you're a witness or accessory to murder.' Finally her patience ran out, deserting her like sea over sand on the ebb tide. 'You can refuse to talk but it won't help you in the end. If you can't – or rather won't – tell us who killed him we'll be forced to charge you.' She stretched the truth for purposes of expedience. 'On the evidence we have you'll be going down for a very long time even though we will never know the full story. Is that what you want?'

She sensed the girl was wavering. Her face had changed to abstraction. She was climbing inside herself as she weighed up the possibilities.

Joanna stood up and had almost reached the door when she heard a sob. Just that one sad sound. She turned around and looked. Bethany's face was screwed up like an animal in its death throes. Joanna made one last appeal. 'We're trying to keep an open mind, Bethany, but we need the truth. You were there. You know what happened. If you don't tell us, we're bound to think the worst. You know that.'

Joanna made her way back to the station to find the officers waiting for a debrief from PC Jason Spark.

Everyone could read the jauntiness that accompanied PCs Kitty Sandworth and Jason Spark as they'd returned to the briefing room. Jason, in particular, couldn't hide his elation or pure happiness. He was grinning from bat-ear to bat-ear. And Kitty, with her big eyes and peachy complexion, looked similarly happy. Romance was definitely in the air.

'Well,' Joanna prompted, 'was your trip to the seaside worthwhile?'

The pair exchanged a look they might have imagined was secret but was patently obvious to all who watched.

When they unloaded their information mentioning Bethany's previous employer in Poole in Dorset, Joanna responded crisply, 'You might think this earns you another trip to the seaside but I think this time we can manage with a phone call. Alan, can you get onto that now?'

DC King went off to make the call and the happy pair didn't even look disappointed even though both had hoped they might have a further trip, this time to the south coast.

Joanna rang Matthew to say she'd be home late and his response was gentle. 'Getting anywhere?'

'Think crawler lane,' she said. 'Baby steps. See you later.'

She could tell he was smiling when he replied, 'Jakob says hi and he'll expect you to be home this evening to read him a story and tuck him up.'

The brief glimpse into the safe world of husband, home and baby boosted her mood up.

'So have we found the gardener? Or Kelvin Shipley?'

Blank faces indicated not yet. 'We're working on it.'

She turned to the forensic team. 'Have you paid attention to the bath taps?'

'We've removed them and have found a partial print.'

'Can you work with it?'

Jack Cornell responded. He was a senior scene of crimes officer with years of experience. 'We think we can,' he said cautiously.

'It's really important.'

'We'll do what we can, Jo.'

'Thanks. And any facial recognition from the body-worn camera footage?'

'Negative,' confirmed Cornell.

'Nothing?' Her tone was incredulous.

Cornell shook his head and couldn't quite stop a smirk spreading like an inkblot across his face. 'There were a couple of marijuana plants in the greenhouse, though.'

That lightened everyone's mood and there were a few chortles around the room.

But she was serious. 'That indicates he wasn't expecting to do a flit but to be at The Cottage for some time.'

She could tell from the blank faces that they hadn't interpreted the evidence in this way. 'So – any good news?'

DC King came over from where he'd been busy at his desk, his thin face lit up with pride. 'The good news is I've tracked down Bethany's previous employers. The Washingtons live along Shore Road, Poole. One of the most expensive postcodes in the country. I've set up a Skype interview with them in . . .' He glanced up at the clock. 'Half an hour's time.'

'Well done. That was quick.' She turned back into the room. 'Anyone else have something to chuck into the melting pot?'

There were a few proffered points but nothing hit home and they dispersed.

THIRTY-EIGHT

10.20 a.m.

King was waiting for her. 'You ready for this?' She came back to reality, stopped aching for past times and faced the screen. 'Yeah. Bring it on.'

She had a somewhat distorted view of a harassed woman somewhere in her forties with a shock of wispy, strawberry-blonde hair.

'Mrs Washington.'

'That's right.'

'I'm Detective Inspector Joanna Piercy of the Staffordshire Police. I'm investigating the murder of a Mr Anthony Newton.'

Dinah Washington, who was possessed of a pair of all-seeing, intelligent, grey eyes, listened carefully while Joanna spent some time explaining why they wanted to speak to her.

'Bethany worked for me for a little over two years,' she responded. 'That was between September 2015 and June 2017. She left because she wanted to travel. At the time the twins were quite a handful.' She laughed and ran her hands through her hair. 'They were one year old, just beginning to walk. And two of them – well, you can imagine. They were three by the time she left and she coped with them really well. While she was a quiet girl' – Joanna couldn't resist a sour smile – 'she was patient and did lots with them – painting and reading. She took them out, down to the beach if the weather was OK. I didn't have any faults with her. Sure, she kept herself to herself. She was a very . . .' a pause, '. . . contained girl but she was pleasant and, as I said. good with the children. We had no complaints about her at all. We would have kept her on but she was anxious to leave.'

'Did you like her?'

Mrs Washington screwed up her face thoughtfully. 'I can't say

I liked or disliked her. She was just there, in the background, and she did a good job.'

'Apart from her being quiet how would you describe her character?'

Mrs Washington took a moment to consider, finally coming up with: 'She was sort of unobtrusive. You'd hardly know she was there. She'd sort of slide into a room unseen and you'd realize she'd been there all the time.'

'That's her physical presence, Mrs Washington. What was her personality like?'

'We-ell. She was naive. Literal.' She gave a chuckle, perhaps forgetting the circumstances. 'You'd suggest something and she'd take it as gospel.'

'Like what?'

'Oh, you'd suggest she went for a walk along the sea front and she'd just do it even though it was blowing a gale. She had a sort of blind obedience. She was gullible. She'd believe anything anybody told her and she was very superstitious – bordering on paranoid. She'd imagine people staring at her, come home early from days out because she felt it was a bad day or something had gone wrong that she felt was an indication that she should come home. She could be a bit overdramatic and she was very tidy.' Mrs Washington frowned. 'Obsessively so. She didn't like me going into her room. But she was quiet and contained and, as I said, good with the children.'

Joanna picked up on something. 'When you say superstitious, do you mean black cats, Friday the thirteenth, stuff like that?'

'No, more than just touching wood. Stupid stuff. She'd refuse to wear certain clothes, go out on certain days. She read her horoscope religiously and would alter her day's plans sometimes if the "omens"' – she scratched the air, at the same time making a comical face – 'looked bad. Used to annoy me no end. But it didn't do any good. She'd argue and cry and I'd feel a bully. I mean' – her irritation bubbled up – 'it got ridiculous. Smearing garlic on the doorframe and sleeping with a cross round her neck. It wasn't quite balanced.'

'But you had no fear for your children?'

'No. If anything she was over-protective. She would have given her life for them. I was out with my job quite a bit so she was alone with them. I had no qualms about leaving the children with her.'

'What about your husband?'

'He's in London most of the time. He's a Lloyd's underwriter. He has a flat in Mayfair. He's down here most weekends but in the week – no. And she had quite a few weekends off so they didn't really have a lot to do with each other.'

'So Bethany was on her own, with the twins, most of the time.'

'That's right.'

'You must have trusted her.'

'*Absolutely.* I couldn't have left the twins with *anyone* I didn't have absolute trust in. I have a very busy beauty salon. I can't just take time off. I needed someone reliable.'

Joanna frowned and glanced at King by her side. So this was the Bethany they hadn't got to know.

'Is there anything else you want to add?'

Mrs Washington looked almost ashamed of herself. 'You say she's connected with a murder?'

'She's a person of interest,' Joanna said calmly. 'We're still investigating and we haven't charged her.'

Dinah Washington was quick to defend her one-time nanny. 'The girl I knew would never have done that. She was sweet-natured and she was awfully good with the twins. She'd do stuff with them, make cakes, painting. She loved painting. They'd show me the messy hands and the pictures. You couldn't tell what they were but they were so proud of them. And she never got cross with them. She never lost her temper or was short with them. She was a good nanny,' she finished firmly.

'OK, thanks for that.'

Joanna gave her her contact details in case she thought of anything else and disconnected the call. For the first time since the girl had been spotted at the top of The Roaches she was thinking about her not as a woman bent on destroying a little boy or even a murder suspect, but as a sort of Mary Poppins character. Good with the children.

So who was the real Bethany Rees? The girl Dinah Washington had described was not someone who masterminded complex scenarios, murdered a man in his bath, took a child to a remote location still wearing bloodstained clothes. Someone else had directed the proceedings. And at the moment her finger was pointing in the direction of the gardener – whatever the reason for his flight was.

But the other question buzzing in her mind was where did

Louisa fit into all this? Had she headed off to Spain leaving her husband dead? If so it had been a poorly thought-out plan. The police had been bound to follow her trail. If she too was dead why leave her husband's body to be found but not hers? But if she was alive then where was she?

The day was spent like many previous ones in fact finding, fact checking, fact collating, trying to track down the gardener. By the early evening she felt her eyes were looking but not seeing. 'I'm heading off for a bit,' she mouthed, waving her mobile at Alan King.

He did a thumbs up in response.

THIRTY-NINE

T he urge to discuss the case with Mike was strong. Less than fifteen minutes later she was facing him, noticing the improvement: he'd walked, with only one elbow crutch, to the door to let her in. There was no sign of Fran or the children.

'Hey,' she said, kissing the prickly, unshaven cheek of her sergeant and glancing at the single crutch. 'Progress?'

He made a face. 'Partially weight-bearing,' he said. 'If all's well I'll be back to fully weight-bearing in a week or so. I go back to see the consultant next week.' He was speaking quickly, sounded excited.

'Brilliant. And when can you go back to the gym?' She was tempted to punch his shoulder. 'Get those muscles back up to scratch?' She would, at one time, have called it 'pulling his leg', but it was something she probably wouldn't ever dare say to him again. He hip-hopped into the sitting room, flopping down onto the sofa and dropping his crutch. 'Bloody exhausting trying to get around on these things.' He regarded her carefully for a moment. 'I know that look, Jo. So?'

She shared everything with him, her doubts and observations as well as the testimony from Dinah Washington, surveying him as she spoke.

'So the girl's still not talking?'

'It's putting us at a huge disadvantage. Even a "no comment" interview usually tells us something about a suspect, whether they're cocky, frightened, but this blanking out is not only annoying, unnerving and uninformative, it's also preventing us making a judgement on her and discovering her role in all this. It's as though she's completely switched off. It's driving me nuts.'

Korpanski's dark eyes gleamed and she could almost read his thoughts. *He'd* have got her talking by now. Detective Sergeant Mike Korpanski had two weapons at his disposal. To men his bulk, height and build displayed a challenge, sometimes a threat. To women he was undoubtedly attractive and she had witnessed a few of the fair sex 'confide' in him when questioned whereas they clammed up when she had put exactly the same questions to them. There was no doubt about it. Women warmed to her sergeant and she could do with that charm by her side right now.

'And she's still at the psychiatric place?'

'Greatbach, yes. Under the care of a forensic psychiatrist.' She felt her lip curl.

'So what does *she* think, this psychiatrist?' Korpanski's scepticism of the psychiatrist was also patently obvious. As usual his manner was blunt, his questions heading straight for the jugular.

'I'm not sure. I think since we found Anthony Newton's body she accepts that the girl has vital information about a murder and we have to find out what she knows.'

'Well, considering the circumstances surrounding her coming to our attention, as well as the crime scene she abandoned, I'd say trauma and anxiety have to be part of the deal, don't they?'

She nodded.

'So will this psychiatrist alter the way she'll treat her now?'

'Probably not. Mike . . .'

Familiar with the tone, he looked up.

'I wonder if Louisa is alive and kicking, somewhere hot and sunny, living it up. But now the gardener's missing . . .'

Korpanski frowned. 'Sort of puts the cat among the pigeons, doesn't it?' He thought for a moment. 'I take it you've checked the channel ports, airports . . .?'

She gave a weary nod.

Korpanski shifted on the sofa. He was obviously still in pain and she felt guilty for bothering him. 'Do you want me to fetch you anything?'

He grinned. 'What? Like a pint of real ale or a couple of painkillers?'

'Something along those lines.'

'I wouldn't mind a cup of tea.'

She was in the kitchen, boiling the kettle and hunting for teabags when Fran Korpanski marched in. And Joanna immediately felt awkward. 'Sorry. I was just making Mike a . . .'

Between the two women there had always been this awkwardness. Joanna wasn't even sure why it had developed in the first place but, like permafrost, it would never melt.

Fran was still observing her, eyes tightly hostile, lips pressed together.

Joanna tried again. 'I just thought I'd like to discuss . . .'

Behind her the kettle hissed and billowed out steam before switching itself off. Fran turned and pointedly dropped two teabags into two mugs before pouring the boiling water onto them.

'Ten minutes,' Fran Korpanski said, holding her fingers up to emphasize the time scale. 'Not a moment longer.'

Mike was smirking as she re-entered the sitting room. She got the impression he'd been enjoying the cat fight in the kitchen, the drama providing a diversion from the boredom of his state. She handed him his mug of tea, sat down again and continued her musings.

'Where's Mrs Newton? Where's the bloody disappearing gardener? Why has he gone? It's only drawn attention to him. And he's clean. No record. And lastly, Mike, was the girl *really* about to chuck the kid over the edge of a cliff?'

'Perhaps she wasn't. Maybe that's just what it looked like. Maybe you're wrong. Maybe you've been wrong from the start. Looking in the wrong direction. Seeing it from the wrong perspective.' He smirked again. He was enjoying this. 'Wouldn't be the first time, Jo.'

And this was what she'd missed – that honest evaluation combined with teasing.

She could hear Fran bustling around noisily in the kitchen and felt the minutes ticking away.

'It's a murder,' he reminded her. 'And to be honest if Matthew says your guy was stabbed in the back while in the bath surely that points fairly clearly to his wife who's done a runner?'

'Or dead,' she said gloomily.

He sat up and she sensed his eagerness and energy. 'Focus on the backstory to the dead man, Jo. That's the real crime. The bit about the baby didn't happen. It was just a drama.'

And now she knew why she'd felt she must discuss the case with Korpanski. He was seeing it as it was supposed to be seen. Putting it into words.

'You'll get your answers, Jo. You always do.' He closed his eyes. 'In the end.'

'Thanks, Mike.'

'You need to find Mrs Newton,' he said.

With perfect timing Fran reappeared and stood in the doorway, unmistakably ushering her out.

But her DS had lit a spark and given the case some clarity, reminding her which path to follow.

FORTY

9 p.m.

She let herself into a blessedly silent house. All quiet in the nursery. Matthew was sitting at the kitchen table, papers, diagrams, pie charts, articles scattered in front of him with his laptop open. He was grinning at her as she walked in, his face as warm and welcoming as a log fire. She bent, kissed his mouth and ruffled the honey blond hair. 'What are you looking so pleased about?'

He handed her an already poured glass of wine. 'I got the full report on the girl's dress as well as the little boy's dungarees.'

She sat down. 'And you're feeling smug? Go on.'

'I was right,' he said.

His grin hadn't faded.

'The boy was in the bathroom when his daddy was killed.'

She'd heard it before but the fact was still shocking.

'He must have been very near, Jo, less than two feet away.'

She took a moment to absorb this.

'And Bethany?'

He shook his head. 'My original thoughts have been confirmed by the blood spatter analysis expert. She picked him up, probably turned his head away, tried to comfort him.'

She nodded. 'The gardener's cottage has been searched. No sign of any bloodstains there.'

'However clever the experts are they can't solve your case for you, Jo,' he said. 'Sorry.'

'Right,' she said. 'Try this for size. Little Stevie witnesses his father's murder. Goes hysterical. Runs for his nanny while the perpetrator escapes. When he's gone Bethany turns off the hot tap, sticks on her cardigan and the coat, grabs the bag that contains money and car keys and runs. Still doesn't explain why she headed for the hills.'

Matthew shrugged.

'Why refuse to speak?'

He put his hand on her arm as though to restrain her. 'I hate to take the medics' side on this one,' he said. 'You know what I think . . . she really was traumatized. A form of PTSD. Whatever happened terrified Bethany so much she took Stevie and ran. She might never fully recover, Jo.'

FORTY-ONE

Tuesday 5 April, 8 a.m.

The day began as usual with a text to the psychiatrist asking if there was any change in Bethany's silence. The psychiatrist's daily reports had dwindled to a brief text message: Sorry. No joy.

To which Joanna responded with a polite:

Thanks. I appreciate it. Let me know if there's any change.

The day's briefing felt as though they were confronted by a brick wall.

But at nine thirty a phone call gave her some more information. It was from Mark Fask, in charge of the forensic examination of the property.

'Thought I'd better let you know,' he said in his gravelly voice. 'Mrs Newton has a walk-in wardrobe.'

'And?' She knew he wouldn't have rung her unless there was some significance to this.

'We've found traces of blood in it.'

'When you say traces . . .?'

'As though someone wearing bloodstained clothes has brushed against the clothes in the wardrobe.' Mark Fask hesitated before adding, 'I don't want to read too much into this but I wondered if it was possible that they hid in there? The blood was found on the hems of some of the dresses and the skirt of one or two long dresses. That's what it looks like anyway. It was in the far corner.'

'Thanks.'

Later that same morning there was another development.

An officer had been posted at The Cottage to guard the scene, but at a little after ten o'clock the officer rang to say a woman (he seemed to use the word advisedly) had arrived and was demanding to be let in.

'Who is she?'

'Her name is a Mrs Traynor and she says she's the cleaner.'

It was the first the team had heard of her.

'Keep her there,' Joanna said. 'I'll come over and talk to her.'

Mavis Traynor proved to be a pleasant-looking lady in her fifties with thick ankles and a mop of curly grey hair. Understandably she appeared anxious.

But the version she gave shed more light on the events at The Cottage.

'They told me they was going on holiday and there was no need for me to come in.'

'Who told you?'

'Mrs Newton.'

'When?'

'Middle March. The Tuesday morning.'

Another one who didn't read the news or listen to the radio bulletins?

'Exactly when?'

Mavis Traynor looked vaguely outraged at Joanna's tone. She squared her shoulders. 'Three weeks ago,' she said finally. 'She said they was going to Spain for three weeks and I didn't need to come in.' She moved closer, in a confiding mood now.

'Very mean they are. If they can save on my coming in they do. And it's only a few quid.' She shrugged.

'They were both going?'

'Oh yeah. That's what she said, anyway.'

'She rang you?'

'Texted me. Look . . .' She pulled out a vintage mobile phone, flipped it open and found the message. It was as she'd said.

Going to Spain for 3 weeks so no need you come in L.

It was dated Tuesday March the sixteenth, eight a.m. Joanna read it through, arguing with herself. But Louisa Newton had not left the country. She looked at Mrs Traynor. 'There's no mention of the little boy?'

'Stevie? I guessed he'd be staying here with his nanny.'

Joanna was incredulous. 'Haven't you heard what has happened?'

Mavis Traynor looked blank. 'I took the chance to have a break myself and went to stay with my sister in Liverpool. Where we've had a lovely quiet time.' And then she realized something was wrong. 'What is it? What's happened?'

'You'd better sit down,' Joanna said and filled her in. Understandably the woman was upset, then faint, before expressing anxiety for Stevie and lastly curiosity as to where Bethany was.

It was obvious she knew nothing about the events surrounding Anthony Newton's murder. In fact, she was more concerned that she wouldn't be able to carry out her cleaning job as the house was sealed up.

It seemed it was going to be a lucky day.

Joanna had recalled something Dinah Washington had said about Bethany being superstitious and reliant on horoscopes, so she'd set one of the newer PCs the task of combing through the horoscopes from the weekend of the thirteenth and fourteenth, and Monday the fifteenth of March.

And, surprisingly, Gino Salvi came up with an answer of sorts.

It was an online horoscope which Bethany had read from one of the apps on her mobile phone. Pale Sister. He called Joanna over, having difficulty suppressing a smirk.

'Do you think this might be what sparked off the trip out to the moors?'

Seek out a place of safety.

She stared at it. The Roaches didn't strike her as a place of safety.

'I don't know,' she said slowly. But her eyes were drawn to the date and time, Sunday March the fourteenth, and she felt that, however unlikely, however strange, this was, at least, a pointer.

Still, why go there?

She picked up the phone and connected with Bethany's mother then put the call on speakerphone. She smothered a grin. Much as they would like to have repeated their jaunt to the seaside there was no need to send Jason and Kitty all the way back down to South Wales. But before she could introduce her reason for calling, Mrs Rees had one question for her. 'Can we come and see her?'

'Your daughter isn't really under my primary jurisdiction,' she explained. 'She's currently a patient at Greatbach under the care of Dr Roget. I suggest you contact her and see what she says. Maybe she'll speak to you.'

She gave her Claire Roget's contact details and asked her to let her know when they'd be visiting.

Then she asked her question. 'We're puzzled as to why your daughter took her young charge up to The Roaches. It isn't particularly close to the house where she was working; neither is it simple to get to. She had to take a bus and would have had a long, steep walk.'

'Oh.'

She needed to prompt her. 'We're wondering why there? Does Bethany have any connection with the area?'

There was a long silence during which time Joanna could hear Bethany's parents murmuring to each other and she wondered about the hesitation. Were they scraping their brains for a far-off memory? In the end it was her father who took over and spoke into the handset. 'We took a cottage near there one year when she was about ten. Took our bikes. There's some trails round there and we hired the bikes and went along the . . .'

'Manifold Track,' his wife supplied. 'We started just outside Leek in a place called Waterhouses and cycled to this pretty little village . . .'

This time it was her husband who supplied the answer. Like many married couples they crisscrossed through a conversation like well-rehearsed actors.

'Hulme End. We had a cup of tea there then cycled back. Oh, it was a lovely day. I think we laughed all the way along. See, it's lovely being on a bike without the traffic.'

'Tell me about it.' Joanna laughed. 'I know that trail well. Bethany was about ten?'

'Maybe she was coming up for eleven? Just before she went to secondary school.'

'Did you visit The Roaches? The Winking Man?'

'We did. Took a picnic up there. Climbed all the way to the top. Marvellous views.' Ben Rees's enthusiasm made his voice sound excited. 'But . . .'

Joanna's pulse quickened. She had heard something in Bethany's father's voice. Something that wasn't enthusiasm. More like a memory he was anxious to bury.

Lynne's high-pitched voice came on the line. 'They never did get on, her and Darren. Always quarrelling. About nothing.' She gave a tight laugh. 'We have a saying in Wales: *chwara fel ci a mochyn*. It means to quarrel like a dog and a pig. Better than the English version, I think.'

'And?' Joanna prompted.

'They'd been fighting. He hit her hard. Her nose was bleeding. She was really frightened. She ran up there, went right to the edge and she shouted. I can still hear it. "You can't get me here." To us it looked dangerous but she felt safe up there.'

In the end the explanation had been ridiculously simple.

By its precarious geography the edge of a drop had been a place of safety. She and Mike had been right about Bethany taking Stevie to The Roaches. It had distracted her away from the real drama in this case.

Ben Rees continued his story. '"Come any nearer," she shouted, "and I'll jump." I'll tell you something, Inspector, Darren never bothered her after that.'

Bethany's mother sighed. 'They just never got on. Chalk and cheese they were. He was very clever. He's done really well. Works for the government, you know, while she . . .'

Even on the end of a telephone line Joanna could hear despair and anger in Bethany's mother's voice. 'Rebelled at school. And look where that's got her. Nannying for other people's children. Hasn't even got her own.'

For the first time since the very start of this case Joanna felt sorry for the girl.

'Did Bethany have any mental health problems?'

This was received with a stunned silence.

'M-mental health?' Lynne stammered.

'Yes. Did she suffer from anxiety or—'

'She had the bloody lot.' Ben almost exploded. 'Everything in the book. Eating disorders . . . thin. Nearly put her in hospital. "Pull yourself together," I said. "For goodness' sake just get a hold on yourself. It's not difficult to eat.".'

Or to speak, Joanna thought.

'And did she?'

'Did she what . . .?' Ben was sounding angry now. 'Did she what, Inspector?'

'Get a hold of herself? Eat?'

'Never well. She was never much of an eater. Probably the stars told her not to.' Lynne's voice was acidic now. 'She has a great reliability on the stars and what they tell her to do.'

'Has she ever had an episode like this before when she's not spoken?'

'We-ell . . .' Lynne had elected to answer this one. 'She'd go quiet like, climb inside herself if something upset her, but those times generally didn't last for long.'

'What would convince her to speak again?'

'Just time, Inspector. We'd just wait for her to start again.' Lynne's voice was gentler this time round. 'What's she charged with?'

'She's a person of interest,' Joanna said. 'We haven't formally charged her with anything.' Something pricked her. 'Is she on any medication for a psychiatric disorder?'

'Not to our knowledge.'

'OK. Thanks. Let me know when you're visiting.'

FORTY-TWO

So she had an answer to one of her questions. Bethany had taken Stevie to The Roaches not to harm him. She'd fled from the killer. It seemed to make sense but it wasn't the full answer. She couldn't or wouldn't speak because she was traumatized. In time her tongue would loosen. It seemed most likely that she and Stevie had hidden amongst Louisa's clothes in the walk-in wardrobe.

It was all fitting together very nicely. To understand is to lose irritation.

Except where was Louisa?

And where was Adam? Were they together now? Had Newton been murdered to facilitate their flight? And so back to the crime. Whoever had killed Anthony Newton in such a precise and cruel way had then felt it necessary to fill the bath with scalding water.

In fact, they still knew little about the dead man. He had accumulated a substantial amount of money in a relatively short space of time. Simply through classic cars? That was something for HMRC to unravel unless it had a bearing on their case.

Feeling a sudden sense of clarity, she knew she must focus the investigation more squarely on Newton's business life. For that she needed to speak to Cindy Mellor's husband.

The team had tracked Damien Mellor down to a small business premises just outside Hanley, so Joanna made her way there. It looked as though he had set up as a rival to Newton. On the forecourt stood a pale blue E-type Jaguar and a Jenson Interceptor, both from the early seventies. There was no price on either windscreen. It reminded her of the dark red Jaguar Mark 2 which was housed in Newton's garage.

She pushed open the door and was met by a smart young Asian woman in cream trousers, a pink sweater and long, straight, black hair that reached almost to her waist. She had large, luminous eyes. Damien Mellor proved to be a slim, balding man in his fifties with sharp blue eyes. He greeted Joanna warily, invited her to sit down and she sensed he was about to ask whether he should summon his solicitor. She reassured him quickly. 'This isn't in any way an interrogation, Mr Mellor,' she said and watched him relax – almost. 'You're not under investigation. We just want to find out a little more about Anthony Newton.'

He bowed his head and gave a strange, sideways smile that smacked of cynicism.

Then he leaned back in his chair and put his palms flat on the desk. 'So what do you want to know?'

'What was he like?'

Mellor's smile widened. 'Truth?'

Joanna nodded.

'Well then. He was a bully. He was dishonest, avaricious. Untrustworthy, even as a partner, someone I'd known for years.' Mellor put his elbows on the desk. 'He would sell his best friend down the Swanee if it meant making a few extra bucks.'

'You were in partnership for years. What finally persuaded you to leave?'

Mellor swallowed a smile. 'You may not believe this but I love classic cars. I really do. Tony was putting fake parts into them. Patching them up in his workshops so badly they looked fine but in reality were an accident waiting to happen.'

'But surely with classic cars the parts are difficult if not impossible to source?'

'These were substandard. They were rubbish. Last a few miles. I'm talking brake pads, clutch, gears. The bloody lot. And the fitters! I watched them ram parts in, fail to test that the engines were running properly. It was a nightmare. I took it for so long but at some point it was all going to blow up in our faces. I decided to split the partnership before it did.'

He stopped speaking for a moment. 'Do you know who killed him yet?'

'We-ell . . .' Joanna decided to trust the man. 'His wife has disappeared along with the gardener who's also done a runner. So we've plenty of leads.'

Damien Mellor nodded.

'Your wife and Louisa are good friends. What did you think of her?'

He shrugged. 'I didn't really dwell on it. I think she liked the high life and like lots of women didn't particularly care how it was financed.' There was a hint of bitterness in his voice which made Joanna wonder whether he was including his own wife in the description.

She decided to step on Mellor's toes a bit. 'The car business certainly did finance the high life.' She made it sound as if she was in admiration but Mellor didn't take the bait.

'It's all put against the business,' he said. 'Sometimes in the wife's name. HMRC have real difficulty catching up with it all. Some of it always slips through the net, gets salted away out of reach.'

He gave her a bland smile and Joanna left, convinced she would not have liked Anthony Newton had she met him alive.

Wednesday 7 April, 10 a.m.

Joanna hadn't, so far, interviewed Anthony's parents, though she doubted they would be able to shed any light on their son's murder.

It was practically a courtesy call. They had already politely declined the offer of a family liaison officer, saying they had each other and they wanted to be left alone. Today, however, she felt was a good opportunity to speak to them in person. They'd agreed to be interviewed and she took PC Paul Ruthin with her.

He looked pleased to be taken away from the mind-numbing checking of facts and statements on a rainy Wednesday when the station held the sad atmosphere of a fairground, shrouded in winter.

'You drive, Ruthin,' she said. 'It'll give me time to think.'

George and Valerie Newton lived in a retirement village near Nantwich on a large complex which included, according to the board outside, a golf course, swimming pool, gym, restaurants, shops, hairdressers and community areas as well as 'extensive grounds'. In sweeping italics underneath it was described as *Community Autumn Living*. Looking on the website the costs were astronomically high for the size of property.

They were buzzed in, the gates opening very slowly and, obeying the signs to limit their speed to five miles an hour, they inched the car along the gravelled area at the front of the building and followed the signs to the Visitors' Car Park before looping back to the front door. The façade was heavy Victorian, the grounds stunning, lawns dotted with trees: beeches and oaks, sweeping down to a lake.

'Let's find Newton senior,' she said as they made their way into the hall. There was, undeniably, something calming about the place, as though once inside you left all the worries of everyday life – work, bills, house maintenance, insurance, keeping a car on the road, fear of theft – outside. It was a safe, secure world behind tall gates which kept the inhabitants in and the outside world out.

FORTY-THREE

George and Valerie Newton were waiting at the top of the stairs of a brick-built contemporary addition at the back of the building containing annexes, three storeys high, with tall windows and tiny Juliet balconies.

Valerie was small, with dark hair, presumably dyed. She looked in her eighties and her face was scored with anxiety but she over-rode that with a bright smile. She moved easily, quickly, with a sprightly agility. Unlike her husband, who shuffled on a Zimmer frame and was bent over. They were let into a flat. George Newton sat and stared gloomily out of the tall window overlooking the man-made lake, but appeared too wrapped up in his own private world to notice the view. The face he turned towards them was strangely expressionless.

His wife twittered around him. 'Parkinson's,' she explained, 'and dementia.' Then, patting his shoulder, she added, 'Poor love.'

She dropped down into a large and comfortable-looking armchair and indicated a padded bench with no back for them to rest on. 'George,' she chided gently. He looked around. The hands on his lap shook slightly. Valerie seemed to think she should explain. 'Drugs,' she said. 'They've really helped. But when George had the diagnosis we decided we should move to somewhere like here. Anthony helped us.' She looked around, her face a mixture of pleasure and sadness. 'It's lovely, isn't it?' And then the truth came out. 'But we'd rather be at home.' Her hand reached out to touch her husband's shaking hand. 'Wouldn't we, darling?'

George managed a brief, confused smile but apart from that his face remained a blank canvas.

Valerie leaned towards them and spoke quietly. 'We've told him' – her voice choked – 'about Anthony but I think he's forgotten. So,' Valerie resumed her normal speaking voice, 'shall we make a start? Obviously anything we can do to help . . .' Her voice trailed away.

'I'm sorry,' Joanna said, not specifying so the apology encom-passed both her son's murder and the mental state of her husband.

Valerie acknowledged the words with a nod before saying, 'Have you found out who . . .?'

'We have a few leads.'

'Have you found Louisa?'

'Not yet.'

'You think she—?'

'We don't know.'

'And Stevie?'

From Joanna's visit it was obvious that Stevie's paternal grand-parents were in no fit state to take him in. 'He's with foster parents.' Joanna felt bound to add, 'He's being perfectly well looked after.'

For a moment Valerie looked as confused as her husband. 'But what about Louisa's parents?'

'We're still trying to track them down. Do you have an address?'

Valerie shook her head. 'We only met them at the wedding.'

PC Ruthin stepped in. 'What were things like between your son and his wife?'

Valerie shrugged. 'Same as any couple. They seemed all right.' She looked upset then. 'Whatever they say Tony was a good boy. He helped us secure a place here. We couldn't have afforded it without him.'

The two officers exchanged glances but said nothing.

'Are you renting or have you bought?'

'We bought two years ago. When we sold our house Tony put the money into a fund. That paid for it.'

Startling them all, George spoke. 'Why are you here? Why are you asking these questions?'

The officers decided it was best to let Valerie answer.

'George,' his wife chided him again but gently. 'They want to know things about Anthony.'

But her husband had lost his thread.

'You have her, don't you? The nanny. It *was* her, wasn't it?' Valerie asked.

Joanna was tired of saying it. 'We don't know.'

But Valerie too was losing patience. 'I don't know how you police work but it seems bloody obvious to me, 'scuse my French. *She* killed our son. I know it.'

She had it all worked out even if they didn't.

'You met her, Mrs Newton?'

Valerie drew in a loud huff. 'I can't remember as I did.'

Joanna skirted round the assumption. 'She hasn't confessed.'

'Well, she wouldn't, would she?' Valerie was angry now. 'So you're waiting for her to confess, are you?'

Joanna didn't dare respond to this.

Valerie's anger grew hotter. 'And you still don't know what's happened to Louisa, our daughter-in-law. She could be dead too. That bloody nanny could have done for her too.'

George was still staring blankly around, his face masked with a slight smile.

Joanna rose to leave. 'We're working on finding your son's killer.' It was all she could honestly say for now.

PC Ruthin had been doing some swift arithmetic in his head. The Newtons had lived here for two years. This two-bedroom flat would then have cost at least £250,000. Their previous address had been a terraced house in Milton which, according to Zoopla, they had sold for £80,000. Which left a shortfall of £170,000. Unless they had had substantial savings that would make Anthony a generous benefactor. With money he actually didn't have – according to his tax returns. It was around a year ago that Anthony and Damien had dissolved the partnership. But Anthony had had a sister they were trying to make contact with.

He voiced the question. 'Did your daughter help you buy this place?'

It was George who responded to this, shaking his head very slowly and answering the question with difficulty. 'Her couldn't afford it,' he said. 'Her had a no-good partner and works all the hours God sends to make ends meet.'

Joanna could feel a slight frisson. She liked the sound of a no-good partner. And by the look of interest on Paul Ruthin's face so did he.

'When you say no good . . .'

Valerie pressed her lips together. 'He's crossed your lot a time or two.'

'His name?'

'Kelvin Shipley.' Said with a venomous glance.

A connection, the circle beginning to close. Shipley, the name on Adam's van insurance and the friend behind his move to The Cottage.

Shipley the petty criminal, the burglar, the car thief.

'They split up years ago. She dropped his name then.'

'But I take it Anthony knew his brother-in-law?'

George was frowning and predictably didn't answer her question. 'Our Shelley and him broke up years ago. Good job too.'

No love lost there then.

They proffered a few more pleasantries but Joanna was anxious to get back to the station and follow up Shipley's current whereabouts. As soon as was decent they left.

Back at the station Alan King was still pursuing the hunt for Louisa Newton as well as trying to track down her parents. At nine o'clock she left him and the rest of the team chasing after Kelvin Shipley and Judd and headed home. She was too tired to think.

She was yawning as she turned into the drive of their Victorian semi. All the lights were on and as she opened the door she could hear Jakob Rudyard Levin in full throttle and Peter and Charlotte doing their best to soothe him. She pushed open the door into the sitting room and immediately it struck her how old and tired Matthew's parents looked. This was too much for them. Jakob, in his grandmother's arms, was wriggling and screaming, but stopped to gawp at her. His plump face registered surprise and curiosity at her entrance. But he did not hold his arms out to her.

She took him from her mother-in-law. 'Hey,' she said, 'little fellow, what's all this about?'

Charlotte was on the defensive. 'He's only just started. I think he's teething.'

Peter looked as though he'd like to go home and slump in front of the television with a glass of whisky. This was hard on them. They were fit and adored their grandson but looking after him almost all of the time was maybe a step too far. But Matthew's career had been hard won after years of study and success and she felt the same about hers.

'Matthew not home?'

Charlotte rallied a little at mention of her adored son. 'He had a road traffic victim that the coroner wanted him to see urgently. A youth knocked off a bike. He felt he should get on with it and do the post-mortem tonight.'

'You look tired, the pair of you.'

Recognizing their cue to go Peter stood up smartly. 'We-ell,' he said.

Joanna took the bull by the horns. 'This is hard on you.'

As usual, Peter spoke for both of them. 'Nonsense. We love having the little chap.'

'I know.' Joanna eyed them both. 'But every day? And such long days?' Joanna knew she'd hit on the truth. 'Have a think about it. You do a brilliant job, both of you. I think you're wonderful. But Jakob's a handful and as he grows it won't get any easier. I can look into having a live-in au pair.' Even as she spoke the words she felt a shudder. They trusted Matthew's parents. Would they really entrust Jakob to a nanny, as the Newtons had to Bethany? She felt them about to protest and held up her hand. What was she doing?

She spoke the words but without conviction. 'You need some time to yourselves.'

And she caught a sense of relief pass from one to the other.

She was aware that Jakob was looking at her wide-eyed, his gaze flicking from grandparents to mother, as though he couldn't believe what he was hearing. She stroked his pale curls, kissed the top of his head and pressed on.

'I'll talk to Matthew about it when he gets in. We are so grateful to you both for everything.'

Charlotte's face turned hard and, sensing her objection, Joanna faced her full on.

'Matthew and I *both* value our careers and we're only too aware that we don't stick to regular hours. Leaving Jakob with you has taken a load off our minds but we need a long-term solution.' She managed a smile and tried to soften her decision. 'Surely you'd appreciate *some time* to yourselves?'

'We moved down here specifically to be near our grandson,' Peter said stiffly.

Joanna walked up to him and put her hand on his arm. 'You'll still be near him, Peter,' she said. 'He'll grow up under your influence.'

'Well, I wouldn't mind the odd round of golf,' Peter admitted and Charlotte winked at her daughter-in-law.

'And I wouldn't mind the odd hour or two of peace. Maybe read a book.'

Joanna ushered them out of the door and took Jakob upstairs. He was still regarding her with Matthew's perceptive green eyes as though challenging her decision. 'And you,' she said severely, 'have been playing up today. How could you be so mischievous?'

He giggled as though he had understood all her words.

And now she felt sick. Could she really entrust this precious bundle to someone like Bethany?

These thoughts plagued her as she bathed him and put on a clean sleepsuit. Having obviously finished with his ill humour Jakob sucked contentedly at his evening bottle, eyelids drooping until his mouth grew slack and she removed the teat and gently placed him on his back in the cot. He didn't stir as she tiptoed back downstairs just as Matthew opened the front door. She put a finger to his lips, eyes and index finger pointing upwards. He kissed her. 'Hi, Jo,' he said, once they were in the kitchen. 'Sorry, I meant to get back a bit earlier than this. But . . .'

She shared her thoughts about his parents as well as her

misgivings about hiring a nanny. 'We need to have a serious think about this.'

He nodded but in his eyes she saw reflected the same doubts.

FORTY-FOUR

11 p.m.

She was dropping off to sleep, making plans, her arm coiled around Matthew who was already deeply asleep, unconscious, even when she whispered to him. 'Night, Matt.' He didn't even grunt a response and so she rolled onto her back and tried to make a list of tasks.

She needed Bethany to talk. The girl knew everything, the answers to all her questions.

In the dark Joanna recalled something the Washington woman had mentioned. 'Painting.' She'd talked about Bethany painting with her twins. Maybe the girl couldn't or wouldn't talk. But what if she was given pens and a pad of paper and encouraged to draw? Would she?

As she dropped off to sleep the image of the girl, frightened by an older brother, seeking refuge on the edge of a drop, imprinted on her eyelids so she could almost feel the chilly wind, the wide expanse of moorland, the sharp shapes of the rocks. Had she really felt safe up there? Believed no one could hurt her?

She finally fell asleep dreaming that Bethany was talking. Speaking in a soft voice with a slight Welsh accent. 'I wouldn't have hurt him, you know. But I had to take him away. He was screaming. I had to go.'

Thursday 8 April, 8.45 a.m.

She'd ridden in with that one thought in her mind: how to get Bethany to talk. The voice she'd heard in her dream enticed her.

'I'm going back to Greatbach,' she said as the officers filed out from the morning briefing. 'Wish me luck.'

A few of them gave her the thumbs up sign and she left, taking

PC Gilbert Young with her. She had hopes for the PC. There was something endearingly honest about him.

'Come on, Gilbert,' she said, chivvying him along. 'We have a job to do. Use your charms on young Bethany.'

'I'll do what I can,' he said, stolidly literal as ever, 'but if you can't persuade her to talk I don't think I'll have much luck.' These were two others of his characteristics: modesty and loyalty, the proverbial 101 per cent.

The psychiatrist greeted her with resignation and reluctance. 'Nice to see you *again*, Inspector.' Joanna could have smiled at the ironic tone. Claire treated PC Young to a nod before issuing her dampener. 'I doubt you'll have more luck today.'

'I have to keep trying. I thought rather than trying to encourage her to talk I'd try with paper and pens?'

She'd picked up a pad and a pack of felt-tipped pens on the way over and chuckled to herself as she pocketed the receipt. £7.11p. Was that all it would take to unlock Bethany's secrets? Hardly going to break even their measly budget.

'We've given her a pad and pen already,' the psychiatrist said acidly, 'in case she felt like writing an account of her adventures but we haven't given her colouring pens.'

'One of her previous employers said she was quite an artist. Do you mind if I . . .?'

'Do what you like.' Claire gave a quick laugh. 'If it works it'll have been worth it.' She chewed her lip and frowned. 'I'm beginning to lose faith in my own methods.'

Me too, Joanna thought but was too polite to voice this sentiment out loud.

'You don't mind if I sit in?' It was a big climb down to which Joanna responded with a smile halfway towards being friendly. She couldn't resist making a point.

'To make sure I don't overstep the mark?'

Claire Roget's response was non-verbal, a smile around her eyes as she logged out of her computer and stood up, saying briskly, 'Let's go, shall we?'

The three of them climbed the four flights of stairs to the top floor and the locked ward. Joanna had been expecting instructions, what she could and could not do, say or prompt. But for once the psychiatrist was allowing her to take the lead.

Bethany was sitting on her bed, in the same small, square room. A wall-mounted television was switched on with the sound off but she wasn't looking at it. As usual she'd been staring out of the window at the people standing in the quadrangle, chatting so noisily that even four floors up they could hear sporadic laughs and sharp chatter. To Joanna it looked as though Bethany was longing to be out there, be part of it.

'Hi, Bethany.'

Her head flew round. She must have been so absorbed in the scene outside the window that she hadn't heard them enter. Her tawny eyes rested on Joanna for a moment before she looked, first at the psychiatrist and then at the uniformed policeman, as her gaze narrowed with suspicion and hostility.

Joanna regarded the girl before pushing the bed table towards Bethany and laying out the pad and the wallet of pens. The girl looked at her, a question in her eyes.

'I brought you a present.'

Bethany still looked puzzled and a bit suspicious.

'I spoke to your ex-employer, Bethany, Mrs Washington. Dinah.' The guarded expression melted from the girl's face. She understood now. The cat eyes were fixed on Joanna, anticipating her next move.

'She told me about your artistic capabilities.'

Bethany reached out, fingered the plastic wallet holding the pens. She selected a red one before opening the pad. And then she folded her arms.

Trying not to betray her exasperation, Joanna continued speaking. 'I've learned a lot about you from other people. I know you were good with Mrs Washington's twins. And your parents told me about the day when you climbed The Roaches to escape from your brother.'

Two fat tears bubbled up in the girl's eyes and spilled down her cheeks. Joanna touched her hand. 'You didn't want to harm Stevie, did you? You wanted to protect him.'

Bethany raised her gaze, looked straight into Joanna's face.

'You wanted to take him. Away from . . .' Joanna paused. 'He saw, didn't he? He was there.'

Bethany nodded, closed her eyes and kept nodding and rocking now, to and fro.

'Was it Adam?'

The words made the girl agitated. She started rubbing her knees, her breaths coming in ragged sobs.

'You're going to have to tell me the whole story one day,' Joanna said, keeping her voice steady and calm. 'I can't put words into your mouth.'

Bethany continued rocking.

FORTY-FIVE

Midday

Joanna now had to make a decision. Did she leave Bethany here where she was safe and the psychiatrist could work on further recovery? Or should she move her to the station? She was wondering that as she faced the girl and watched the drawbridge slowly drop. The bleak, unhappy look was returning. She needed to act quickly. 'Who killed Anthony Newton? Adam?'

No response.

She tried the second name. 'Kelvin Shipley?'

No response to this either yet Joanna felt the girl was puzzled. And sensed Bethany didn't know Shipley.

She tried, 'Louisa?' next and sensed Bethany relax.

'What went wrong?' Joanna asked very quietly though she had an idea.

Everything, the look on the girl's face seemed to say.

'You hid in the wardrobe, didn't you?'

This provoked an alert. Joanna explained, 'We found blood smears on the clothes. You hid there. Who from?' And when the response was the expected silence she continued, 'You kept him safe.'

Bethany's head was down.

'Who killed Mr Newton, Bethany?'

Bethany shrugged. A casual *how-should-I-know* action*?*

But Joanna wasn't put off this time. Bethany's silence was a key factor in Newton's murder staying undiscovered, allowing Adam to abscond, Louisa to vanish, Kelvin Shipley to cover his tracks. She was puzzled by why Adam had initially stuck around The Cottage instead of running. The police have a reputation for fingering the nearest collar so why risk it? His running now had only drawn attention to him.

They could probably track Shipley down with relative ease. But Louisa was proving evasive.

And Joanna felt cold. She was silent for a minute. Then she pushed the paper and pens towards the girl. 'It might help to clarify events if you draw things as you remember them.'

Bethany's hand gripped the red pen and looked mutinous. Then she changed her mind, put the red pen down and picked up the black pen. Joanna tensed. Could this be the breakthrough? Bethany drew an outline of a bath, then a man sitting in it. After a moment she swapped the black pen for a brown one and, her face absorbed, coloured in a shock of thick brown hair. She studied that for a moment before reverting to the red pen and drawing blood spurting from the man's back. It was naive, childlike, but there was no mistaking what it portrayed.

Joanna peered down without making a comment. Bethany was watching her. The girl swallowed, put down the pen and looked at her before clamping her mouth shut.

On the way back down Joanna spoke to the psychiatrist. 'I don't know,' she said. 'I don't think Bethany's guilty but I'm not sure I believe that her silence is the result of PTSD.'

'Well,' returned the psychiatrist, 'she witnessed a pretty horrific crime and when they hid in the wardrobe they must have been terrified. PTSD under those circumstances is perfectly understandable.' She gave a small smile. 'Don't you agree, Inspector?'

FORTY-SIX

Thursday 8 April, 2.30 p.m.

True to form DC Alan King was locked into his computer when she returned. 'Hi,' he said and waited, presumably for her to pass on any information. When she didn't he prompted her. 'Did you get anywhere?'

'Yes and no. We've squeezed a sort of confession out of her.'

'She spoke?'

'She spoke, yes. Well, not in words. In a drawing. Whether she actually told us anything new is a different matter. How about you?'

'I think I've found your gardener.' She drew up a chair. 'Facial recognition was no good,' he said. 'He was too tech savvy, either wearing a hat or turning his head away. He did a pretty good job of cleaning up the cottage too.'

'But . . .?'

Determined to extract a moment of drama King held up an index finger. 'Not quite hopeless,' he said and pressed a few keys. 'I factored in his build, height and probable age and came up with this guy.'

'Joachim Saveloy?' She looked at him, puzzled.

'An alias. He was based in Hong Kong. Wanted by the police over there.'

'On charges of . . .?'

'Fake designer goods.'

It rang a bell. 'Car parts?'

'No, mainly fashion stuff. Big names. Looked as good as the real thing. Logos, packaging, everything but the price. He vanished from the island two years ago.'

'How did you find him?'

'Partial fingerprint. Interpol. Narrowed the field.'

'Last known address?'

'Spain,' he said. 'Looks like he skipped there from Hong Kong.'

'Which bit of Spain?'

'Santander. On the north coast.'

'Anywhere near where Louisa's parents live?'

'Just over a hundred kilometres.' DC King was thoughtful. He swivelled round in his chair to meet her eyes.

'Just give me a couple of hours,' he said. 'I want to run some checks.'

'OK.' Her curiosity got the better of her. 'You don't want to share them with me?'

He held his hand up. 'Just an hour or two.'

'All right.'

She hesitated for a moment but DC King was absorbed in the world of the computer, his fingers flying over the keyboard, extracting information.

* * *

The next piece of information trickled in from an unlikely source.

At three, Karen Murphy, the social worker, came on the phone. 'Joanna,' she started, her voice uncertain, 'I'm not sure whether this will be of any help but Sandra Clowes has just been on the line.'

Karen anticipated her response. 'It's really crazy,' she said, 'but since he's been at Sandra and Michael's he's begun to talk.'

'Really? So what's he saying?'

'Why don't you pop over and see him for yourself?'

'Yeah.' Joanna was stuck with the idea. 'All right. I think I will.'

The comfortable, homey, relaxed atmosphere at the Clowes's house was unchanged. Sandra opened the door, filling the space with her generous frame. 'Hello, Inspector,' she said. The little boy at the centre of the storm toddled behind her. Joanna hunkered down. 'Well, hello, little man,' she said.

His big blue eyes gazed into hers and he clung to Sandra's leg as though it was his life support.

Joanna straightened up. 'So he's been talking?' At the same time she was thinking: have I descended into questioning two-year-olds?

Stevie was hardly recognizable as the shivering toddler she'd first seen. He was laughing and chatty. Pink-cheeked, even a little plumper?

'Daddy,' he said, looking at the door, pointing.

If only he could answer the question *where's Mummy?*

The small finger went into the little boy's mouth and he looked at Joanna as though wondering. She showed him the photograph of Bethany and he looked at it without expression then back at her before he started to cry, his small shoulders shaking with noisy sobs.

Sandra gathered him to her. 'She must have frightened him.'

Joanna nodded. 'Perhaps.' Inwardly she was cringing. No judge in the entire world could convict on the very shaky evidence of a two-year-old child.

She tried again. 'Where's your mummy?'

The child looked at her as though he didn't understand the question.

Sandra was watching them both very carefully. Hands on bulky hips, she addressed Joanna. 'So, Inspector,' she said, 'what are you going to make of that?'

'I'm not sure.' Joanna had no option but to be honest. 'Nothing really.'

Her face creased and she echoed Joanna's thoughts. 'You can't be getting very far with your case if you're having to resort to the testimony of a two-year-old child.' But there was a kindness in her tone that robbed it of any spite. 'She still not speaking?'

'She's starting to . . . communicate.'

Sandra Clowes's smile broadened and she held the child tighter, pressing his face into her arm as big as a ham. 'Well, one thing you don't have to worry about is little Stevie. He's safe enough here. No one will get to him here.'

'I don't doubt it, Sandra. Thank you.'

As she left Joanna was struck by a feeling of happiness. In the police force one meets little altruism. It is rare to meet goodness and generosity, people who give without counting the cost, people who share the love they seem to have in bucket loads. Real kindness in twenty-four-carat gold. In her job she usually encountered the other sort. Sandra Clowes's character helped the sun to shine all the way back to the station.

And then she had another idea.

What if she were to reunite Bethany with her charge? A two-year-old child with his nanny? Supervised, of course.

She contacted Karen Murphy who was, predictably, not in favour of the idea.

'You're joking,' she said. 'Aren't you? I really can't see what good that'll do.'

Joanna felt she needed to push it. 'I think it's worth a try.'

'So you're not getting very far in your search for Mrs Newton?' Karen's voice was scornful.

'We're working on it,' she said shortly.

Even on the end of a phone she could tell the social worker was astonished. 'What earthly good do you think it will do to reunite them?'

'It might encourage our girl to talk. I want to observe the dynamics between them. Since we've found Newton's body the emphasis has shifted away from Stevie and his nanny. His mother is still missing. I want to know what part that original little scenario played in this.'

Karen's response was a long, drawn-out and troubled sigh. 'You're scraping at barrels here.'

'It'll be a supervised interview, Karen. He'll be at no risk.'

'But it could be traumatic for Stevie. He hasn't seen her since . . .'

'He won't be in any danger.'

'But it might evoke a bad memory.'

'We'll be with them all the time. If he seems to be upset by being reunited with Bethany we'll stop the interview.'

Karen cleared her throat and Joanna made an ultimate attempt. 'Sandra Clowes will be with him. We can bring the psychiatrist too to keep an eye on Bethany if that'll put your mind at rest. We still haven't found Mrs Newton and her husband is still dead and unburied. Stevie will be at no risk.'

'I'll have to check with my superiors,' she snapped. 'If they say it's OK I'll get back to you.' Her voice was tight and still reluctant.

'I'll keep my fingers crossed,' Joanna responded with more than a hint of irony.

She returned to the main office.

FORTY-SEVEN

Thursday 8 April, 4.30 p.m.

DC King's most valuable commodity was his dogged persistence. The task he had set himself was to track down Louisa Newton. So far he was getting nowhere but it wasn't putting him off. He'd run down her list of known associates and drawn a blank. None had seen her since early March when all claimed she had appeared 'perfectly normal'. Slightly worrying was the fact that there had been no activity on any credit or debit cards in her name, or mobile phone records. It was a dead end. She was not on the police database apart from two SP30s. He'd tracked down contact details of her parents but he was getting no response from them either. They also seemed to have vanished into thin air. He sat in the corner of their office, fingers flying over the keys as he checked out one theory after another. DC King was a silent type, but what he lacked in communication he made up for in intelligence and his skill with computers. He had a secret ambition which he had shared with no one. Not even Kylie. He wanted to impress his DI the way Korpanski had.

Joanna, needless to say, was completely oblivious to this ambition.

King suddenly let out a loud whoop.

She was at his side in a nano-second. 'You've found her?'

He turned around to savour the excitement in her face and nodded slowly.

Joanna peered into the screen to what looked like a jumble of names.

'Passenger lists,' he said proudly. 'Just a hunch. I just wondered whether our missing lady might have hopped off to join her parents.'

'And?'

'I thought I'd check the passenger lists for the Plymouth to Santander ferry.'

'Bu-ut surely we ran a check on her?'

'Yeah,' he said. 'But this is the clever bit. You asked me to check whether she'd used her nanny's ID, so I wondered whether she might have used her nanny's passport.'

'Really? What about all the checks? Iris recognition?'

'At the airports. So I looked for a low-tech means of leaving the country.'

She drew up a chair.

'The ferry,' he said, 'crosses from Plymouth to Santander. It takes just over twenty-four hours and crosses the Bay of Biscay into the north of Spain. I conjured up the passenger list. And bingo. There she is.' He touched the screen with his finger. 'Bethany Ann Rees, travelled Tuesday March the sixteenth.'

'Except she didn't.' So Bethany's silence had enabled her employer to make a break for it.

'Exactly.'

'But they look nothing alike. And Louisa's forty-three. Bethany's twenty-seven. And the height.'

King swivelled around in his chair and he was grinning, a wide, goofy grin which showed almost all of his big white teeth. 'Good complexion, sunglasses? Flat shoes. She's there, Joanna,' he said, moving the cursor now and highlighting the name. 'She's there while Bethany was here. Clever really, because by the time we did start looking for Louisa Newton, we were not searching for Bethany Rees. Mrs Newton crossed the day of the little drama on The Roaches.'

'Why? What would be in it for Bethany?'

King drew in a deep, thoughtful breath. 'I don't know,' he said. 'Maybe that's the real puzzle?'

Joanna was silent, chewing over this new scenario, testing it against various explanations. None was strong. There was not one theory which could mean any possible advantage to Bethany. There was nothing in it for her. Unless . . .

What part had Adam Judd played in this? And Kelvin, Newton's brother-in-law? How did they all fit in?

Was Bethany what she appeared, the fall guy left holding the baby – literally in this case a decoy, to shoulder all the blame in her blood-spattered clothes? Had her role been to set up a tableaux? Was she now silent to indicate a mental diagnosis? Or avoid answering any questions? Joanna still couldn't decide whether their nanny was a complete victim. She would have to speak at some point, explain away a murder scene and account for her actions. Had Louisa's plan been to vanish and leave Bethany to take the rap? Again Joanna sensed that Louisa Newton had achieved what she had wanted. An initial delay. But what about the child? It appeared that she hadn't been over-endowed with maternal affection. But to abandon him altogether . . . Surely she would have realized the police would never stop looking for her? Had she thought she could vanish only to reappear as someone completely different? Had she gambled that Bethany could have been found guilty? Perhaps, rather than following an instruction and without a clear tale to tell, Bethany realized the precariousness of her position and kept her lips sealed. But yet again Joanna felt this was not the full story. There was another angle to this. The gardener. And Shipley, Anthony's brother-in-law and Adam's friend.

She turned back to Alan King. 'What about Judd?' she said. 'Have you found him yet?'

He shook his head.

Even DC King's magic fingers couldn't find the gardener.

'OK,' she said, 'let's finish the job, King. Set clear objectives. Let's start with finding Mrs Newton and keep looking for the gardener and his mate.'

She left Alan King speaking in fluent Spanish and silently thanked the ex-girlfriend who had schooled him so well in both Spanish and French. Criminals don't respect borders or politics. They needed to work together.

Joanna wasn't relishing the rest of her afternoon. Karen Murphy had returned her call to say that her team leader had 'reluctantly' given permission for Stevie and Bethany to be reunited under 'strict' supervision. And she insisted that the psychiatrist be present.

Joanna agreed to all the conditions without demur, though she was fast losing confidence that anything would be gained through this engineered encounter.

But anything that helped them find the truth and the missing key players was welcome.

She rang Dr Roget to set up the meeting for the following morning and sensed that the psychiatrist was as eager as she was to find some sort of explanation. Maybe, Joanna reflected as she hung up, the psychiatrist was getting as bored and fed-up as she was with her patient's silent state.

FORTY-EIGHT

Friday 9 April, 10.30 a.m.

Joanna arrived first.

After twelve long minutes a car slid in behind hers and Claire Roget and Bethany climbed out. The girl still looked pale and apprehensive but it was immediately obvious that a rapport had grown between psychiatrist and patient. Bethany stood by the car until Claire Roget encouraged her forward with a smile and held out her hand, which Bethany took.

Today the girl was dressed in a pair of neat, dark trousers and a pale pink sweatshirt which looked too big for her. But her step was light and confident and as she passed Joanna she gave a tentative smile and her tawny eyes looked unwaveringly into Joanna's, which almost led Joanna to hope this meeting, which had seemed so ill advised, might achieve something.

'Hi, Bethany, I expect you're looking forward to seeing your little charge again.'

Bethany's eyes flickered. And there was a wariness about them and shame. Sandra Clowes must have been watching through the

net curtains because she opened the front door right on time, just
as Joanna's hand was poised to lift the knocker.

Sandra's smile was wide and genuine. Her eyes scanned the
three women and she picked Bethany out correctly. 'Hello. You
must be Stevie's nanny. I'm so glad to meet you.' Her welcome
was so warm that, turning around, Joanna was anxious to see
Bethany's response.

The girl was taken aback. Then she extended her hand to Sandra
and smiled too.

Mouthed, *Thank you.*

Sandra's greeting to Joanna was equally warm. 'Hello again,
Inspector.'

'Thank you for agreeing to this and, again, for helping us out
with little Stevie.'

Sandra Clowes's smile almost split her face. 'It's my pleasure,'
she said. 'He's a lovely, sweet little boy, isn't he, Bethany.'

To both Joanna and Claire's shock Bethany's eyes filled with
tears. It was the first real emotion either of them had seen her
display. So far she had held everything in check. Sandra seemed
not to have noticed. Or if she did she ignored it, turning her
attention instead to Claire.

'So by a process of elimination you must be Dr Roget.'

Claire nodded and held out her hand too.

Sandra stood back. 'Well, come in. Come in.'

She led them into a long room – two knocked into one, it
seemed. A sofa was at one end and at the far end was a small,
gate leg dining table. The floor was littered with toys – building
bricks and plastic towers of graduated tumblers, cars, lorries, a
soft vinyl ball . . . So many toys it was hard to see more than
a few spare inches of carpet. In the centre of this virtual toyshop
sat the small, solemn-faced toddler who looked up curiously as
they entered. His eyes scanned them all and stuck on Bethany.
Joanna watched his response carefully. Was he glad to see her?
Frightened? She watched as he stood up and again there was that
catch in the girl's throat.

Stevie ran across the room and wrapped arms around Sandra's
plump leg, peeping around at Bethany who was standing quite still.

Bethany hunkered down to the child's level, smiling.

But the little boy didn't relinquish his hold on Sandra Clowes's
leg.

Joanna looked across at Claire who was also taking it all in.

Sandra took charge. 'Well, look who's here, Stevie.'

Was it because a two-year-old has a very short memory? It had been more than three weeks since they had been together. He was watching his nanny warily. Was it because he didn't recognize her?

Or was there a more sinister reason? Had she frightened him in the past? Joanna looked from one to the other. It seemed that while Stevie was now shrinking away from his nanny, Bethany's face was transfixed. *Stevie*, she mouthed, over and over again until they could almost hear a sound, almost a whimper, but not quite there yet.

Claire appeared to be coldly observing. The three women stood, waiting. And then Bethany took three swift steps and scooped the little boy up, burying her head in his bright curls. And this time they heard it. 'Stevie.'

It hit Joanna with a thump. Bethany loved the little boy – as Dinah Washington had assured her that Bethany had loved her twins. With that came a conviction. She could never have hurt this child. But she would have risked everything to protect him.

Another theory was worming into her brain. Something . . .

Joanna watched for Stevie's reaction. Difficult to gauge as his face was pressed into Bethany's shoulder. Bethany finally released the little boy, set him down on the floor and searched around the room before hunkering down. And Joanna picked up on something. Bethany was afraid. For herself? Or for the child? She was even watching the windows nervously as though she expected to see someone there. Who? Louisa? Adam? Kelvin?

Joanna had never been more aware that inside Greatbach the girl was protected by the staff and her locked-in status. But locked-in can also mean locked-out. Bethany had felt safe in the institution. The psychiatrist was still watching with detached observation. Joanna could imagine her notes. Patient appeared . . . emotional, affectionate, apprehensive.

Sandra's gaze moved from person to person until she came to a decision. 'Where's my manners? Anyone want a cup of tea?'

It broke the silence. Claire responded first, shaking herself away from the observed experiment. 'That'd be nice. Thank you.'

Joanna joined her. Bethany was too busy building a tower of

coloured bricks and watching Stevie knock it down to respond. And the little boy? He was gurgling and chatting. 'Again, again.' Like a dog with a stick he was thriving on repetition.

While Sandra bustled around in the kitchen, Bethany continued building the tower of multicoloured plastic for Stevie to knock down while Joanna and Claire watched and waited. Once they exchanged glances, Claire nodding as though to acknowledge that this meeting had been a good idea. There was no denying the bond between child and carer.

Sandra returned with a tray of cups, a milk jug and sugar bowl and handed them round. Bethany spooned in one teaspoonful with a shaking hand. The tears on her cheeks had dried leaving faint tracks down her face.

She eyed the psychiatrist, even risking a ghost of a smile and looking at peace, her face sinking into relaxation. She shared that with Joanna for the briefest of moments. She and Claire watched surreptitiously, while Sandra made small talk.

Bethany finished her tea, reached out and Stevie left his bricks to climb onto her lap, snuggling into her. The action spoke further volumes.

Sandra Clowes made sympathetic noises, *aaahs* and *ooohs* as they all watched.

Joanna stood up. She had some answers now though they didn't seem to have reduced the number of questions. 'OK, Bethany,' she said finally. 'Time to go now.' The girl let Sandra peel the child away from her while she stood, like a statue, neither helping nor hindering the separation.

They both thanked Sandra again for the work she was performing and left. Joanna watched as Claire loaded her patient back into the car. She faced Joanna and conceded reluctantly, 'You were right, Inspector. Seeing Stevie has helped. Good for my patient and good for the little boy, I suspect. And it's good to see him safe.' Her face broke into a wide smile and she patted Joanna's shoulder in an almost maternal gesture. 'Life is strange,' she said. 'People's behaviour is strange. The longer I work as a psychiatrist the more I realize that. People's behaviour is unpredictable. Human nature is by its very definition unpredictable.' Her smile was mischievous now. 'That's what keeps me in a job.' She paused then removed her hand. 'I'll be seeing you before long.'

'I don't doubt it.'

FORTY-NINE

2 p.m.

The instant Joanna arrived back in the office she sensed that DC King had more news for her. He was grinning and there was only one reason that DC King grinned that broadly. He was pleased with himself and expected the same response from her.

'Go on then, King,' she said. 'Hit me with it.'

'I tracked Louisa down to the port of Santander where she hired a car. Interestingly using her real name now which made it a bit easier. The Spanish police were really helpful. They promised to help find *Senora Newton* and they've just got back to me. She's with her parents,' he said, excitement inserting an embarrassing squeak into his voice. 'The Spanish police will be paying them a visit any time' – he glanced at his watch – 'now.'

'Then we can extradite her.'

He expected a pat. In fact, she was tempted to tousle his hair but substituted a tap on the shoulder. 'Well done, King.'

He bent back over his keyboard to hide his face and his feelings.

'Keep up the search for the gardener too,' she said.

Another one who had vanished in plain sight along with his crony.

While they waited for the Spanish police to make contact Joanna decided to return to The Cottage. She wanted to see for herself the place where Bethany and the child, and possibly Louisa, had hidden.

It was a bright day, everywhere endowed with the fresh April green. There was a scent of newly mown hay and the distant birdsong as she turned into the drive, windows open.

Fask greeted her on the doorstep and took her upstairs. The place was marked out, platforms to step on, everything but a chalk outline of a body. He led her into the walk-in wardrobe and pointed out a couple of smears of blood on the sides and explained about the clothes they'd removed.

'Not a crime scene, Joanna. They'd brushed past. Blood on the clothes and—'

She butted in. 'The nanny and the child? Or was Mrs Newton with them?'

He was thoughtful, guarded in his response. 'Hard to say, Joanna. Could have been the three of them.'

'Were they here for long, do you think?'

'They'd made a little bed for the boy using a fur coat so I would guess a few hours. I found a wet nappy in the corner.'

Joanna could picture it, the three of them cowering behind coats and dresses, sweaters, pairs of trousers. And she realized the implication. It was an indication that neither Bethany nor Louisa was Newton's killer.

She let herself out and wandered into the garage. The cars stood there, the Tesla Model 3.

'Fifty-six grand,' Mark said, having followed her out, 'if you're wondering.'

'No, I wasn't.' She rested her hand on the Jaguar Mark 2. 'This is much more my taste.'

'Morse,' he said. 'Inspector. Same car. Lovely piece of work.' And he too let his hand run down the paintwork.

She returned to the station just as the phone rang and she indicated to King that he should answer it. Moments later he replaced the receiver. And even from that one slow gesture Joanna knew the bird or birds had flown.

'House empty,' he said. 'No sign of them.'

Even more confusing. Flight usually indicated guilt. But there was no way Bethany could have hidden from her employer in her own wardrobe.

She could have torn her hair out.

'OK,' she said, 'leave the Spanish police to find them and we can focus on finding Adam Judd and Shipley.'

It was almost nine o'clock when she arrived home but Eloise's car was in the drive.

Eloise was Matthew's daughter by his first marriage. Her devotion to her father was inversely matched by her hatred of Joanna, the woman she blamed for breaking up her parents' marriage. And there was an element of truth in this. Matthew might have stayed with

Jane, his first wife, whatever the state of their marriage, had he not met up with Joanna and something had sparked between them, leading to an affair which she had put an end to. But not he. Matthew's love for her had intensified rather than died down. He had left Jane – and Eloise – and finally Joanna had capitulated.

Eloise was now almost twenty-three years old and in her final year as a medical student, a fact which endeared her not only to her father, as a pathologist, but also to her grandfather, a retired GP and now almost fulltime childminder. Medics are a strange breed when together. They speak their own language unintelligible to a lay person. They have their own jokes and gallows humour. Eloise was nearing her graduation, firing through her final year exams. She was a bright, sparky young woman. So it was natural that her arrival, probably to announce yet another success, would delay Peter and Charlotte's departure. But it was a fitting end to an imperfect day.

Their prime suspect had slithered through their fingers, using a not particularly clever ruse; the villains of the piece had disappeared and the one witness they had in custody was being no help at all, while the child was obviously unable to help. And they still had a dead man to account for.

And now she had her stepdaughter's hostility to deal with too and that odd feeling of exclusion when Peter, Charlotte, Matthew and Eloise were together. Even Jakob was part of that inner circle.

As she pushed open the front door of Briarswood she could hear Eloise's voice, high-pitched, excited. Joanna entered the sitting room where they were all standing up, champagne flutes in their hands. She was right. Another success. Matthew spotted her and found another glass. 'She's passed Medicine *and* Surgery.'

'Wow.' Joanna tried to sound suitably impressed.

Eloise turned to face her. Stick thin with her mother's eyes, cold as Arctic ice, pale skin and long, straight, white-blonde hair. 'And Paediatrics and Obstetrics,' she announced. 'I'll be graduating in the summer.'

'Congratulations.'

As though to join in the celebration the baby speaker emitted a loud wail. Matthew set his glass down and was almost instantly out of the room, returning with Jakob in his arms. The child's face was red and he was still heaving out irregular hiccupping sobs. Matthew was holding him very close, his mouth nuzzling the top of the baby's head, murmuring, 'What do you think of your big sister? Clever girl. Going to be a doctor soon.'

'Half-sister.'

Joanna's eyes moved to Eloise. What she read there was hatred. Red-hot hatred to which Matthew was oblivious. He was still speaking to his son in a soft, indulgent voice. 'And are you going to be there when she graduates?'

'He can't,' Eloise snapped. 'They don't allow babies, Daddy.'

She always called him Daddy when she wanted to call him to heel.

'Besides, Mummy will be there.'

Joanna found it unbearably sad that, at the age of nearly twenty-three, Eloise still tried to glue the family together, Mummy, Daddy, Gramps and Granny. But Joanna had quickly realized she never called Jakob her brother. Not even half-brother.

She looked around the room.

In true baby appreciation fashion, once they had all (except Eloise) cooed over him, Jakob, having broken up the party, was handed over to Joanna. She fed him, changed him and sat in the nursery she and Matthew had painstakingly designed. 'She doesn't like *you* either,' she said to her son, nuzzling his head and touching his button of a nose with her forefinger.

Later she heard their guests leave, doors slamming, cheerios and then silence.

FIFTY

Saturday 10 April, 7 a.m.

She'd awoken with a feeling of vigour and sudden clarity. This was a simple case of tracking down three people. The diversion had been Bethany's silence. She was still unclear exactly what the girl's role really had been in all this.

And it was this that stayed with her as she gave Jakob his morning bottle, taken quickly and greedily, changed him, showered, pulled on a pair of leggings, brushed her hair, sat in front of the mirror to do her make-up and cycled into the station. Riding a bike is a great time to put your thoughts in order. It was still early and, it being a Saturday, with many people appreciating extra time in bed, the traffic was, for once, light.

King was at his usual station. A murder warrants plenty of overtime. And they could all use the money.

'What do we know about Adam Judd?'

King brought up his past. 'Clean. Nothing there.'

'And Shipley?'

'The usual lowlife. A couple of stretches, mainly for burglary, TWOC-ing, drunken bar stuff. One really nasty one where a bloke lost his eye due to a glassing.'

'So why would they suddenly veer off course and commit a major crime?'

King stared into the screen but failed to find an answer there.

'Exactly. And Louisa?'

King shook his head. 'Nothing there.'

'And I take it Bethany was also clean.'

King nodded. 'Absolutely,' he said. 'Nothing there either.'

He didn't see what she was getting at. Neither did she for that matter. But a new thought was slowly hatching.

She left King to his screen research, headed for her office and shut the door. Then picked up the phone. 'Matt?'

'It's a Saturday, Jo,' he complained.

She had her answer ready. 'Crime doesn't respect weekends.'

'Oh, OK. What is it?'

'How long would Newton have bled after he was stabbed?'

'We-ell . . .' As though he was in a court of law, he was not going to rush his answer. 'Judging by the scald marks he lived – or rather his heart continued to beat – for around ten to fifteen minutes.'

'During which time?'

'Blood would spurt from an artery, ooze from a vein with diminishing force as his cardiac output reduced.'

'I thought so. He hadn't moved or tried to get out of the way.'

'He couldn't, Jo. He was paralysed.'

She took a while to absorb this before asking, 'All well at home?'

'Yeah.' He sounded proud of himself and so was she. She had a new theory.

Someone else had stabbed Newton in the bath and they had all split. His wife, the gardener, Shipley and Bethany who had leaned across to turn the tap off before scooping up little Stevie on her way out and hiding. They were all frightened. Terrified of the person who had murdered Newton. They were all hiding from him in their different ways: Louisa fleeing the country; Bethany rushing to a place where she felt safe; Judd and Shipley dropping out of view. They would stay hidden until the police had custody of the killer whose partial thumbprint was on the hot tap when they turned it on and made sure the water was hot enough to hurt. They'd wanted to punish Newton.

But who and why? She felt that the answer lay very near Kelvin Shipley.

But . . .

Criminals tend to stick to the same MO, the same level of crime, and Shipley was a hanger-on, a minor felon. There was no murder in his past and Newton's murder was cold-blooded and cruel. Sometimes murder is an accident but that didn't seem the case here. An assault can have unforeseen results. An arson attack escalates but death is a by-product. The intended crime was to burn and watch it burn. Not to kill. A burglary can turn nasty because the homeowner is at home and prepared to defend his 'castle'. But the intended crime was burglary, not murder.

But this wasn't one of those instances. This was deliberate.

She went through the names, everyone connected with the case, male and female. The office was quiet as she pondered.

Prints on the hot tap in the bath. It was easy to assume that the person who had stabbed Newton was the same person who had wanted to watch him suffer. She crossed the room and spoke to Jason Spark. 'The prints on the hot tap,' she said. 'Have we tracked them down yet?'

'Came through last night, Joanna,' he said. 'A man called Patrick Walker.'

She looked at him, bemused.

'Stockport police want him,' he said. 'He's a nasty piece of work.'

She brought up Walker's details and quickly realized he fitted the facts as well as a handmade glove. He was connected to organized crime in Manchester. He was violent, vindictive and had plenty of people around him happy to carry out his instructions or else become another statistic. People around him tended to die violent deaths: car 'accidents', drownings, assaults, unexplained injuries. Or else they simply disappeared.

Walker was a pugnacious, violent criminal. Capable of murder and extreme cruelty.

The trouble was that there was no known connection between Anthony Newton and Patrick Walker.

Joanna set a team on the task of finding that connection. They worked all day Saturday and Sunday and came up with nothing.

But the fact remained stubbornly present, staring her in the face. It was Patrick Walker's thumbprint on the hot tap in the bath where Anthony Newton had been stabbed. And it made no sense at all.

The temptation, Joanna knew, was that when you had a fact that you couldn't explain, you ignored it. Brushed it under the carpet and hoped it would go away, dissolved in a plethora of other forensic detail. But she knew this was not policing.

Monday 12 April, 9 a.m.

She shared the thumbprint with the officers in Monday morning's briefing and saw her own puzzlement reflected in their faces. They were missing something.

One of Joanna's mantras was: worst first. If there is something you really dread, put it at the top of the list, and so she telephoned Chief Superintendent Gabriel Rush. As she spoke and, fair play to him, he listened, she couldn't help but picture his face: the thin, humourless gash of a mouth, eyes flint hard, seeing everything she didn't want him to see, i.e. that having a dead man, a mute woman and all the suspects having fled, with so many threads of enquiry she was tugging at all of them blindly in the vain hope that one of them would prove a solution.

Rush was silent when she shared Walker's thumbprint with him. He harrumphed and she knew that he, like her, recognized a dangerous man. One who would happily have stuck a knife in the back of anyone he didn't particularly like. Naked or not.

He quizzed her about the so far missing connection before, surprisingly, focussing back on the girl. 'Is she speaking yet?'

'No, sir.' She felt bound to add, 'I only know, for certain, that she's frightened.' And she shared the evidence Fask had unearthed in Louisa Newton's walk-in wardrobe.

He could read it as clearly as she did. 'That would fit in with Walker storming the castle.'

'Yes, sir.'

The direction he took then really surprised her. 'Have you discussed this with the psychiatrist?'

'Not so far, sir. The thumbprint has only just been identified.'

'It might be an idea for the psychiatrist to have a handle on the girl's fears.'

She couldn't disagree with that one.

There was a brief silence while she held her breath. 'I'll approve any budget you need, Piercy. If you're right about this man Walker it could be a very useful conviction. He's a villain. Liaise with Stockport. Get to the truth of this, Piercy, and it could be a feather in my cap. And in yours of course,' he tacked on hastily. 'It could be quite a coup. Maybe this time he's made a mistake.'

She decided to share one of her misgivings with him. 'What I don't understand, sir, is why would Walker do such a rash act? He's got plenty of henchmen to do his bidding. Any one of a dozen men would have liquidated Newton or broken his legs or something. It doesn't make sense that he would head down to Congleton to go for Anthony Newton himself. Newton was a bit of a cheat but he wasn't a big-time guy. He was just a chancer. An opportunist. He wasn't the organized crime sort.'

She sensed Rush was getting bored. 'Sort it, Piercy.' He couldn't stop himself from adding a note of caution. 'Just don't go over the top.'

'No, sir.' As she put the phone down she was smiling.

The Walker connection gave her an opportunity to set a couple of PCs onto checking traffic camera footage in and around the area of The Cottage. They would watch until they became fish-eyed. In the past she'd done it herself and gone to bed after a long shift still seeing grainy images of car after car after car. It sent you to sleep better than counting sheep.

Next she made contact with David Rothman, a DI with the Stockport police, who sent over a photograph of a classic criminal face. Pugnacity beaming out from a bullet head, tiny eyes and a scar that reached from his left eye lifting up the corner of his mouth to a permanently sardonic grimace that exposed one canine tooth, a gap either side. This was a face which had been assaulted and in turn had retaliated ten times for every blow he'd received. Like Simon and Garfunkel's boxer.

As he glared at her from the picture she wondered. Why?

Even villains have their reasons. What was Walker's? Newton hadn't felt unsafe. He'd been enjoying a bath in his own home. He couldn't have felt more relaxed. But he had been hunted out by a furious and vindictive criminal. There was no security at The Cottage apart from the obligatory gates which had been standing open, the back door presumably unlocked.

The more she studied the picture the more she wondered. She picked up the phone again.

DI Rothman agreed with her. 'It doesn't sound like him,' he said. 'He's generally careful to hide his tracks. We've only managed to convict men on the very outside of his operations. Anyone close to him is well protected. And as for him, I'm surprised he hasn't joined the church choir he's so squeaky clean. He's so sure of himself too. Used to drive past the station in a flashy car, bright green.' He couldn't quite erase the envy in his voice. 'Two fingers up to us.' He laughed then. 'Was really pleased when I heard he'd come a cropper in it. But you're right, Inspector Piercy. This doesn't sound like him.'

And Joanna too felt doubts. But that thumbprint remained stubbornly present. She read through the report, saw the evidence for herself, even rang the forensic lab and checked though she knew they'd be insulted at her questioning their integrity.

DI Rothman couldn't help voicing both optimism and doubt. 'I really hope you can pin something on him,' he said, 'but . . .'

And Joanna could provide the sequitur.

Cold-blooded murder? Not Walker's style. He doesn't get his hands dirty. But there had to be . . . *Unless* . . .

And if Joanna knew anything about felons it was this: criminals stick to a pattern. Their crimes were like a tattoo. Impossible to erase or change. Their felonies were embedded somewhere in a vicious twist of their DNA, present since birth.

She dug a little deeper. 'Has he done time?'

'Short bursts,' DI David Rothman said, sounding glum. 'Stockport's a safer and cleaner place when he's inside and there's nothing I'd like better than to put him away for a nice long stretch. Catch up on our overdue leave and give us all an annual holiday. But I'm not optimistic.' He gave a sour laugh.

'Thanks,' she said. 'Do me a favour. Keep an eye on him. Just in case he slips up . . .' she couldn't resist adding, '. . . again,' provoking a grunt from the DI.

'Are you planning to interview him?'

'Not yet. But if you can find a link between Newton and your resident villain, get in touch, will you?'

'Sure. And good luck.'

'Thanks.'

'Keep me up to date.'

'I will.'

Ten minutes later she was facing her assembled officers, passing on this titbit, pinning the picture of Walker onto the whiteboard and bringing them up to speed.

'So we're looking for a connection between Walker and his operations and Anthony Newton.'

She could tell by the ripple that passed around the room combined with a few happy glances that this new strand to the enquiry felt more like a breakthrough to them than it did to her.

But she didn't want them to focus solely on this aspect.

'The Spanish police are currently on the lookout for Louisa Newton,' she said. 'They have an address for her parents but they are not at home.' She glanced at DC King to elaborate.

He took over. 'The house was locked up. They'll keep on the lookout so we can leave that aspect of the investigation to them. They'll extradite her when – if,' he substituted, 'they find her.'

She turned to her side. 'Louisa slipped through because she was using Bethany's passport. Well done, King,' she said, 'for coming up with that idea.'

King started to look like Bashful out of Snow White, his face flushing an embarrassing shade of pink.

One of the officers sitting at the front asked, 'Have we any more forensic results come through?'

'No, except the evidence that Bethany and the little boy, and maybe Louisa, hid in her walk-in wardrobe for some length of time.'

She paused, visualizing the scene, Walker charging in, panic, terror, the household hiding and then Walker leaving the inhabitants with a dead body and a state of panic.

She singled out Jason Spark. 'Gather up a team, Jason.' He looked eager.

Something was pricking her conscience. 'Look into Anthony Newton. Find out all you can. See if there's a link between Walker,

Kelvin Shipley, Adam Judd and our dead man. Look into business associates, see if you can find the connection. It must be there somewhere.'

Something else had occurred to her. Walker had erupted. According to DI Rothman in the past Walker had largely managed to steer clear of the law or at least under the radar. He didn't make mistakes. For a hardened criminal this crime scene was careless. So something had happened that had made him break his own rules. Had the origins of this been personal? Close to home? She needed to talk to DI Rothman again. But first she'd check a few more facts.

FIFTY-ONE

'Matt.'

'Jo?' He sounded surprised.

She launched straight in. 'How long did you say Newton lived after he was stabbed?'

'Judging by the scalding I would say ten, fifteen minutes.'

'During which he wouldn't have been able to move.'

'That's right.'

'There were no signs of defence wounds, were there?'

'No.' He gave an indulgent little chuckle. 'I can't tell you the exact sequence of events, Jo, because they happened in quick succession. My instinct is that the stab wound in the neck came first, paralysing him because there were no defence wounds and no evidence of evasion, twisting, et cetera, in the subsequent incisions. And of course the final wound in the back still had the weapon embedded in it.'

She was silent for a moment, unsure how to phrase this next question. 'Would it have taken a lot of knowledge?'

'Yes and no. A certain amount of determination and – yes, Jo.'

'Was the assailant practised?'

'I guess so. There was' – he hesitated – 'confidence in the assault. Cruelty in adding scalding water to Newton's bath. I doubt this was the assailant's first murder.'

She recalled the layout of the bathroom. Newton would have

had his back to the door. The mirrors would have been steamed up. He wouldn't have seen whoever came in. Might well have imagined it was his wife. But it wasn't.

'That first wound severed his spinal cord, Jo. He wasn't able to move. The pathology on Newton's buttocks and arms indicate that he lived for some minutes after being scalded. There were signs of inflammation visible to the naked eye and damage to underlying tissues supporting this. What's your thinking?'

'Just trying to visualize the scene. The sequence of events.'

She knew he would be considering this question from all angles before responding. It was Matthew's way to be cautious in venturing an opinion. He would be frowning, running his fingers through that honey blond hair, hardly knowing he did it, while he would also stick strictly to his remit. As a pathologist he trod very gently and kept within professional parameters. She had learned to be patient during such moments.

Finally he spoke. 'Considering the blood spatter around the bathtub combined with the fact that the wounds were straight – no twisting, I *think* . . .' Again he was exercising extreme caution, tiptoeing around the facts. 'I think . . . that the sequence of events was *likely* to be this. Newton is in the bath when our assailant enters. I don't think he even turned around to see who had come in.' He surmised the same scenario as Joanna. 'He might have assumed it was his wife – or else someone he was familiar with. Your assailant incapacitates Newton with a stab which severs the spine at C6. He or she then turns the hot tap on. This person,' he continued, 'was very angry. Furious. He drove the knife in right up to the hilt.'

'But Matt,' she appealed, 'why didn't Louisa or Bethany call the police?'

'At a guess,' he responded, 'they would have been terrified. If you're right and it was Walker he could have stayed in the house rather than make a quick exit. You say they hid. It's even possible he threatened them. Shouting.'

'Thanks, Matt,' she said. 'I think I get it,' she said, 'except the reason. What made Walker so angry he broke all his own rules, came himself instead of relying on henchmen? And what part did Adam Judd and Kelvin Shipley play?'

He chuckled. 'I can't do all your work for you, Jo. But I'm glad I've left you some things to puzzle out. Tell you what,' he said, 'I'll take another look at the crime scene photographs and go over my notes. If I have anything to add I'll call you back. Is that OK?'

'Perfect,' she said, suddenly overcome. She remembered the first time she had seen him, blond hair escaping from the Jay-cloth hat, green eyes resting on her as his mouth, visible over the mask looped below his chin, curved into a smile. She had been 'unwell' (puking into a sink) after watching the post-mortem of an elderly woman who had been bludgeoned to death in the course of a burglary. When she had raised her head she had seen the patholo-gist watching her in the mirror, the light in his green eyes displaying gentle mischief.

He was still holding on. She could hear his breathing, possibly sharing the same memory. 'Matt.'

'Mmm?'

'I love you,' she whispered and he laughed.

'Say it louder.'

Now it was she who was laughing but the talk had lifted her day.

She connected with DI Rothman and asked him again about Patrick Walker.

'Why was he careless? He has people who could have done his dirty work. Why risk it?'

'I don't know. It doesn't make sense. Walker is one of those criminals careful not to get his hands dirty. How about I do a bit of research into him? I have a couple of officers who've followed his exploits pretty closely. I'll get back to you.'

And she had to be satisfied with that.

It was six o'clock, coming to the end of yet another unsatisfactory day. There were still holes in her theory.

This was the point where she and Mike would usually hunker down in the office, spread out every single photograph of the crime scene, play through the video recorded by the forensics team and toss ideas from one to the other. She tried to do it alone, focussing on the crime scene as they had first seen it, reliving the starkness of the bathroom, as she'd first entered: bloodstaining on white floor tiles, white bathroom suite, white walls, white towels. Big mirrors. Stark and theatrical, a chill crime scene more than two weeks old. But she was uninspired. Mike wasn't here. She couldn't bounce ideas across to him. Feeling that sudden impulse which drives us to action before thought she slipped on her jacket and headed for the car park. She felt guilty, knowing she was abandoning ship, but she needed a dose of Mike's blunt philosophies and common sense. She left her bike at the station and took a squad car to Mike's house.

There was no sign of Fran's Fiat outside the house and it looked ominously quiet and deserted. She knocked on the door and listened but was greeted with silence. It didn't take a detective to realize that no one was home. A neighbour pulled up next door with bags of shopping as Joanna returned to the car and explained that Mike and Fran were at the hospital, where the doctors were 'taking some pins out or something'.

Frustrated, she considered her next move. She still had a whole cast of missing people – Louisa, Adam Judd and Kelvin Shipley, and the one witness she did have safely ensconced in Greatbach secure psychiatric unit was saying nothing. And she did not dare make a move against Patrick Walker until she had more evidence. And an explanation.

Impulsively she decided to make another visit to Cindy Mellor. It was evening now and she hoped that Damien would be home.

A Jag and an Audi in the drive boded well.

Damien himself opened the door. 'Inspector Piercy,' he said. 'Nice to see you again.' He shook her hand warmly. 'Was it Cindy you wanted to speak to?'

'Actually no, Mr Mellor. It was you I hoped to catch.'

He grinned. Open but guarded. 'So how can I help you, Inspector?'

Damien Mellor was a likeable chap. He would have been an asset to any business.

'Tell me more about Tony's dodgy dealings.'

Mellor chuckled, perhaps momentarily forgetting his onetime partner was dead.

'He was fun. Ambitious. Wanted to make it big quickly.' Mellor's face darkened. 'Too quickly. He cut corners, reduced costs when he shouldn't have. And to be honest the stuff he was importing from the Far East was pure crap. He got away with it but at some point the shit was going to hit the fan. It was going to implode on us. I could sense it coming. We'd been lucky but it wasn't going to last. There was going to be an accident. One of the cars was going to let its owner down.' His face changed and he gave a mischievous, rather endearing grin. 'But it was good fun while it lasted. Tony was full of shit, but he was also full of ideas. When it worked, Inspector, it worked well. We made money, a lot of it, and very quickly. We sold cars worldwide. Crated them off all over the world. UAE, China, Japan, Australia. Anywhere there was a classic car petrol head with money enough to afford our prices. Rescued some phenomenal cars, rare sets of wheels. It was both our passions. We loved it. As I said. When it worked it worked well.'

'But you split up.'

'Before everything caught up with us.'

'Were you ultimately rivals?'

He saw very quickly what she was getting at and instantly his friendly, open manner changed. He closed down. 'If you want to know whether I killed him, no I did not. Yes, we were rivals. Our onetime close friendship withered away to just our wives. Socially we didn't mix anymore.'

'Did you ever expose him on social media?' She didn't even know why she'd asked this.

Neither did Damien Mellor. He shook his head, slightly confused. 'I was tempted, I can tell you. I wanted to expose him for what he did before one of those lovely cars ended up a heap of junk. But I didn't.'

His words were planting a seed of suspicion. 'If you had he might still be alive.'

Mellor stared at her. 'How so?'

Joanna didn't answer but watched him steadily as she asked her next question. 'Does the name Patrick Walker mean anything to you?'

'Oh.' And she saw from his face that to him at least things were slotting into place.

He was nodding as he worked his way through and then put a hand up to his forehead. 'I see,' he said.

Her instinct was to prompt him. *Come on, Damien.*

But she didn't. She remained silent.

He took a few deep breaths, presumably to steady himself, and then his mind must have moved on a pace or two and his face blanched.

'He was a customer,' he said. 'He was a classic car fanatic. I warned Tony he was playing with fire. I told him not to let him buy any of the classics we'd cobbled together. But Tony was a chancer.'

'Tell me about Walker,' she said quietly.

Damian Mellor leaned back in the chair as though he had a long story to tell. He half closed his eyes. 'How much do you know?'

'Probably not all of it,' she admitted. 'But enough to know that he has connections in the criminal world.'

'Tony usually dealt with him,' Mellor continued. 'I gave him a wide berth. We sold him a few classics, an Austin Healy from the sixties, an E-type Jag from the early seventies, a couple of Lotus Elans and a beautiful 1911 Rolls-Royce Silver Ghost. That,' he said, 'was a dream come true.'

'He paid cash?'

Mellor looked at her with a glint in his eyes. 'You're thinking money laundering, aren't you? Well, who knows? The deals were done, as I say, through Tony. We made our money and I didn't ask.'

But Mellor's confirmation of what she had suspected was enough.

She rose and Mellor looked surprised. 'Aren't you going to quiz me more?'

'Not at the moment. I just wanted to know about Patrick Walker and I think you've told me enough. Thanks.'

FIFTY-TWO

Tuesday 13 April, 10.35 a.m.

She had another meeting with Gabriel Rush and outlined her next steps. 'We need to bring Walker in.'

He was silent, his thin face moving through various emotions, mainly frowning and folding his arms. 'You need to track down your witnesses first.'

She didn't want to confess it to Rush but she was worried about the gardener and Kelvin Shipley. Maybe Rush sensed this because he was watching her and his next statement confirmed this. 'You're wondering why the gardener, whoever his name was, stuck around?'

She nodded.

'And I take it Mr Shipley hasn't presented himself to the station either?'

'No.'

'Is your silent girl beginning to speak?'

'No.'

'And the child is still with the foster parents?'

At last an affirmative. 'Yes, sir.'

'And Mrs Newton?'

'We're having a bit of trouble tracking her down but the Spanish police are on board.'

'Good. I take it you'll work with the Stockport police on bringing Patrick Walker in?'

'Of course, sir.'

'And have you a motive, a connection between Newton and Patrick Walker?'

'I believe so.'

He scrutinized her with a sharp stare. 'Believe so, Piercy?'

'I just need to confirm something with the Stockport police.'

'You need to head up there,' he said testily. 'They have Walker under surveillance?'

'Yes, sir.'

'Then get to it, Piercy. You need to tie this up.' He started to shuffle papers around which she took as dismissal. She stood up and was almost at the door before he spoke again with a merest hint of sympathy. 'Difficult case, eh?'

'Frustrating,' she admitted and left, still wondering whether that thin mouth had just bent into a smile.

She drove up to Stockport to speak to DI Rothman. She'd filled him in on Newton's dark business in classic cars and asked for more details about Walker's car crash.

A tall, slim, balding man with warm brown eyes, he greeted her with a firm handshake and a broad grin.

'I was looking forward to sharing this with you,' he said, ushering her into a small office, handing her a file and switching the computer on, the smile hardly leaving his face.

'The date is Saturday March the thirteenth. The time is six p.m.'

She opened the file. Inside were photographs of a car wreck. Difficult to say what sort of car it was or rather had been. But the colour was a metallic lime green. The bonnet was crumpled, the windscreen smashed, doors opened with something like a tin-opener and it sat at an angle facing down a bank.

She looked at Rothman for explanation.

'Walker's,' he said. 'His beloved Jensen. The one he used to ride past here, two fingers stuck in our eyes.' He rested his fore-arms on the desk. 'Walker,' he said, 'is a classic car enthusiast.'

Joanna waited.

'He had this accident. The throttle stuck. So there he was, riding high, revving up from the golf club. He comes up to a junction and can't stop, shoots straight over. Hit on the side, ends up down the bank. He was lucky to survive. We didn't have much trouble identifying the vehicle. We'd seen it often enough.'

'And I think I can tell you where he bought the car from.'

They looked at one another.

'I want to bring him in,' Joanna said.

'On the thumbprint alone?'

'Just let me check that this car came from Newton. Keep watching him.'

'I think you need your dumb girl to talk and the wife to give evidence. If she will.'

She looked at Walker's picture again and sensed cruelty behind his glare. It made sense now why Louisa had put herself so far from harm's way and Bethany's voice had been silenced.

'One more thing,' she said. 'Kelvin Shipley. Does the name mean anything to you?'

'Can't say it does. Maybe one of his minor henchmen. I'll dig around if you like.'

Their eyes met for a moment. Both knew they needed to time their arrest of Walker so they had enough to charge him and make it stick. And even with the connection of the car, one thumbprint was thin. She could do with corroborative evidence.

She thanked the DI but as she drove back to Leek Joanna focussed on the tasks ahead. She thought back, full circle. Right back to the beginning and that chilly morning, the girl silhouetted against a lightening sky, the little boy in the pushchair, perhaps sensing something was wrong but with no real understanding of what it could be.

A statement from Bethany, or witness statements from Louisa, the gardener or Shipley would have clinched it. But she didn't have any of those . . . yet.

Walker would have a smart lawyer to defend him. She needed more.

She still had no lead on the missing gardener or Kelvin Shipley, who was, after all, Newton's brother-in-law.

She decided to interview Shelley Newton to see if she could shed any light on the connection between her ex-husband, her brother and Adam Judd. Shelley had separated from her husband ten years ago. There were no children and she currently lived in Derby.

Brother and sister, it seemed, were not close. Newton had been dead for four weeks but she hadn't appeared. They had tried to contact her, with little success. While Anthony's parents had come forward his sister had stayed out of the picture. There had been none of that badgering the police every five minutes to arrest someone for his murder. They had heard nothing from her and Joanna's repeated request for an interview had finally been met with grudging acquiescence.

Joanna took DC Danny Hesketh-Brown with her. She wanted to leave Alan doing what he was best at – tickling the computer keys.

The A50 was a dual carriageway which headed due east, ultimately ending up in Hull. Derby was halfway along, less than an hour away and a straight drive. Joanna drove at a steady sixty miles per hour and eventually they pulled up outside a dingy terraced house, whose front doors opened out onto the pavement. Obviously Newton's generosity to his parents hadn't extended to his sister which might explain her detachment. The house was near the university and the entire street had the uncared look of houses rented out to students.

They parked up and knocked on a dusty door painted dark green. Behind it they heard a heavy tread and then the door was tugged open and they were face to face with the dead man's sister.

FIFTY-THREE

helley Newton turned out to be a large woman with a pale, doughy face and small, suspicious eyes which studied them both for a moment while her frame blocked the doorway. She was wearing black leggings, stretched, surely, to their limit, slippers and a loose tan-coloured sweater over the top.

Joanna presented her ID card and Shelley gave a sniff and a tight smile before glancing at Danny as though he was an unnecessary extra. 'Come in then,' she said grudgingly. 'I have to go to work in a bit so best we don't waste time.'

The front door opened into a small, square room with a couple of wide armchairs facing a large TV. One picture hung on an adjacent wall. A print of Millais' *Ophelia*. Interesting but a bit morbid. Shelley's eyes followed her gaze and she looked pleased with herself.

'You'd best sit down,' she said.

Danny stood in the doorway but Joanna accepted the offer.

Shelley gave them both a toothy smile, possibly trying to charm them. 'I take it you want to know about my "dear" brother?'

Not much affection there or respect for the dead.

'Anything that might help in our investigation.' Joanna kept her tone neutral.

'I don't know as to that. We didn't have a lot to do with each other. As he went up in the world I got stuck here . . .' She waved her arms around the room before adding, in a spiteful tone, 'I suppose you want the dirt on him.'

Joanna satisfied herself with an encouraging smile.

'I don't – didn't,' she corrected, 'have a lot to do with him. We're different sorts. Nothing like brother and sister. He's the greedy one.'

And you're the lazy one?

When Joanna failed to respond Shelley continued. 'He's ambitious. He's always wanted to get *somewhere in life.*' She scratched speech marks into the air self-consciously. 'He'd keep his foot on your head if it helped him climb the greasy pole. Ambitious but most of all my little brother wants – wanted – to be rich. Flashy rich. He always was a show-off. That's why he had to have money.' She swallowed. 'Our parents always worried about money, you see. They fretted, did endless sums and equations always worrying how they would manage to pay the bills. It made him . . . obsessive about it. Greedy.'

It went some way to explaining Newton's grasping character – to some extent.

'Tell me about your husband.'

Shelley looked startled. 'Kelvin? What's he got to do with it?'

Joanna decided honesty might be the best policy. 'We don't know.'

Shelley held her hand up in defence. 'Now look. I think Kelvin's a bugger but murder, oh, no. He wouldn't have done anything to hurt Tony. They got on well together. They were mates.' It provided a link, albeit a loose one between Newton, Shipley and Patrick Walker. Joanna felt the knots tighten.

And more was to come. She produced a photo of Adam Judd. 'Do you know this guy?'

'Adam? Yes. He and Kelvin were old friends. They were at school together.' She laughed. 'Egged each other on to do mischief.'

She looked at Joanna then, a reluctant question on her face. 'What's Kelvin . . .?' Her voice trailed away. And then she looked miserable.

How often does this happen? An estranged couple who aren't really.

Shelley looked expectantly at Joanna. Waited for her cue.

'What were they doing at Anthony's house? Adam was employed as a gardener there. But the van he was driving was registered to your husband.'

'Ex,' she said automatically, but there was no heat behind it. Instead she looked thoughtful. 'I don't know,' she said. 'I don't know. Adam's dad was a farmer. I suppose he'd know about gardening.' But her voice sounded dubious. And now she looked even more unhappy, her face sagging and older than her years.

She pressed her lips together. Like Bethany she was keeping schtum. But it was a less involved silence. Joanna read something else in her eyes.

'You must have your own theory as to your brother's murder.'

'Take your pick,' Shelley said, folding her arms, summoning up strength from somewhere. 'You've a nanny who by all accounts is not quite right in the head. You've got Anthony's shady business practices. You've got Louisa who is as cold a woman as I've ever met. And into that you want to chuck in Kelvin and Adam. As I say. Take your pick.'

'You've been following the papers,' Joanna observed.

'He is my brother,' Shelley snapped.

'Has your brother enemies?'

'Well, he had one, didn't he?' She'd scored a point there.

'You mentioned Louisa. How did you get on with your sister-in-law?'

Shelley leaned as far forward as her belly would allow. 'She was a greedy, lying, cheating little—' She stopped. 'She'd have sold her own grandmother for a pair of Louboutins.'

Joanna couldn't help but look down at Shelley's feet, bulging out of a pair of worn slippers. *Quite a contrast*, she thought.

'Have you any idea who might have murdered your brother?'

Shelley shook her head and they felt they would get nothing more out of her.

It wasn't long before Shelley started to fidget. 'It's time I went to work,' she said, rising from the chair. 'I really do have to go.' But as she stood she faced Joanna. 'I don't know who killed my brother,' she said calmly. 'If I did I would have come forward. Right is right, Inspector.'

'Do you have a current address for your ex-husband?'

'I had one in Nottingham but it's from almost a year ago.' She smiled. 'I doubt he's still there, knowing Kelvin. He likes to move around. Shiftless. Never stays anywhere for long – or with anyone for that matter,' she added as an afterthought.

Joanna waited but there was nothing more and she sensed this was as much as Shelley was going to say.

She stood up too. 'Thank you for your time.'

However, Shelley hadn't quite finished. Before Joanna had reached the door she put a hand on her shoulder. 'I saw very little of my nephew so didn't really know his nanny but Tony thought a lot of her. He said he trusted her. Bethany wouldn't have done it. She wouldn't have hurt Stevie. Neither, for all her faults, would Louisa. She wasn't the most caring of mothers. She'd leave every-thing to the nanny.' She chuckled. 'I don't think Louisa even knew how to change a nappy. Whoever killed my brother it wasn't one of them and it wasn't Kelvin either – or Adam. Thick as thieves they were.'

The opinion struck Joanna as genuine. 'Thanks.'

And they left.

On the way back she suggested to Danny Hesketh-Brown that they take a detour and drop by Newton's Classic Cars, take a look for themselves.

He pulled up outside large premises in Macclesfield. An extensive forecourt with gleaming cars temptingly lined up and at the back workshops with mechanics hard at work on various car parts. The sound of hammering combined with a smell of engine oil filled the air as Joanna climbed out of the car. 'I hadn't realized it was such an extensive operation,' she remarked to Danny. 'It's big business.'

He was at her side. 'Oh yeah. Lots of people go for classic cars,' he said, admiration in his voice. 'It's the shape, the bodywork. It's an obsession. My neighbour's got a seventies Triumph Stag. H reg. He loves it. Paid over twenty K for it. Keeps it in the garage like a treasured possession and only takes it out on fine days with the roof down.' He laughed as his eyes roved the gleaming bodywork. 'Think he values it more than his wife to be honest.'

Two mechanics were working in the main area, a large, noisy place with a deep inspection pit. One of them approached, wiping his hands on an oily rag. 'Can I help? Were you interested in . . .'

He was silenced by Joanna's ID card. Gave a little grunt. 'Not here about a car then?'

'No. You're still working though?'

'What else is there to do?' The mechanic was sunburnt with a pair of bright blue eyes. The other guy was too absorbed in his job to take any notice of a couple of strangers who weren't buying.

'What'll happen to the business?'

The guy shrugged. 'Who knows? Go to the highest bidder. Me and Clem are just hoping they take us on too – as part of the business.'

She had a hint of light then. 'Do you have a list of customers?'

The mechanic grinned. 'We do. Because people who like old cars don't just like them. They love them.'

Now Joanna loved her bike (21 speed Shimano gears, saddle tailor-made to fit her butt protected by padded shorts, handlebars and pedals adjusted to perfection) but she'd never felt the same about cars. She just wanted to get in and drive to wherever she was going. Matthew was fond of his BMW but it was, in no way, an obsession. Nothing like this. But this description perhaps explained why a hardened criminal like Patrick Walker flew into a rage when his 'sweetheart' died because ultimately it had died because of a badly fitted part. And so Walker had flown into a rage, broken all his rules about being too close to his crimes, had driven to The Cottage and stabbed and tortured the man who had probably assured him, when he'd spent nearly £100,000 on the car, that all was kosher.

And there it was, neatly listed on the list of sales with a refitted engine and replacement Dunlop disc brakes. Jensen Interceptor FF. Crystal green. First registered 1970. Anthony Newton's nemesis, bought on December of the previous year, mileage 53,000. And he'd paid £123,000.

For a moment she stood still, realizing this brought the case round full circle. She had nearly everything. And just at that moment her phone rang and she was transported to her other world.

'Any chance of you cooking tea?'

'You are joking, aren't you?'

'Sorry . . .' Though he wasn't. 'Forgot you'd be solving major crime. Have you cracked it yet?'

'Not quite. But I'm getting close, Matt.'

'Good.'

'All OK at home?'

'Absolutely fine. Mum and Dad have taken Jakob to Rudyard Lake again on that little train they have there.'

For a moment she was in that other place, watching her son's excited face riding in the little train along the side of Rudyard Lake. She felt a pang. She should be there. Not here.

DC Danny Hesketh-Brown was watching.

'Better go, Matt,' she said. 'See you later.'

And she rang off.

FIFTY-FOUR

Back at the station DC Alan King had some good news to add to the growing file.

The Spanish police had Louisa in custody and were currently organizing a flight to bring her back. 'Her parents had a holiday place in Mojacar,' he said, 'in Almeria. They'd gone down there.'

Far enough away from Patrick Walker.

She risked a high five with the DC. 'Well done,' she said. 'And thank you. Your knowledge of Spanish has come in really useful.'

The tip of King's ears turned red. She gave him the Nottingham address Shelley had given her for Kelvin Shipley and left him to track him down from there.

Joanna wished she could share this triumph with Mike, that he had been part of it. But she wanted more. She still wanted to find the gardener and his mate and understand their involvement. It was even possible that they could provide further evidence, fill in a few of the gaps. And the horrid phrase that snags us all lay at the back of her mind, *pride goes before . . .* made her pick up the phone and speak to Rothman who was reassuring.

'He's still here, Inspector Piercy.'

'We're nearly ready to bring him in. Just waiting for our girl to talk and the victim's wife is on her way back from Spain. I want some corroborative testimony and I have to know my witnesses will be safe.'

'Fair enough.' Rothman sounded jaunty. Maybe he was looking forward to the Staffordshire police bringing a case against a man they had recognized as a villain years ago but had failed to convict.

When a case begins to unravel it happens almost too quickly to appreciate each single piece of evidence that finally solves it.

She couldn't wait to tighten the drawstrings.

9 p.m.

It was late when word came through that Louisa had touched down at Manchester airport. Joanna had already dispatched two officers to bring her to Leek. This was the time when a case took over your life and the best you could manage was a quick phone call home to apologize – again – and explain your absence without giving out any idea when you might actually arrive home. Joanna suspected it would not be tonight or even possibly tomorrow. She left Alan King still trying to track down Kelvin Shipley and the missing gardener.

She drew breath and recapped.

Stockport police had Patrick Walker under observation ready for the Leek force to swoop. Another whoop from DC Alan King told her he'd found another address for Kelvin Shipley and was pursuing this lead. He did a quick fingers crossed and bent back over the keyboard.

She'd made a quick phone call to Greatbach partly to bring Claire Roget up to date and partly to find out how Bethany was, but the psychiatrist had already left and the nurse in charge wasn't giving away any secrets whoever was on the end of the line. She simply conveyed the meaningless news that Bethany was 'well and comfortable'. In response to Joanna's query whether she was ready to talk yet the nurse seemed confused.

No matter. It would wait – for now.

Joanna finally met up with Louisa Newton at ten thirty p.m. when she arrived under escort. Louisa was tall, statuesque – and still frightened.

After offering the almost obligatory sandwich, cup of tea and a caution as well as the services of a duty solicitor, which Louisa declined, Joanna began by reassuring her about the safety of her son – though Louisa hadn't actually asked.

Next she described the police's involvement beginning with Bethany on the edge of the drop.

Louisa was calm. 'I knew I could trust Bethany,' she said. 'She would never have hurt Stevie.'

She appealed to them then, eyes flashing out a warning. 'You have no idea,' she said. 'It was a peaceful Sunday evening. Tony was in the bath with a bottle of whisky. Bethany was somewhere or other with Stevie. I was watching television and this man is just there. I didn't know he'd come in. I didn't know *how* he'd come in. We have electric gates and . . . There was a voice behind me. "Where is he?".'

She met Joanna's eyes. 'I have never seen anyone so furious. He was practically foaming at the mouth.'

Joanna didn't ask for a description of the man. She already knew it. And besides she didn't want to interrupt the flow.

Louisa's eyes appealed. 'I was so frightened I couldn't speak. I just pointed.' And now she did just that, finger shaking as she relived the moment.

'I heard some splashing, running water. I tried to tell myself it would be all right. Then I heard Stevie screaming and Bethany running into the bathroom. She was terrified and Stevie was inconsolable. Bethany just said Tony was . . .' Louisa put her hands over her face and her shoulders shook.

'I was so frightened. We hid for ages, until we were sure he'd gone. I had money. I just wanted to run. I thought he'd come after me. I told Bethany to take Stevie somewhere safe, to take the car and to give me her passport and made a run for it. Adam took me down to Portsmouth and I caught the ferry using Bethany's passport. I knew I could trust her with Stevie. I thought I'd be safe in Spain with Mum and Dad but I didn't feel safe so we went to their holiday place.' She smiled. 'That was when I began to feel better. I knew I'd have to face you some time.'

'Do you know where Adam is now?'

She shook her head. 'Not a clue. I told him to hang around for a bit. He thought of texting Mavis and telling her we'd gone away and not to come in for a couple of weeks. I didn't want her to find the body. I thought it would buy us a bit of time to think.' Her voice was thin now, doubting the wisdom of her decision. 'You have to understand. We were in a blind panic.'

Joanna turned her laptop around to show Walker's face and she blenched. 'That's him,' she said. Joanna didn't insult her by asking whether she was sure. Patrick Walker's face was pretty memorable.

They put Louisa in a local hotel and Joanna looked around the room at some very tired officers who soon perked up at her next statement.

'Time to arrest Walker.' She watched as shoulders tensed and eyes widened. Even a muted cheer.

Always a sweet moment when you charge a suspect knowing you pretty much have it in the bag. She had a word with DI Rothman and warned him they were about to bring Walker in.

'Be careful,' he said.

Walker lived in a huge Victorian semi in Stockport. He answered the door, scowling at them but saying nothing when she cautioned him and they slipped on the cuffs.

FIFTY-FIVE

2 a.m.

Facing Walker, she breathed in his defeat. He knew that after a lifetime of being careful this one fit of fury would lose him his freedom. Joanna was ready to face him with Louisa's statement as well as the evidence of the thumbprint. But instead she showed him the picture of the wrecked car and watched his face tense.

He reached out to touch it with the tenderness of the touch given to a newborn. The look of grief on his face might have melted polar ice caps but Joanna had witnessed the crime scene, the girl driven by terror to the top of a cliff, her lips stuck dumb, the blood spatter on a little boy's dungarees, Louisa's flight as well as the catalogue of crimes DI Rothman had failed to pin to this man's chest. And she recalled Colclough's words. 'In the end they pay. And what sits opposite you in the Interview Room is someone whose self-confidence is about to be crushed. However much they bluster and deny, inside they are squirming because they are frightened to go to prison, to lose their control and power. Thugs are thugs and inside they will be amongst their own, surrounded by criminals with their own cruelty, greed and inhumanity. Remember that and in any interview you will come out on top.'

Walker had small, pale eyes, hooded by sad, drooping lids. When he looked at the photograph it wasn't anger she saw but grief as though looking at a picture of a murdered son. 'You don't understand,' he said. 'This isn't just a car. It's a work of art as well as science. The engine. The Ferguson Formula is the pioneer of four-wheel drive systems. Less than 300 of these made. 6.5 litres engine. Steel body, walnut interior.' He reached out and touched it again. 'That bastard.' His eyes locked onto Joanna's. 'Fucking throttle stuck. Accelerator on full. I was belting along, knew I was going to have a big accident and I knew this car . . .' He reached out again to touch the picture of the car wreck. 'This beautiful car was going to end up like this. And I swore I would make him suffer.'

She waited until the morning before picking up the phone and punching in Claire Roget's number. 'You can tell Bethany,' she said, 'that we have the man in custody. She's safe.'

'Oh.' The psychiatrist sounded surprised, just remembering in time to add her congratulations. 'I'll pass your message on, Inspector.'

Joanna put the phone down and then she made her way to interview rooms two and three.

King had tracked Adam Judd and Kelvin together, in a small rented house in Birmingham. Mates to the end.

They already knew Judd's part had been to drive Louisa to the ferry port. And Shipley had had £5,000 in cash paid anonymously. He claimed to have thought it could be connected to a burglary, which gave them a clue as to why the gates had been opened together with the unlocked back door to The Cottage. The best they could hope for was to pin the word accessory to Shipley while it hardly seemed worthwhile pressing a charge of obstructing a police enquiry to Adam Judd's chest.

Two days later, Joanna felt a sense of relief that this would be the last time she would be parking outside the psychiatric hospital.

Claire was waiting for her just inside the main door. She wasn't smiling and Joanna guessed that even though they had Walker in custody Bethany was still mute.

Claire stopped her just outside the girl's door. 'Please don't upset her,' she said. 'The poor girl has been through so much.'

Joanna came back fighting. 'I understand perfectly. But look at it from my perspective, Doctor. Bethany's silence has delayed our investigation, made it so much harder. Man hours have been wasted uncovering details she could have given us herself. And all that time a crime scene was undiscovered and slowly degrading. I don't doubt that you're right. Her silence is the result of trauma but it has had an impact – and a cost.'

Bethany's eyes were wary when they walked in but she straightened up and Joanna knew she was engaged.

Joanna sat down. 'The first thing I want to say to you, Bethany, is that we have the man who murdered your employer safely in custody.' She reached out and touched the girl with her hand. 'He can't hurt you or Stevie or Louisa.'

Bethany dropped her chin and Joanna continued.

'So what I want to ask you is this. Now will you talk?'

Bethany smiled.

Joanna finally rolled in late on the following evening, and to her surprise Peter and Charlotte were peering through the window as she pulled up outside. She gave them a wave, at the same time acknowledging with a sense of guilt how much she, Matthew and little Jakob owed this couple in their seventies.

She let herself in. Peter put a finger to his lips. 'Sssh,' he said. 'He's taken an age to settle.' He looked exhausted.

'Where's Matthew?'

'He got delayed. Something came up at the hospital and he had to go through some tissue samples. He said he'd be late.'

Joanna nodded. 'Thank you,' she said and tried to lighten the heaviness that lay between them. 'You and Charlotte have been so good. I don't know how we'd have managed without you.'

Peter put a hand on her shoulder and gave her the smallest of smiles. 'We know that, Joanna.' He spoke slowly, hesitantly. 'Maybe if your job . . . Couldn't you put it on hold – just while he's so small? Go part-time?'

'It doesn't quite work like that. It's all or nothing, I'm afraid, in the police – at this level.'

'Hmm.'

Charlotte had joined him and from the looks they exchanged Joanna could guess this was a conversation they'd already had. More than once.

'We'll head off now.' Peter spoke awkwardly. Charlotte already had her coat on.

Half an hour later Matthew turned up. She had had a shower and was in her pyjamas. 'Hey,' he said, as she descended the stairs. He too looked exhausted. She put her arms round him. 'Busy day?'

He kissed her back. 'Tissue samples.'

'Yeah, your mum and dad said.'

'When does it stop, Joanna?'

'It's the same for both of us.'

'Yeah. But now we have Jakob . . .' He didn't need to finish the sentence.

'Fancy a nightcap?'

'Yeah,' he said again. 'A whisky would be nice.'

And so they sat in the kitchen, she with a glass of wine and he with a whisky. 'Matt,' she said, 'are we rotten parents?'

For a while Matthew didn't answer. He was always honest – always had been. And so she waited for his response with anxiety. Whatever he said would be what he truly believed. He took her hand. 'We do the best we can under the circumstances.'

And then he lifted his head. 'What about having a nanny?'

She stared at him until he broke into a smile. 'I'm still thinking about it,' was the best she could manage.

FIFTY-SIX

Ahead lay the construction of their case to satisfy the law, the logging of every sample, the recording of every statement. They charged Walker with first degree murder and Adam Judd and Kelvin Shipley with being accessories, but with less confidence of success.

Mike was in the garden and must have heard her car pull up. He came round the side of the house. And her heart lifted. He was walking without crutches. Standing straight as a soldier and grinning at her in a way she hadn't seen since before the accident. His steps were maybe not quite the confident stride he'd once had. 'Mike,' she said and was tempted to hug him, at the same time worried she would bowl him over. He took the decision from her. Two steps and his arms were around her in the biggest of bear hugs. 'I'm going to make it, Jo,' he said. 'I'm going to be OK. I saw the doctors yesterday and they're really pleased. They've advised me to start doing loads of exercises to build up the muscles and walk and walk and walk. Which is exactly what I'm doing.'

She extricated herself and felt her face fold into a beam. 'I am so happy. Thank goodness. I was worried.'

'Hey.' He stopped her. 'We were all worried. I thought I'd be . . .' He tried to make a joke out of it. 'Long John Silver or Captain Ahab. But,' he said, grinning even broader now, 'it wasn't to be.'

'No.'

He had something more to say. 'I know this sounds barking mad,' he said, frowning, 'but I'm almost glad it happened. I never appreciated having two functioning legs until this . . .' He looked down. 'Maybe illness is a lesson for us to appreciate what we have?'

She smiled warmly. 'I can't wait for you to come back to work, Mike. I'm missing you. I can't help thinking we would have got here quicker had you been around.'

'I won't be back to complete active duty for a couple of months,' he warned, 'but I should manage desk duties by June at the latest. In the meantime I'm working up to capacity.' His smile was rueful. 'I'm missing it too,' he said. 'It's shit being at home all day, every day.'

The hardest part of a major investigation is sleeping – without your dreams being invaded. She wasn't really sleeping but lay alongside Matthew, listening to him breathing while she fitted the facts together. And came back full circle. Straining to hear Bethany's silent voice. Soft, musical. 'I had to find sanctuary. Be safe. I had to protect Stevie.'

Maybe, Joanna thought, a nanny wouldn't be such a bad idea after all.